Sugar and Spite

Also by Carol J. Perry

Haunted Haven Mysteries
Be My Ghost
High Spirits
Haunting License
The Spirit Moves

Witch City Mysteries
Caught Dead Handed
Tails, You Lose
Look Both Ways
Murder Go Round
Grave Errors
It Takes a Coven
Bells, Spells, and Murders
Final Exam
Late Checkout
Murder, Take Two
See Something
'Til Death
Now You See It
Death Scene

Anthologies
Halloween Cupcake Murder

SUGAR
AND SPITE

CAROL J. PERRY

Kensington Publishing Corp.
kensingtonbooks.com

First Printing: November 2025

ISBN: 978-1-4967-4368-8
ISBN: 978-1-4967-4369-5 (eBook)

10 9 8 7 6 5 4 3 2 1

Printed in the United States of America

The authorized representative in the EU for product safety and compliance is eucomply OU, Parnu mnt 139b-14, Apt 123
Tallinn, Berlin 11317, hello@eucompliancepartner.com.

For Dan,
my husband and best friend.

"To me the word *Witch* is a delicious word, filled with the most ancient memories . . ."

Laurie Cabot

When I
day at
show my
keep
pany
tresses

Chapter One

"Don't forget to get some free samples!" My boss, Bruce Doan, the station manager of Salem's WICH-TV, leaned out of his second-floor office window with the shouted reminder. Waving my hand to show that I'd heard him, I climbed into my almost-new Jeep and backed out of the reserved space in the company's harborside parking lot that had my name on it: "Lee Mondello—Program Director." The lettering was fairly new. Until about a year ago, my name on that same sign was Lee Barrett.

Thirty-six years ago I was born Maralee Kowolski. Orphaned at the age of five, I was raised by my aunt, Isobel "Ibby" Russell, in the old family home on Salem's Winter Street. Maralee Kowalski became Lee Barrett when I married NASCAR driver Johnny Barrett, but sadly I became a young widow when Johnny died in an auto crash. Now, once again, I'm happily married. My husband is Pete Mondello, a detective in the Salem police department. We've bought a comfortable little home on Winter Street—the same street where I grew up, and conveniently located for O'Ryan, the large yellow gentleman cat whose custody my aunt and I have agreed to share, to commute between the two houses. Pete and I also have a dog—a wonderful black lab named Toby—who, believe it or not, used to belong to a famous movie star! He has O'Ryan's complete approval.

Pete and I were both over-the-moon happy when we learned that we were expecting our first baby—and my ultrasound had told us that we were going to have a little girl! At seven months pregnant I still felt wonderful, and my coworkers at the station told me I'd never looked better, so Doan, who prefers that all of his employees "wear more than one hat," decided that there was no reason I couldn't take on a "small extra assignment." Our city, Salem, Massachusetts, is known the world over as "the Witch City." Halloween is a very big deal here—and since Halloween is the biggest holiday for candy sales—around six *billion* dollars' worth—a citywide candy promotion seemed like a money-making idea, not just for the merchants involved, but for a hefty helping of TV commercial revenue.

"It's an easy one," Doan insisted. "You'll just grab a videographer and visit all the candy stores and sweetshops you can find. Interview the owners. Get some free samples. Take your time. Find out what the most popular candies are." I could tell he was in love with the idea. "Heck," he said, "we even have the oldest candy shop in America right here on Derby Street."

He was right. Ye Olde Pepper Candy Companie was less than a block away from WICH-TV. I wasn't ready for the videographer yet, but I decided to drop in unannounced. I'd been a customer for their old-fashioned treats since I was a kid, and folks in Salem have been savoring their goodies since 1806. It seemed like a good idea to run the plan by the staff of a place who'd been in the candy biz for a couple of centuries.

To put it briefly, they loved it. I did a quick interview with a longtime staff member, left with rave reviews of Doan's brainstorm and, as instructed, plenty of free samples—all neatly packed into a canvas bag emblazoned with their trademark horse-drawn carriage. I'd already stashed one of the famous Gibralters in my handbag, to be sure I wouldn't miss out when my coworkers descended on the sugary haul. I added a package of watermelon licorice twists for my best friend, River North. She wouldn't be at the station until after the rest of the crew had gobbled up all of the samples. She does the midnight to two a.m. show, *Tarot Time with River North*, where she reads the beautiful tarot cards for callers during breaks in the scary midnight movie.

I made a quick switch back to my program director hat when it occurred to me that *Shopping Salem*, one of my personal favorite programs, could use a feature on the old-timey candies too. See? Multitasking. Doan would love it. I added another go-see. Christopher Rich at Christopher's Castle was always good at coming up with novel ideas for another of my programming responsibilities—the station's morning kiddie show, *Ranger Rob's Rodeo*. Rob's "little buckaroos" love anything Western, and Chris had a brand-new shipment of kid-sized cowboy boots. I grabbed a couple of photos with my phone and promised that videographer Francine Hunter would come by later for a proper shoot. While I was there I told Chris about Doan's idea for a Halloween candy feature. His eyes sparkled with interest.

"Have you ever been to Casa de Chocolatte?" he asked. "It's kind of new and it's not far from your place, over on Washington Square on the east side of the Salem Common in one of those big, old brick mansions. They make all kinds of chocolate candy in the basement, and there's a showroom on the first floor that's so gorgeous it ought to be featured in one of those fancy home decorating magazines. I understand that the good-looking grass widow who owns the place lives upstairs." I had to smile at Chris's use of the term *grass widow*. Salem people still use the old term to mean a divorced woman—and not always in a flattering way.

"It sounds interesting," I told him. "I'll definitely check it out. They make the candies right there in the house?"

"They do. I bought a box of them and I plan to order some to sell here in the castle. Wicked good stuff."

"I'll stop by there soon—maybe even this afternoon if I have time—since it's just across the common from my place. I hope I'll get some samples. Doan is seriously into the free samples thing."

"Good luck. And thanks for stopping by. I look forward to seeing Francine. I miss the days when you two used to work together doing field reports," he said.

"Sometimes I do too," I admitted, "but working nine to five instead of all hours of the day and night chasing news stories around the city is much better for married-lady me."

I knew the more traditional schedule was going to be better for mommy-me too, but that didn't mean I wouldn't miss the excitement and the immediacy of those field reporting days—and yes, even the danger.

Chapter Two

Once again I parked the Jeep, crossed the parking lot, and, clutching my canvas bagful of goodies, climbed the granite steps to the WICH-TV building. Inside, I crossed the black-and-white tile floor to the vintage brass-doored elevator affectionally known as "Old Clunky." As was a long-standing habit, I tried to avoid looking directly at those shiny brass doors. Not many people know this about me—only Pete, Aunt Ibby, and River—but I'm what's known as a *scryer.* That's a person who sees things in reflective surfaces that other people cannot see. River calls me a "gazer," and says that the ability is a special gift. I don't think of it as a gift. Almost all the visions I've seen, in mirrors, windows, silverware, hubcaps—anything reflective—have had something to do with death.

The ride up to the second floor was no bumpier than usual, and Rhonda, the way-smarter-than-she-needs-to-be station receptionist, greeted me with a big smile. She leaned across the curved purple Formica-topped reception desk, pushing aside an improbable arrangement of glitter-sprinkled lavender tulips, and reached for the bag.

"Samples?"

"Yep. Lots of them." I handed over the bag.

"Any root beer barrels in here?" She dipped a tentative hand into the stash.

"I'm sure there are, but we'd better let Doan have first dibs, don't you think?"

With a small sigh, she stood and joined me on the other side of the purple counter. "Let's go."

We crossed over to the partly open door marked "Station Manager," where I tapped lightly. "Mr. Doan? I have some samples," I announced.

"Come in! Come in!" he boomed. "How many candy stores did you hit?"

"Just the one, so far," I admitted. "Ye Olde Pepper. I have another one lined up for this afternoon though." I sort of white-lied about the lined-up part and hoped it would be open when I arrived. "It's a big new one. Casa de Chocolatte."

"Sounds good. Let's see what we've got so far." He reached for the bag and dumped the contents onto the top of his desk. "Mrs. Doan is particularly partial to their purple jelly beans."

Buffy Doan is partial to *all* things purple—explaining the purple to lavender to lilac décor prevalent in the WICH-TV offices. "I asked particularly for them," I told him. "I think you'll find several packages."

"Excellent." He deftly removed three plastic envelopes of the desired beans. "You can take the rest down to the break room and tell the gang it's on me." Bruce Doan likes to be generous with his employees—especially when it doesn't cost him anything.

Rhonda and I scooped up the remaining candy and put it back into the bag. Rhonda managed to liberate a package of the desired root beer barrels, and I carried the remaining loot down the ramp and past the newsroom to the employee break room, where I placed it on the table with a sticky-note invitation to *Help Yourself*.

Chris King's sketchy bits of information about a grass widow who makes candy in a mansion basement had intrigued me enough that I'd promised Doan a feature on it. I was pretty sure that since said mansion was just across the common from Winter Street, my Aunt Ibby would know all about it. I told Rhonda I'd see her later and ducked into my glass cubicle of an office and called my aunt.

"Oh my, yes," she said. "I know Shirley Parker. I'd heard that she was reviving the old family candy business. Good for her."

"Casa de Chocolatte was an old family business? Chris didn't mention that."

"Is that what she calls it now? A long time ago, before you were even born, the Parkers owned a whole chain of candy stores. I'll bet every town in New England had a Penny Parker Candy Shop." Her voice took on a nostalgic tone. "They all looked alike. White front, the name "Penny Parker" spelled out in black script on a white sign. There were even white ruffled curtains in the window." Deep sigh. "Oh, those chocolates. Buttercream, maple walnut, almond bark, orange cream, strawberry caramel. I guess they must have sold the name along with everything else when the business failed. Casa de Chocolatte, huh? Well, at least she still has the house."

"Do you know her well?"

"We went to school together," she admitted. "She's in her sixties, like me, but we've never kept in touch."

"Why not?"

"Well, Shirley was what they call a trust fund baby. She's always had plenty of money. Fabulous clothes. Her own car when she was sixteen. After high school she went to a fancy finishing school in New York. She was—well, *different* from the rest of us. We had nothing at all in common. Shirley was never what you'd call beautiful, but she was attractive in a stylish way. She married the handsomest man in Salem—Bernie Bingham. Some people said that she'd bought herself some eye candy. They had one child, as I recall. A boy. They're divorced now, and he's moved up to New Hampshire. Betsy says *she* still pays *him* alimony!" Betsy is one of my aunt's closest friends—the one who knows everything about anybody who is anybody anywhere north of Boston.

I told her about my new assignment. "I'm going to stop in over there this afternoon and try to make an appointment for Francine and me to do a video. I think they'll enjoy the free publicity. Most places do. Shall I mention your name?"

"I hardly think she'd remember me at all from school, but she probably has a library card. Sure. Go ahead. Mention my name. Let me know how it turns out."

"I will. I promised Mr. Doan I'd try to bring back some free samples. Do you have a Penny Parker favorite in case they're using the old recipes?"

"Maple cream, for sure," she said.

I said I'd either beg or buy some maple cream candies for her. I was glad to have the backstory about the Penny Parker stores, and since I didn't have an appointment at Casa de Chocolatte, the fact that I was related to one of Shirley Parker's classmates might give me a foot in the door of the Parker mansion.

Pete likes to know if I'm apt to be working past five o'clock, so I called to let him know about the planned candy caper and headed the Jeep toward the common. It's not far from Derby Street to Washington Square, so in minutes I pulled up in front of what one might describe as a stately brick home. A discreet black-and-gold sign over what was quite probably a genuine Samuel McIntire carved doorway identified it as Casa de Chocolatte. I climbed the stairs to the exquisite front door and, following instructions posted on the glass inset, entered the first-floor showroom without knocking or ringing.

Chris King had been correct in his assessment that the place ought to be featured in a top-tier home decorating magazine. A cushy oriental runner in muted reds and purples on a polished hardwood floor led to a massive mahogany desk, where a dark-haired, slim woman wearing what was surely an Armani suit welcomed me with a smile. I looked beyond her, trying to take in the scope of the spacious room. Not too long before, one of the extra hats that had been bestowed on me was "Historical Documentary Executive Director." This had involved documenting the Salem International Museum project, which had included some amazing furnishings, paintings, and other décor, much of it loaned from private collections in Salem homes. I'd learned to recognize Hepplewhite, Sheraton, Chippendale—lots of big names in the antique furniture world—and a goodly amount of it was on display in the first-floor showroom at Casa de Chocolatte. There were delicate candy dishes, complete with assorted chocolate candies displayed on most of the tables, and a stack of the boxed products on a Victorian pastry cart. A large glass showcase displayed trays of the individual flavored pieces. Thinking of Aunt Ibby, I made sure there was one marked "Maple Cream." I even spied a large framed photograph of one of the Penny Parker Candy Shops that my aunt had described.

"Good afternoon. May I help you?" The smiling woman greeted me from behind the desk. I handed her a business card—one of my new ones that identified me as *Lee Barrett Mondello, Program Director.*

"Oh, yes." She peered closely at the card. "Lee Barrett. Of course. I've seen you on TV. You're Isobel Russell's niece, Maralee." She offered her hand and I shook it.

"You have a good grip," she said. "Tennis?"

I'd had some tennis lessons as a teenager at the Salem Country Club, but rarely played anymore. "A little bit," I admitted. "You know my aunt Ibby?" I wasn't surprised. In her position as head research librarian at Salem's main library, I think my aunt has met everybody in Salem who has a library card.

"Yes, indeed. We were high school classmates." She

offered her hand across the broad expanse of desktop.
"I'm Shirley Parker."

I was pleased by her immediate recognition of my
name, and at the same time surprised by her high school
memory of Aunt Ibby—who I was quite sure would be
surprised by it too. I dove right in with my unrehearsed
pitch about WICH-TV doing a video of Casa de Chocolatte as part of Bruce Doan's pre-Halloween citywide
candy promotion.

"It's a lovely idea. Thank you for including us. We're
quite new in the candy business, you know—even
though the Parker name has been associated with fine
chocolate for many years." She gestured to the Penny
Parker Candy Shop photo. "You're too young to remember Penny Parker."

"My aunt Ibby has told me about the shops," I said.
"I wish I could have seen one—with the white ruffled
curtains and all."

She pointed to another framed photo. "Here's a picture of our current crew. I'm proud of each and every
one of them for upholding our tradition of excellence."
The group shot showed a dozen or so men and women,
all wearing identical white jumpsuits with a "CdC"
monogram embroidered on the breast pockets. "I guess
Penny Parker has gone forever, but we're using the
exact same recipes for our candies that they used back
then." She stood, and I realized that she was quite tall.
"We're what you'd call a boutique candymaker. Everything is handmade—with appropriate machines, of
course. We have commercial melting machines, enrobing
machines, chocolate molds. We package our handmade
chocolates in three sizes—twelve-piece, eighteen-piece,

and thirty-six-piece. We only need a few workers at a time, but they're all expert at what they do. We're not working today—we're on a four-day workweek at this time of year. It'll pick up later in the fall. Would you like to see where we make them? It's right downstairs. There's no one down there today except the cat, but you're welcome to wander around and take a look."

"I'd love to. Thanks for inviting me."

She glanced at my very round tummy. "Is your baby coming soon?"

"A couple of months to go."

"Is it a boy or a girl?" she wanted to know.

"A girl," I said.

"A little girl will be fun." She smiled. "I only had one child. My boy, Hugh. He's my manager here at Casa. Maybe you'll meet him while you're here." She handed me a soft cashmere wrap. "You'd better put this on. It's chilly down there, especially in the fancy climate-controlled, air-conditioned, oxygenated walk-in that keeps the candy cool."

I accepted the wrap, tossing it over my shoulders, and approached the stairway. It was every bit as pleasing to the eye as the rest of the room, with graceful white-painted spindles supporting the polished wooden railing. I pulled out my phone and began to click a few photos. Doan would like to get an idea of what the place was like. There was a gentle curve to the staircase itself, and it ended on the kind of bleached wide board flooring rarely ever found in newer housing. The long room was a study in white cleanliness. There were several large machines in varying shapes, all of bright stainless steel—the commercial helpers Shirley had talked about, I assumed. There were several tools laid out in neat rows—long-handled forks and pointed spoons, large and small shears, an assortment of knives in graduated sizes. I smiled when I recognized, along the side wall, what had to be a conveyor belt beside stacks of candy boxes in varied sizes, bringing immediate thoughts of Lucy and Ethel popping candy into their mouths. More spots of brightness on long counters of white marble were neatly spaced round copper basins, and the delectable rich aroma of chocolate was everywhere. I approached the nearest counter, where the copper containers reflected the gleaming overhead lights, then looked away quickly, fearing an unwelcome vision—the kind a surface like this often initiated, complete with flashing lights and whirling colors.

I focused instead on a sleek black cat rounding the corner of one of the counters. "Why, hello there, pretty kitty," I said. The cat seemed friendly, approached me, and allowed my tentative pat on the head. I focused the camera on the pretty, long-whiskered face. "I have a nice cat at home," I told it. "His name is O'Ryan."

The cat graced me with a gentle lick on my fingers, then proceeded to creep away from me, nose close to the ground, following a series of spots on the immaculate wood floor. I bent, looking closely at what appeared to me like drops of dark chocolate leading to a doorway covered by a heavy white curtain. I pulled the curtain aside and felt a blast of cold air. "This must be the climate-controlled cold room," I said aloud to the cat, while gathering my cashmere wrap closer. "She wasn't kidding about keeping the candy cold." There was another marble counter in there, piled high with boxed candy marked "Casa de Chocolatte" in gold lettering on a chocolaty brown background. Much different in appearance, I thought as I snapped a photo of the boxes, from the long-ago black script on shiny white boxes of Penny Parker chocolates—but elegant in their own way.

The cat rounded the corner of the counter, and I followed it. I dropped the camera. I didn't have to touch the man in the middle of a pool of that dark stuff to know that he was dead. And cold.

Chapter Three

I picked up the phone and raced for the stairs. I'd already hit 911 before I'd reached the top of the pretty stairway. Shirley Parker was still at the desk. A dark-haired man sat in the chair I'd vacated. Shirley frowned, looking startled. "What's wrong, Lee? Are you all right?"

"There's a dead body in the cold room. I'm calling for help." The man stood and ducked around me, heading for the stairs.

"Don't go down there, Hugh!" Shirley commanded. The man stopped. She stood, starting toward me. "Dead? Who is it?"

I held up a warning hand. "I don't know. It's a man. The police are on the way."

She stopped then too and stood, as if frozen herself. "You don't know who he is? You don't recognize the man?"

"I don't."

"Nothing but bad luck in this damned place," she muttered. The man, her son I presumed, put a steadying arm around her shoulders. I leaned toward her, straining to make out her words. "Now a dead body. Nothing but bad luck from the beginning."

"We'll wait for them here," I told the two. The man gave me a questioning look, while Shirley seemed near tears. "I'm Lee Barrett," I told him. "WICH-TV. I'm doing a documentary on candy."

"Hugh Bingham," he said, as calmly as though this was a normal business meeting, and offered his right hand, his arm still protectively around his mother's shoulders. His grip was firm. "I'll be glad to assist in any way I can."

Assist with the chocolate story? Or with the dead man downstairs?

Shirley silently moved toward the desk, shrugging his arm away, and resumed her seat. Then absently, almost automatically, pushed a pewter candy dish toward me.

"Chocolate?"

I waved the candy away, focused on the front door of the place, anxious for the police—anybody—to arrive. It didn't take very long. A uniformed officer entered first, following the same instruction posted on the door that I had. I shouldn't have been surprised to see Pete right behind the uniform. I'd told him I was headed for Washington Square. He showed Shirley his badge, spoke to her briefly, nodded to her son, then—in an un-cop-like move, took me into his arms. His voice was gruff. "Are you all right? My God, Lee. What's going on here?"

"I don't know. There's a dead man downstairs in the walk-in. I don't know who he is."

By then there seemed to be a sea of blue uniforms in the room. Two of them carried a stretcher between them. Pete said, "You told the dispatcher that there's a body downstairs. Has anyone else gone down there since you called?"

"No," I said. "Not unless there's another stairway somewhere."

"Stay here." He gave my hand a comforting pat. "I'll need to question you. I'll talk to Ms. Parker first." Once again he spoke to Shirley, Hugh Bingham still hovering protectively at her side. Together the three moved to where the police had emerged carrying the stretcher, where a blanket now covered its contents. I watched as Pete moved the top of the blanket. Shirley looked down, nodded briefly, her expression not changing, and said something to Hugh. The police moved out of the front door with their burden while Pete, Shirley Parker, and Hugh Bingham walked toward a small grouping of more fine furniture—a couch and chair and a coffee table—and sat down. Pete pulled the notebook he always carries from his inside breast pocket.

I did as he'd asked. Sitting still in a very comfortable chair within sight of my husband was all I wanted to do at that moment anyway. It isn't every day that I see a dead man in a pool of what I soon realized was a puddle of congealed blood. Was the sight of something so undeniably shocking harmful to my unborn baby? I'd seen awful things before—both in everyday life and especially in the visions produced by my unwanted scrying ability. I thought of the bright brass doors on

Old Clunky and of the shiny reflective copper bowls in the basement of this place. Neither had produced the flashing lights and whirling colors that always preceded the visions.

It hit me suddenly. I hadn't experienced a vision in months. Not since just before we'd found that I was pregnant. Was the pregnancy preventing them? It seemed likely—but it's hardly a question I'd be comfortable asking my obstetrician. But what about what had just happened to me? Could witnessing something that frightening harm my little girl? I could ask my doctor about that. As soon as Pete came back and sat beside me again, I shared my fear with him.

"Women have had healthy babies during slavery and during wars," he said. "Our baby can handle this. But if you don't feel up to answering a few questions about it right now, we can wait a little while."

"I'm sure you're right," I told him. "What do you need to know?"

"Just walk me through it," he suggested. "From when you came inside the house until we arrived after you called 911."

That's exactly what I did, carefully, taking my time, trying to remember every detail. What had Shirley said? What had I noticed?

"Chris King told me what to expect, but even so I was amazed at the beauty of the showroom," I said. "Well, you've just seen it yourself. This furniture alone is museum quality. Anyway, Shirley Parker was sitting at this desk." I pointed. "She recognized my name on my business card and she remembered that she and Aunt Ibby were high school classmates." Pete raised an eyebrow but didn't comment. "Shirley told me that there was no one working in the basement today but that I could go downstairs and look around. She said no one was there except the cat. She gave me this wrap because it was cold down there." Once again, I pulled the soft cashmere around me.

"Did you see anyone downstairs? Anyone at all?" he asked.

"No one, except for . . ."

"Except for the body," he finished the sentence for me. "Description?"

"Yes. I saw him. A man, of course. White shirt. Tan slacks." I closed my eyes, trying to bring back the scene. "Gray hair, neatly trimmed. A little mustache. He looked like somebody who might have worked out regularly. He has—had—a tan."

"Go back to when you first went down the stairs."

"Right. They're curvy, so I walked slowly. My first impression was how clean everything is."

"Tell me what you noticed particularly."

"The shiny things. Stainless steel machines. Copper kettles. I was worried about . . ." I dopped my voice. "You know."

He nodded. "But you were okay with them?"

"Yes. That—thing—hasn't happened to me in a long time."

"Go on."

"There were some tools there that I guess they use for making the candy. Forks and knives and spoons and scissors. I'm sure you noticed those too. And the smell of chocolate. And the conveyor belt."

He smiled. "Lucy and Ethel. What else?"

"I followed the cat. Is he still down there? He was sniffing at what looked like spots of dark chocolate. I followed him. He went behind a heavy white curtain. I guess it's what they call a walk-in cooler. There was a table full of candy boxes in there. The cat moved around the corner of the table and that's when I saw him. The man. Then I ran up the stairs and called 911."

"Did you tell Ms. Parker what you'd found?"

"Sure I did."

"What was her response?"

I paused, thinking about that. "She asked if I knew who it was. I said I didn't. That I'd never seen him before."

"And then what?"

"Her son was with her by then. Hugh. He wanted to go downstairs but she told him not to. She seemed almost—well, almost angry. She said there'd been nothing but bad luck here. *Nothing but bad luck from the beginning.* That's what she said."

"Interesting." He glanced back to where Shirley still sat on the couch beside her son. "She seemed to me to be mostly concerned about her help. Whether they'd want to work where there'd been a body found. I had to tell her they wouldn't be working there at all for a while," he said regretfully. "It's a crime scene."

"That *is* more bad luck," I said, "for her candy business. Does she have any idea who the man is?"

"Oh yes. She identified him right away. He's her ex-husband. Bernie Bingham."

I looked around to see if anybody was listening. Shirley was still across the room, and the police officers seemed to be congregated around the staircase. As

I watched, one of the officers appeared at the head of the stairs with the black cat in his arms.

"Oh, looks like they've found Blackie," Pete said.

"Is that his name?" I was somehow disappointed.

"I don't know. We've been calling him that. Ms. Parker didn't mention a name."

Another officer began to unroll the yellow plastic tape that spells out "CRIME SCENE," festooning it around the lovely white spindles, draping it across the polished wooden railing. I didn't see Shirley there anymore. I hoped she wasn't all alone somewhere in this big, old building.

"Aunt Ibby says that when Shirley and Bernie Bingham got divorced he moved away," I added the gossipy detail. "Aunt Ibby says that Betsy told her that Shirley has to pay *him* alimony."

"I've heard of that before," Pete said. "When the woman has been the main breadwinner, she's supposed to keep the man 'in the manner to which he's become accustomed,' as they say."

"She won't have to worry about that anymore." The words slipped out before I'd had a chance to think them through. I was glad no one heard me except Pete. I had another thought. *Is that a good enough motive for murder?* That one remained unspoken.

The next unspoken thought was about Bruce Doan. Under the circumstances, he could pretty much kiss goodbye any idea of getting free samples of Casa de Chocolatte today.

Chapter Four

Shirley Parker and her son had voluntarily gone in one of the cruisers to the police station to give their reports and the medical examiner's van carrying the body of Bernie Bingham had just pulled away from the curb in front of the Parker mansion when Scott Palmer came through the gorgeous front door. Scott is the current top field reporter for WICH-TV—a position I once held (and sometimes still missed). He spotted me immediately, made eye contact, and started across the room. "I think this would be a good time for me to head for home," I told Pete. He followed my line of vision and stood, effectively blocking Scott's progress.

"Hi, Scott," he said. "You're the first press to get here. I can't give you much information just yet. The chief will be doing a presser from the police station shortly."

"Hi, Pete. Hi, Moon." When I first joined the staff of

WICH-TV I had a brief stint as a call-in psychic named Crystal Moon. Some of the station long-time employees still call me "Moon." "It was on the police band," Scott said. "I came right over. What's up? Who's dead?"

"You'll have to wait for Chief Whaley for the official report," Pete answered, using his stern cop voice. "It's above my pay grade."

"Come on, Moon?" Pleading voice with wide-eyed stare. "Just a hint? I need something. Anything. You understand how this works."

I understood. I looked at Pete for approval and received a slight nod. "A male was found unresponsive at the Parker mansion." I spoke cautiously, guardedly.

"When? Where?"

I looked at my watch. "About half an hour ago. He was in the downstairs area where chocolate candy is made."

Pete held up a warning hand. "I'm about to take my wife home now, Scott. Wait for the presser." He motioned to a nearby uniformed officer. "See Mr. Palmer out and secure the premises."

"Moon?"

"I have to go home and feed O'Ryan, and it's time for Toby's afternoon walk," I told him. Scott knew how important the animals in my life are. "Wait for the chief. He'll have the details." Pete grasped my elbow and we headed for the door as the officer signaled for Scott to leave. The three of us left at the same time. Scott headed for the nearby WICH-TV mobile VW at a run.

"I saw the Jeep out front," Pete said. "Drive straight home. I'll be there as soon as I can."

I didn't have to hear it twice. Home was where I wanted to be. I drove the short distance around the Common to where Winter Street begins on the west side of Washington Square, passed my Aunt Ibby's house, and gratefully turned into the driveway behind our half of the cutest duplex on the street. It wasn't exactly true that I had to feed O'Ryan just then, but Toby was going to need a walk pretty soon. Even though my aunt and I share custody of the big cat, he decides for himself where he wants to reside at any given time. Besides, there's always a bowl full of dry cat food available—if he's really hungry—at both houses.

Once inside I waited in the sunroom for Pete's cruiser to round the corner into our backyard parking spaces, then realized that I was holding my breath. The swishy sound of the cat door opening as O'Ryan strolled in reminded me to breathe. He passed by me with barely a sniff of acknowledgment and headed straight on into the living room. "Okay, cat," I said. "We'll wait for Pete in there." I followed him. Toby was already standing impatiently in the narrow entryway beside the front door.

I sat in a dark blue armchair facing the window. O'Ryan got a better view by sitting on the windowsill. That's another good thing about old houses that newer places don't have: wide windowsills with plenty of room for plants or tchotchkes or cats.

A glance at the banjo clock over the mantelpiece told me it was almost time for the early news—and probably time for the promised presser from Chief Whaley. I turned on the TV, still keeping an eye on that window. Scott opened the show by reading the breaking news headline, starting with one of his trademark long stares into the camera. I recognized the Salem police station behind him. "There's been an unexplained death at one of Salem's most famous Washington Square mansions," Scott intoned. "Chief Tom Whaley will join us shortly with details. Meanwhile, here's the scene in front of the Parker estate, now the home of the Casa de Chocolatte candy business, taken earlier today." A video of the beautiful old home with police vehicles in front of it and a police presence of uniformed officers standing guard on the granite front steps to the place filled the screen. I could see a tiny bit of my blue Jeep at the very edge of the shot. "A 911 call from this house in late afternoon reported a man found unresponsive in the basement of the building, the part where the actual manufacturing of the chocolate candies takes place." The camera zeroed in on the covered area in front of the police station where these pressers usually happened. "Here comes Chief Whaley."

The chief doesn't enjoy doing these things and always keeps them as short as he can get away with. Media interest in this death had grown. I recognized two reporters from Boston stations. The chief, tall, distinguished, and handsome in a dress uniform and a chest full of medals, approached the microphone. "Thank you for coming. I'll attempt to update you on the matter of the death of the man identified as Bernie Bingham." A split screen showed a studio portrait of a handsome gray-haired man with a neat, narrow mustache. I knew it was the man I'd seen on the floor of the candy shop. "Mr. Bingham was found unresponsive in the basement of the Parker Estate," the chief continued. "Mr. Bingham was once married to Ms. Shirley

Parker, owner and operator of a candy company. Mr. Bingham has lived in another state for many years." He consulted a sheet of paper and read the exact address of the mansion. "Our investigation indicates foul play. The deceased died from a wound in the back of his neck inflicted by a sharp instrument. We are continuing a thorough investigation into the circumstances of Mr. Bingham's death. There has been some significant progress in the case, the details of which will be forthcoming later. Certain materials have been turned over to the forensics unit for further analysis. Thank you." He turned away from the mic and the shouted questions began.

"Do you have the weapon that killed him?" The question came from one of the WBZ-TV reporters.

"There have been several items collected and sent to the forensics lab," the chief said. "I'll have no further comment on that at this time." I thought immediately of the display of tools I'd seen. Several of them could have inflicted a deep wound. Scissors, knives, even a pointed candy thermometer. I thought too of the pool of blood. Scott managed to get in a question. "Do you have any suspects?"

Chief dodged the question. "A state forensics team is working on new evidence we've gathered. That's all we have for now. I'll notify the press as soon as there is any further relevant information. Good afternoon." He moved quickly toward the entrance to the station, looking relieved as he pushed the door open and escaped into the building.

O'Ryan gave a purry meow from his perch on the sill as Pete's cruiser came into view in front of the house and moved toward the driveway leading to the yard. "Here comes Daddy," I told the cat, easily slipping into the new term for my husband. "Daddy's home."

I turned off the TV and clipped Toby's leash to his collar, and with the cat in the lead, we hurried to the sunroom. We watched as Pete backed the car into his usual space and climbed out. He saw us there behind the glass, gave us a smile and a wave as he locked the vehicle, and hurried toward us. I pulled the door open, so glad that he was home, safe here with me and our baby and the pets—realizing in just that moment how extremely stressful my day had been. "I love you," I said.

"I love you," he answered, holding me close

I felt baby girl kick. He felt it too. "She wants her name," he said. I handed him Toby's leash and put a plastic bag into my pocket, and together we walked around the house and back onto Winter Street.

"Yes," I agreed. "Which grandmother gets the honor? My Grammy Eleanor or your Nana Lana?" We'd already agreed on the namesakes. We just hadn't figured out the order. We knew her middle name would be Marie, for Pete's sister—because we both love her so much and Marie goes beautifully with just about any first name. Would it be Lana Marie or Eleanor Marie? We were almost ready to simply toss a coin and let fate decide. "Lana Eleanor, Eleanor Lana" I singsonged as we approached the grassy area behind the Civil War memorial that had become sort of a mini dog park.

"Wait a minute. Do that again." Pete's eyes were wide. I did. "Lana Eleanor, Eleanor Lana?"

"That's it," he announced with conviction. "They'll have two letters apiece. *E L* for Eleanor and *L A* for Lana. Ella!"

"Ella," I echoed. "Ella Marie. I love it."

He bent and spoke to my belly. "Ella Marie Mondello," he said. "How do you like your name?"

She gave a hefty kick. "She likes it," I said. Toby woofed his approval too. I deposited the doggy litter bag into a tall gray receptacle. Baby's name decided upon, I brought the conversation back to—well, back to murder. "So can you tell me what happened with Shirley and Hugh? Are they suspects?" I'm never sure how much information Pete can share with me when he's working a case. When I was a field reporter he couldn't tell me much of anything, but neither a program director—nor even a documentary executive—deals with hard news, so he's quite a bit more lenient with details these days.

Anyway, I was the one who found the body this time!

"We'll know more once the ME finishes his examination," Pete said. "We don't know for sure how long Bingham's body was there, because of the refrigeration, but it may have been more than an hour. Doc says that the dark color of the blood you saw was caused by the oxygenator. Then we need to figure out who might have been in the house at the time of his death. Conversely, we'll want to know who *wasn't* in the house at that time. For now though, to answer your question, yes. Shirley and Bingham's son were in the house, so they are theoretically suspects."

"When the ME finishes, who do they release Bernie

to? To Shirley? She'll probably have to pick up the tab for his funeral anyway." I wondered aloud, "Or will his son have to deal with it?"

"Shirley says there's a girlfriend in New Hampshire," Pete said. "We're trying to contact the woman. Trisha Violette. We'll need to talk to her too. She may have come here with him. If she did, by now she's heard of his death."

Chapter Five

Bernie Bingham's girlfriend, Trisha Violette, had indeed come to Salem with him. She'd shown up at the police station as soon as she'd heard that he was dead. Pete got the call right in the middle of dinner and had to go back to work.

I got the rest of the story after midnight when Pete climbed into bed beside me. O'Ryan was curled up at the foot of the big bed. I turned off *Tarot Time with River North* just before the late movie started. River was showing *The Conjuring*. Pretty darned scary. I'd already seen it. "What happened with the girlfriend?" I asked.

According to Pete, she'd stormed into the station demanding that they give her the contents of Bernie's wallet so that she could catch a bus back to New Hampshire. She and Bernie had come to Salem to tell Shirley that they needed a bigger allowance. Prices had gone up on everything, Trisha had insisted, and since Bernie only worked for a few months in the winter as a ski instructor and sometimes gave tennis and golf lessons, they'd lived almost entirely on his alimony. Now that he was gone she was penniless.

"She's quite a piece of work," Pete said. "Mad as all get-out at him for dying."

"Is she a suspect too?" I wanted to know.

"Sure she is. They came to Salem by bus and she was still in Salem when he died, and she let fly quite a few uncomplimentary names for Bernie. "*Dumb old SOB* was about the mildest one." He smiled. "She has quite a vocabulary."

"Mad at him for dying?" I asked, surprised by the statement.

"I don't think she meant the things she said about him. The names she called him. I got the distinct impression that she was very fond of the old guy."

"Yes. People mourn in different ways," I said. "Was he a lot older than she is?"

"I'd say quite a lot," he answered. "She's maybe in her late twenties, early thirties. She's pretty in a Barbie doll sort of way."

"Aunt Ibby said that Bernie Bingham was the handsomest man in Salem when he married Shirley," I told him. "And if that portrait of him on the news is recent, he was still darned good-looking."

"You saw him."

"Yeah, but he wasn't at his best right then."

"True that. Let's get some sleep. I have to go in early again. You?"

"I'm meeting Francine at nine. We're going to do

the video at the Pepper Company, then scoot over to Curly Girl Candy Shop. They have all the nostalgic stuff. Sky Bars. Necco Wafers. Sugar Daddies." I thought back to some of my own old favorites. "I wonder if they still have those clear barley candy lollipops? They used to make a red one in the shape of a lobster."

"If they do, you should treat yourself to one."

"I will. Good night." I rolled over for his kiss.

It seemed like no time at all had passed before the smell of coffee brewing and the sound of country music coming from the kitchen radio told me that morning had dawned and Pete was up. I made the bed and selected stretchy jeans, a loose shirt, and low-heeled shoes—casual enough for candy shopping, but professional enough for some on-camera commentary—dashed to the bathroom, and prepared myself for the day. Pete, of course, was dressed, groomed, looking good, and had already walked the dog.

"Gotta go, babe," he said. "Chief's all over this Bernie Bingham case. He arrested Bernie once years ago on an armed robbery charge. Seems that Bernie wanted a Rolex watch, so he pulled a gun on a jeweler. Shirley hired a big shot lawyer and got him out of it. She paid off the jeweler and got him to say he was mistaken about the gun. Chief says Bernie got to thinking he could do anything he wanted to and Shirley and her money would always bail him out."

"He must have been like a big, spoiled kid. Good looks and an endless stream of money can be a bad combination, I guess." I almost felt sorry for the man. Sometimes having money can bring problems. Between the significant inheritance from my parents, Johnny's insurance, and some excellent advice from Aunt Ibby's financial advisors, I am what might be considered a fairly wealthy woman. It took me a long time to work up the courage to tell Pete—I was afraid he'd be uncomfortable about it. But his reaction had made me love him even more. "Great," he'd said. "Now I don't have to worry about college for our kids." It's nice to know there's money if we need it, but I surely don't throw it around.

We agreed that if we both had time we'd meet for lunch. "That is, if you're not full of candy by noon," he joked.

"One lollipop is my limit," I promised

"I'll text you," he said. "We can figure out time and place."

Francine Hunter is a top videographer and we always enjoy working together. Back when I was doing real news, we found ourselves in some tight spots more than once. It was fun to climb back into the mobile unit with my old friend. "Candy shops, huh?" she said when I told her about the assignment Doan gave us. "We can't find a much more pleasant destination than that, can we?"

"Hey, I've already found a dead body in a chocolate factory," I reminded her.

"Oh, well. That. Yeah. But that kind of lightning probably doesn't strike twice in the same candy bar, right?" She grinned.

"That's kind of a mixed metaphor," I said, "and I'm not an expert on lightning, but let's do the job Doan expects from us and hope for the best in the dead body department."

"So do we still get to do the video in the Parker mansion—I mean after they clean up the body mess?" she wondered.

"I'll have to check with Shirley Parker," I said. "But I should think that after being closed while the investigation goes on, and with Halloween candy season coming on, they could use a nice promotional boost—especially when it's free. Of course, some people might think doing it so soon after somebody died there is in bad taste," I worried.

Francine smothered a laugh. "Since when does bad taste bother Doan?"

"True. Let's start with Ye Olde Pepper Candy Companie," I said. "It's a good story, and the shop is really pretty."

It is a good story, and I was sure the viewers of WICH-TV would like to know how, back in 1806, Mary Spencer used a donated barrel of sugar to create Salem Gibralters—a peppermint-flavored confection so pure that it remained fresh in all climates—and that a woman in that day could start and own a business. She bought a wagon and peddled the candies through the streets of Salem. The company was later sold to John Pepper, who created America's first "stick candy," the Black Jack, a hard candy made with molasses that some say tastes like the top of a crème brûlée. Both confections are still made with the same ingredients today.

We did the video, came away with a second goodly haul of Doan's coveted freebies, and moved on to Curly Girls. It's always a nostalgia rush there with all the old-time favorites. We filmed our way through the cute shop, where they have Halloween candy year-round. I bought my lollipop, tucked it away to savor later, and accepted a generous bag of old-time penny candies for Doan.

We arrived back in the WICH-TV parking lot with a satisfactory amount of samples and nary a dead body to report. Francine dashed inside to get going on the editing of our day's work. I dropped off my stash of treats with Rhonda and headed for my glass office cubicle—partly to make sure that all the t's were crossed and i's dotted on my program director schedule, while at the same time getting a bird's-eye view of the next-door newsroom and Scott Palmer's desk.

I'd barely had time to sit in my swivel chair when Scott tapped on the glass and gave me the familiar thumb-and-pinkie "call me" sign. I tapped in his number on my phone. "What's up?"

"Have you met the girlfriend yet?" he wanted to know.

"What girlfriend?" I asked, assuming that he was talking about Trisha Violette, but not sure. You never know with Scott.

"Bernie Bingham's most recent," he said. "I thought you might have run into her at the Parker place. She was over there this morning, pounding on the door, demanding to see Ms. Parker."

"I'm sure they didn't let her in."

"They didn't, even when she ran around to the back of the place and tried to get in through the bulkhead entrance to the cellar."

So there is a second entrance. I knew there had to be one in a house that size.

"I'd love to get an interview with her," Scott went on. "Do you know where they lived?"

"In New Hampshire," I told him, thinking about both Trisha Violette and that second entrance at the same time. *She could have been in the basement before I even arrived there.*

"That's what I heard too," he said, "but a cop friend told me that she was trying to get hold of Bernie's wallet so she could get bus fare home."

"I heard that too," I agreed.

"They don't want her to leave the state though," he went on. "So they've put her in some kind of 'approved facility,' whatever that means. I thought you might know where she is."

"I don't, Scott," I said honestly. "I knew about her trying to get money to go home, and I didn't know she was still in Salem. But if you *do* get a chance to interview her, be sure to have the bleep button handy. I hear she has quite a colorful vocabulary."

Chapter Six

Pete's promised call came shortly after noon. "If you're free right now I can pick you up out by Ariel's bench and we'll grab a sandwich someplace," he said. "Ariel's bench" is a comfortable, sturdy wooden bench, a pleasant place to sit overlooking one of the prettiest parts of Salem Harbor. It's located at the edge of the WICH-TV parking lot, next to the low granite seawall. It was placed there by a local coven in memory of Ariel Constellation, a witch who once hosted a late-night show called *Nightshades*. O'Ryan (she'd named him Orion) had been Ariel's cat—some say her familiar. In Salem a witch's familiar is always respected and sometimes feared. As it turned out, I inherited her excellent cat—and my bestie, River North, wound up with that late-show slot.

Pete's unmarked Ford was already in the lot when I stepped out of the darkened studio, blinking in the bright sunlight. He waited beside the bench, holding the passenger door open for me. "What do you say?" he asked. "Grilled cheese indoors at Red's or roast beef on the deck at Bill and Bob's?"

I opted for the always-good roast beef sandwich. We drove across the Beverly Bridge, picked up our sammies, fries, and drinks at the drive-through, then parked on the deck out back overlooking the water. It wasn't until then that I noticed a manila folder on the dashboard in front of Pete. I pointed. "What's that?"

"It's a kind of dossier on your friend Bernie. Chief is really ticked off about all the times Shirley has rescued him. Apparently, it continued even after the divorce." He shook his head. "Weird, huh? Old Bernie burned a lot of people, and Shirley never stopped buying his way out of trouble."

"Not my friend." I fake-pouted. "Am I allowed to see it?"

"I brought it because you have some street contacts we don't have. People who might know some of the folks mentioned," he said. "Chief knows what I'm doing."

I knew right away who he was talking about. "Aunt Ibby and Betsy Leavitt and Louisa Abney-Babcock." I recited the names of my aunt and her friends, who think of themselves as a cross between *Charlie's Angels* and *The Golden Girls*. "You're right," I said. "Betsy knows everybody who is anybody and Louisa knows everybody's net worth and Aunt Ibby claims to have a 'master's degree in snooping.'" More than once, the over-sixty trio had been able to help the police with some hard-to-find information. "I'll call my aunt and find out when the next meeting of the Angels is scheduled so we can run this by them." I tapped the folder. "If anyone can figure this out, it's those girls."

Lunch finished, we headed back to Derby Street. With a quick kiss goodbye beside Ariel's bench, I tapped my code into the keyboard next to the studio door and moved from the bright sunlight into the cool darkness of my workday world. River's set was lit, which surprised me because River doesn't usually get there until the eleven o'clock news is on. I walked toward the set and saw that some redecorating was happening. The starry sky and silver moon backdrop now featured some recognizable constellations instead of the random arrangement of heavenly bodies that had been there since Ariel's days. I liked the effect, and I was sure River would love it. I complimented Therese, the set designer, and thought about the many changes that had happened since the first day I'd arrived at WICH-TV expecting a job as an experienced field reporter and winding up as a very amateur psychic. Now I had my own office, an occasional stint as a field reporter, a responsible job as program director, and even my little-used title as "Historical Documentary Executive Director." I pushed open the metal door at the back of the studio, passed the newsroom, and, with the manila file under one arm, unlocked the door of my cubicle. With my back to the busy room on the other side of the glass, I dialed my aunt's number.

I explained as briefly and succinctly as I could what I guessed was contained in the folder and what Pete thought the Angels might be able to do with it. "He thinks there are probably names you three will recog-

nize and situations you might know something about—
things that police methods would not ever be able to
ferret out from those involved."

"I wouldn't be a bit surprised," she said, not unex-
pectedly. "As it turns out, we have a regular meeting
planned for tomorrow—remember, we meet when *Midsomer Murders* is on, and we relate Investigator Barnaby's crime-solving expertise to whatever *our* current
puzzle might be. In this case, we'll try to put together
the pieces of Bernie Bingham's misspent life. I like the
similar names, don't you? Bernie and Barnaby? If you
can drop the folder off on your way home this afternoon, I'll make some copies for the others. We've decided to invite Michael to join us for the ferreting. For
the murderer's point of view, don't you know?"

Michael Martell is the owner of the other half of our
sweet duplex and has proven to be an excellent neighbor. He is also a well-known mystery author; as Fenton
Bishop, he writes the bestselling *Antique Alley Mysteries*. Also as Bishop, he teaches creative writing at the
Tabitha Trumbull Academy of the Arts ("the Tabby").
Besides all that, he served twenty years in prison for
killing his wife—a terrible act that he has since sincerely repented. He insisted on serving the full twenty
years even though he could have been released sooner.
Scott Palmer enjoys referring to him as "your friendly
neighborhood murderer." I didn't mind at all if she invited Michael to join in the ferreting, and I promised to
drop off the folder later. In fact, I realized that I wouldn't
mind being part of that meeting myself.

I busied myself with a to-do list, which involves
writing tasks that need doing on varicolored sticky

notes and placing them onto the glass wall beside my desk where I can't miss seeing them. Works for me. I'd written about half a dozen, winding up with a reminder to buy a gift for Wanda the Weather Girl's upcoming birthday, and another note—on a hot pink sticky— telling me to buy the gift from one of the *Shopping Salem* show sponsors.

The folder on my desk was too tempting. Pete hadn't told me not to look at it. I opened it. There were names and addresses of people Bernie had cheated, stolen from, or otherwise wronged. There were stapled copies of arrest warrants, bonds posted, receipts for attorney's fees, and paperwork indicating that many cases against Bernie had been dismissed. That man had owed a lot to Shirley for sure.

Or maybe not.

Maybe she could have encouraged his strengths instead of his weaknesses. I thought of the child growing within me—and of my own wealth. *Bernie*, I thought. *If nothing else, you'll serve as a horrible example of what harm too much love mixed with too much money can do to a person.*

Ella Marie Mondello, I promise you that we will always encourage your strengths.

Another thought—a bad one—popped into my head.

Dear God, I hope Shirley hasn't raised her son, Hugh, to be an adult spoiled brat too.

Chapter Seven

At a few minutes before five I checked Rhonda's whiteboard to see if there was anything special lined up for me on the next day. I assumed that if there was to be some reporting on the "Chocolate Shop Murder"—that's what local media had tagged Bernie's death—Scott would have the assignment. That was perfectly fine with me. Being the body-finder was more than enough involvement to suit me, and I'd already told Mr. Doan that considering my condition, I'd just as soon somebody else covered the nitty-gritty. The only note on the board for me suggested that I visit some more candy shops.

I texted Pete that I intended to stop at Aunt Ibby's on the way home. He answered that he'd meet me there. That made sense. I was sure he had some special instructions for the girls to go along with the printed material. Although I still had one key to Aunt Ibby's front door, when I arrived on Winter Street and parked the Jeep in front of the house, I chose to ring the doorbell. I heard the chime ringing out "The Impossible Dream" and saw my aunt through the glass side panel as she approached the door. O'Ryan wasn't at the window, so I figured that he'd greet me at my own house later.

She pulled the door open wide. She looked younger than the sixtysomething she admitted to in a royal blue silk blouse and gray-patterned palazzo pants. "Come in, come in, my dear Maralee. You look beautiful. You so remind me of your dear mother when she was carrying you." She embraced me in a warm hug, then pointed to the street. "Look. There's Pete's car pulling in right behind yours." We stood together on the front steps and welcomed Pete.

"It sure smells good in here" was Pete's first comment when we stepped into the foyer.

"Beef Burgundy," she said. "Rupert is coming over for dinner. I made plenty. Would you like to join us?" Rupert Pennington is one of my aunt's favorite "gentleman friends," and he's the executive director of the Tabby as well.

"Thanks anyway," I said, not wanting to intrude on her dinner date, "but I just wanted to drop these papers off."

She accepted the folder and, probably noting the disappointment on my husband's face regarding the rejected beef Burgundy, smiled. "How about I just ladle a bit of the stew into a plastic container and you take it home with you? I'll save you making dinner."

"If it's not too much trouble—" I began.

"That would be just great." Pete was enthusiastic. "Thank you."

I like to think that my cooking has improved since Pete and I first met—and I'm sure it has—but it's no-where near up to Aunt Ibby's standards. "Thank you," I echoed gratefully.

"About the information in the folder," Pete said, "it's confidential, of course."

"Of course," my aunt agreed. "The girls know that."

"Any information any of you have about the people mentioned will be most appreciated—by the chief, and by me."

The doorbell chimed again, and I moved aside—which placed me smack-dab in front of the vintage hall tree with its full-length mirror. I looked away quickly and turned my back to the shining reflective surface. That mirror, far too many times, had produced the flashing lights, the whirling colors, and the unwelcome visions that had plagued me since childhood. Fortunately, this time, it had shown only a brief glimpse of a very pregnant redhead before Mr. Pennington's arrival.

It was one of those moments when everyone spoke at once. There were "How're you doings" and "Good to see yous" and "Fine, thank yous."

When the hall grew silent, Aunt Ibby rested her hand on Mr. Pennington's tweed-jacketed, leather-elbow-patched arm. "You're looking well, Rupert," she told him.

He smiled broadly. "You like me because I'm a scoundrel," he said.

What an odd thing to say. Pete and I looked at one another.

My aunt put one fist under her chin and appeared to be concentrating. She returned his smile. "Harrison Ford to Carrie Fisher," she announced. "In *The Empire Strikes Back*!"

It's a game the two movie buffs have played almost from the first time they met, and it still takes me by surprise just about every time they do it.

"I understand that you're doing another documentary. On confectionary treats." Mr. Pennington, still smiling, addressed me.

"Not exactly a documentary," I explained. "It's more of a promotional piece for the Halloween candy season. But how did you know about it? None of it has aired yet."

"I stopped at the Pepper company for my occasional Gibralter. They're very excited about the TV publicity. I told them that you're a friend of mine and they threw in a Black Jack." Big grin. "It pays to have friends in high places."

Aunt Ibby had reappeared by then with the promised offering of beef Burgundy.

"Jacob's doctor to Jacob in *Jacob's Ladder*," she said.

"Good one, Ibby." Mr. Pennington offered a high five—ignored because her hands were full. "We weren't even playing the game!"

"It was almost cheating," she apologized. "River showed that one just a few days ago. Scary horror stuff, but that line just stuck in my head."

Movie line cheating or not, I was seriously impressed. Pete accepted the plastic box. Aunt Ibby accepted the high five.

"Thanks for this, Ibby," Pete said. "We'd better go right along home before it gets cold." With his free hand, he opened the door. We were about to step outside when O'Ryan bolted into the foyer and zipped out the door ahead of us.

"I think he wants to go home with you," my aunt said.

"Maybe he's following the stew," I suggested. We said our goodbyes and got back into our individual cars while O'Ryan trotted away in the direction of our house. When I pulled into our driveway he was already sitting on the back steps. As soon as he saw me there, he pushed open the cat door and went inside.

I saw that Pete had backed into his space. I expected that he'd carry the stew directly to the kitchen in a hurry. I put soup bowls and silverware on the table, and O'Ryan waited beside his empty red bowl. Toby waited beside his blue one. I opened the refrigerator and selected their individually packaged fresh food. Several minutes passed and still no Pete. No beef Burgundy. The animals and I retraced our steps back to the sunroom just as Pete unlocked the door.

"I ran into Michael Martell in the backyard," Pete said. "He wanted to talk about Bernie Bingham."

"Everybody wants to talk about him lately. What did Michael say?"

"Well, you know, I guess, that considering all the time he spent in prison, Michael has met some pretty shady people," Pete said.

"I know," I said. "He told me once that he uses some of them as characters in his books."

"Michael says that, according to his sources, Bernie made some really bad enemies." Serious cop voice. "He burned some of the wrong people. He wanted me to know that it isn't a good idea for you to get involved with this chocolate factory mess. He wouldn't want you to get in the way of some professional killers." He put the plastic box on the table. O'Ryan looked up from his empty bowl and gave it an impatient nudge with one big paw. We know that beef Burgundy is not included in the proper diet for cats and dogs, but we allowed a spoonful of the liquid on top of each of their regular food so they wouldn't feel left out.

"I promise I won't. I'm working on the Halloween candy piece. Nothing else." I crossed my heart and put the rapidly cooling beef Burgundy into the microwave for a minute.

"We've finished the on-site investigation at the candy factory. Can you stay away from there from now on?"

I hesitated. I knew he wanted an unqualified "yes."

"Francine and I still haven't done the video we promised. Doan will be expecting it. Hugh Bingham has offered to help us with it." My voice sounded very small, even to me.

Chapter Eight

It turned out that between my program director duties and the remaining candy shop calls I didn't have time for revisiting Casa de Chocolatte anyway. My Saturday morning business guy called in sick, so I had to cobble together a "best of" presentation from his old shows. Then one of Ranger Rob's little buckaroos turned up with the measles, so the whole set had to be sanitized in a hurry. A couple of the smaller sweetshops that sold candy along with snacks and sodas wanted to be included in the Halloween special, so Francine and I did some quick filming and not a little nibbling in those places. One of them sold doughnuts and had my favorite powdered sugar ones. I tried to use restraint, with minimal success.

The Salem Common is at the end of our street—a big, beautiful oasis in the middle of a busy city, lovely at every time of year. Flower beds, bright with seasonal flowers, provide flashes of color among grassy paths. The old-fashioned popcorn wagon was in place and happy kids crowded around the swing sets and monkey bars while young moms, ever watchful, chatted together. I looked forward to being part of that group before too long. Stacia, the pigeon lady, was seated on her usual bench, tossing treats to her expectant audience of cooing gray birds. A man's voice interrupted the "cobweb clearing" aspect of my stroll.

"Mrs. Mondello?" Hugh Bingham approached from a row of benches on the south side of the common, almost in the shade of the Hawthorne Hotel. "I thought that was you." He fell into step beside me. "It's a great day for a walk, isn't it?"

I nodded agreement. "Yes, it certainly is."

He smiled. *He has a nice smile. Orthodontically perfect.*

"I have to get away from the smell every so often." He waved in the general direction of the Parker mansion. "It gets to you after a while."

The smell?

"Chocolate," he said. "As nice as it is in small doses, breathing it in for eight or ten hours will give you a headache. I try to get outside at about this time every afternoon."

"I've never thought about it," I admitted. "I had a friend once who worked in a perfume shop. She said the same thing about the smell giving her a headache."

"She was right."

Where was this conversation leading? I had nothing to add, so I remained silent, wishing he'd go away.

"I just want you to know I'm sorry," he said.

"Sorry?" It was an odd statement.

"I mean, about what you found. What you saw. My father. Dead. I'm sorry." The smile was gone. "It must have been terrible for you."

I appreciated the thought, but wasn't crazy about continuing the conversation. Would a simple *Thank you* suffice? I tried it. "Thank you."

"Can I offer you a year's supply of chocolates?"

He was starting to creep me out. I patted my belly. "No thanks. I'm watching my weight."

"Oh, well. I'll tell Mother that I tried."

"Yes. Tell her thank you for me. I appreciate the thought." *And please go away.*

"I'll do that. I expect we'll see you again soon when we set up a date for the Halloween candy shoot." The smile was back. "I'll call you."

"Yes. Let's do it soon so Casa de Chocolatte will get a good spot in the rotation." *Let's get it done ASAP* was my silent thought. *My detective husband doesn't want me anywhere near the place.* I walked a little faster.

"We appreciate the publicity."

"Okay. We'll be glad to have your help with it." We were getting close to the break in the fence right across from the corner of Winter Street. I was almost jogging. I raised one hand in a ladylike wave and headed for the exit.

"I'll call you," he said again.

"Okay." I headed for Winter Street and didn't look back. *This is like trying to get rid of an unwanted high school boyfriend*, I thought.

It felt good to be back on Winter Street. There's something calming and comfortable about the tall, old trees lining the street, the sturdy Civil War memorial on the corner, the brick sidewalks, the graceful street-lamps, the rows of attractive homes on both sides. Aunt Ibby's house came before ours. I'd already decided to pop in there for a minute, just in case Hugh Bingham had followed me across North Washington Square.

I rang the bell, then used my key and ducked inside. "It's me, Aunt Ibby," I called. Trying not to be seen, I peeked out of the tall, narrow window beside the door. The well-trimmed bushes in the side yard blocked my view to the right. I didn't care about the left side, so I looked straight across the street.

"Hello, Maralee." Aunt Ibby joined me in the foyer. "What in the world are you looking for?"

"N-nothing," I stammered. "I mean . . . I'm not sure."

"Come into the living room and sit down," she ordered. "You're upset about something. You can't fool me." She moved closer, looked down at my tummy. "Are you all right?"

"Oh, yes. Ella Marie and I are both fine. I was walking home from work—walking off the effects of a powdered sugar doughnut I ate earlier—and I ran into Shirley Parker's son, Hugh—who is probably a perfectly nice man—but for some reason—maybe because I'm pregnant—I don't like being around him." I peeked out that window again. "I thought he might be . . . well, following me."

"You just sit down and relax. I'm going to call Betsy. I'm sure he moves in the same circles she does—you know—the beautiful people." She picked up her phone. "Let's see what she knows. As you say, he's probably a perfectly nice man."

I sat, as ordered. "The beef Burgundy was wonderful," I said, belatedly remembering my manners.

"I'm glad you enjoyed it. Hello, Betts? I'm checking up on a man." She paused, and then laughed. "No. Good heavens, no. Not for me. It's for Maralee. You know Hugh Bingham, don't you? Shirley Parker's boy?"

There was a pause, during which my aunt nodded her head frequently, uttering a few "Uh-huhs" and "No kiddings" and the occasional "Wow!" Finally she said, "Thanks, Betsy. I'll pass that on to Maralee."

I could barely wait for the report. "What did she say?"

"She knows him. She says he was sent to all the right prep schools and summer camps and a small Vermont college, so when he arrived back in Salem to join the Parker family's candy business he knew hardly anyone here." She frowned. "Poor kid."

"A poor little rich kid story, isn't it?" I commented.

"It is. Betsy said that since he got back he's become something of a social climber. Of course, the Parkers have a pedigree as long as your arm, but that Bingham last name has been a curse around here. His late daddy burned a lot of people—and a lot of important bridges to the movers and shakers in the community."

"I can imagine that happening," I said. "'The sins of the fathers' and all that."

"Exactly. Betsy checked with Louisa about the financial situation. Bernie Bingham left a lot of debt, even beyond the many bills that Shirley has already paid."

"That's not helping him socially either, I guess."

"That's right. Money is important in the circles he wants to move in," she pointed out. "But on the positive side, he's good-looking and he has impeccable manners. He drives a fine car—a late-model Range Rover, thanks to his mama's generosity—she drives a vintage Bentley, by the way—and he lives at the Parker Mansion's excellent address."

"That's true—I mean about his looks and manners. He's offered to be helpful in producing the video Doan wants. He's probably quite likable," I told her. "There's just something off-putting about him. I don't know what it is."

"Maybe it's just the Bingham last name," she offered.

Chapter Nine

I had several things to think about as I left Aunt Ibby's house and proceeded along Winter Steet to our place. First of all, I needed to get the video date with Shirley Parker firmed up. I needed to get over this creepy feeling about Hugh Bingham too. Completing the video would take care of both problems and Pete wouldn't have to worry about my being associated with those people anymore. One more problem that had to be solved pretty quickly was the creation of a proper room for Baby Ella Marie. The room we'd designated as a spare room was on the second floor. That would not do, since the master bedroom is on the first floor and baby must be close to us. Pete's den would need to be moved upstairs and the resulting empty space would soon be turned into a pinky, lacy, pretty room for our soon-to-arrive little princess.

We'd already contacted my favorite handyman, George

Washington, who'd been so helpful in getting the Salem International Museum looking shipshape, to do the painting. Pete had told me that Michael Martell had offered to help move the den furniture upstairs when the time came.

I parked in my regular space under the maple tree. Pete hadn't arrived home yet. I glanced over at the adjoining property—Michael's backyard. It looked very different from ours. Other than a few potted geraniums, there was nothing other than the lone maple tree in the expanse of neatly trimmed grass behind our half of the house, while his was a veritable sea of vegetation. Banks of flowering annuals in shades of orange and yellow bordered neat rows of pole beans, varicolored squash and pumpkins, lacy carrot tops. There were even window boxes full of herbs. I recognized basil and thyme because Aunt Ibby grew those in pots in her kitchen, but Michael had many more on display. The gardener himself, in white overalls, waved to me over a trim wintergreen box hedge.

"Good morning, Lee," he called. "It's a beautiful day in the neighborhood, isn't it?"

"It certainly is," I told him. "I'm just admiring what you've done with your yard. It looks wonderful and it even smells good."

"It's getting there," he said. "It's kind of a new hobby for me. I made the mistake of dropping in on a new class on urban farming at the Tabby and got totally hooked on it. I'm learning as I go along."

"It's perfectly beautiful," I said, meaning it sincerely. O'Ryan, seated on the back step, gave a purry meow of agreement. It was good to be home. O'Ryan scooted through his cat door while I unlocked the French door entrance to the sunroom. Although the front door entrance to our house is lovely, it's the back door entrance that always makes me smile. My beautiful carousel horse is there, forever proudly prancing as he once did on a long-ago merry-go-round. There's a bentwood bench I acquired from an old friend of Aunt Ibby's, and just above it, there's a framed photo of Aunt Ibby and my mother, Carrie, sitting on that very bench. There are lots of indoor plants too, all enjoying the sunny exposure through the many windows.

Pete had offered to bring home take-out pizza and salads from the Pizza Pirate. Maybe I'd need to walk to work and back again, to exercise the pizza pounds off. I'd plan to leave the office a bit earlier or later too, so my time wouldn't coincide with my recent unwanted walking partner's schedule.

I set the table with paper plates for the pizza slices and wedding china bowls for the salad. I filled O'Ryan's red dish with his favorite refrigerated food and Toby's blue one with his. I kept an eye on the front window, watching for Pete's car from around the large cat on the windowsill. As soon as he spotted the unmarked Ford, O'Ryan gave another of those purry meows and scooted toward the sunroom. I stood to follow him. At the same time, the front doorbell chimed. It was one of those moments where you stand still as you try to decide which way to go.

Pete would let himself in, but the front door wouldn't answer itself. I hurried to the narrow entryway, stood on tiptoes, and peeked through the tiny peephole—the only visual access to the outside. I thought about the tall side window on Aunt Ibby's house. I would trade my wide windowsills for a skinny glass window beside the front door any day. All the peephole showed was a fluff of blond hair. There was a short blonde on my doorstep. A Girl scout selling cookies? Only one way to find out. I opened the door.

My caller was not a Girl Scout for sure. The blonde was petite and pretty, with a curvy figure and T-shirt and shorts both tight enough to show it off to advantage. She smiled, flashing dimples. "Hello, Mrs. Mondello," she said.

I'd never seen her before in my life.

"What are you doing here?" Pete's voice came from the living room at my left. In another instant he was by my side. "What are you doing here?" he asked again. I looked from one to the other.

Who is this person? And what IS she doing here?

Sensing my confusion, Pete explained. "This is Trisha Violette," he said. "She was Bernie Bingham's— um—friend."

The woman focused a blue-eyed gaze on me. "I think maybe you can help me, Mrs. Mondello. I've seen you helping people on TV before."

Pete had one hand on the door, as though he was preparing to close it. I covered his hand with mine. "I'd like to hear what she has to say."

"Okay. Keep it brief, Ms. Violette," he cautioned. "And keep it clean."

She spoke rapidly then, almost running her words together, as if they'd been pent up inside her for a long time. "I was living with Bernie up in New Hampshire, you know? We'd been together for a couple of years. He got these checks from his ex-wife every month. I didn't think much about why he got them. He just said she owed him money. It was quite a lot—I mean, enough so he didn't have to have a real job. He gave tennis lessons in the summer, ski lessons in the winter. I had a little part-time job in a bar. The rich ladies liked him to teach them stuff because he was so handsome, so he got a lot of tips. I didn't mind. He always shared everything he had with me." She took a deep breath. "Then he went and got himself killed, so I have no money at all. We have a paid-up year's lease on our little apartment up in New Hampshire, but the damned cops—oops, sorry, Detective—the doggone cops won't let me go home. They liked me at the bar. I could get more hours and take care of myself. All I need is bus fare. Bernie must have had some money in his wallet. That's all I'm asking for. Friggin' bus fare. Big deal. They've stuck me in a women's shelter here full of crying babies and sob stories. They think I'm a suspect. Like I'd kill him! He was my meal ticket. Besides, I really liked the old fart."

I knew there must be a good reason for Trisha Violette to be kept in Salem. I wasn't about to question Pete's judgment. But her story made a certain amount of sense to me.

"It's true that you're a suspect, Trisha." Pete used his Nice Cop voice. "That's why we don't want you to leave the state. It's for your own protection too, you know. There have been no arrests made in Bernie's murder.

We've made sure you are in a safe environment and that you have three meals a day."

She dabbed at her eyes with the back of her hand. "I miss my cat."

That got my attention. "Where is your cat?" I asked.

"One of the girls I worked with has been taking care of her, but her landlord says no pets. She's going to send Bathsheba to animal control." Real tears rolled down her face. "She's only two years old. If they don't have room for her they'll kill her, or else, once they see how beautiful she is, they'll sell her. She's an all-white Siberian. Do you know what that is?"

"I don't," I admitted.

"Bernie bought her for me. I know she was really expensive. Bernie told me that her daddy was imported all the way from a cattery called the White Witch in the Czech Republic."

"Can't she have her cat at the shelter?" I asked Pete.

"One of the women has a dog there," Trisha insisted, wiping tears with the back of her hand.

"I'll look into it," Pete promised, "and as soon as an arrest is made in Bernie's murder you can return to New Hampshire. I'll give you a ride back to the shelter now. How did you leave without anyone noticing, anyway?"

"I hitched a ride with the guy that delivers the diapers." She shrugged as though walking away from an approved shelter was no big deal. "Mrs. Mondello, I know you love cats too." She reached for my free hand and held it. "You used to talk about your cat on TV. Please try to convince the detective that I need my cat."

I squeezed her hand and didn't make a verbal commitment—but I'd already decided to do as she'd asked.

"I'll look into it, Trisha," Pete said again. "You wait right here while I get my car," he ordered her. "I guess you'll have to reheat the pizza," he told me, and with a quick kiss on my forehead he headed back to the sunroom.

Chapter Ten

The pizza reheated nicely and the salad had stayed crisp in the refrigerator. I opened a bottle of Diet Pepsi, sneaked a piece of pepperoni under the Lucite table to O'Ryan and another to Toby, and waited for the rest of the Trisha Violette story.

"Didn't they notice that she was missing at the women's shelter?" I wanted to know.

"She'd rolled up a blanket under the covers on her bed so it looked like she was sleeping," he said. "They'd just figured that out and had put in a call to headquarters when we got there. I spoke to the chief and told him I had her with me, and meanwhile, she somehow sweet-talked the matron at the shelter into letting her back in—a sad story about her place in New Hampshire and how she'd meant to come right back as soon as she'd made sure her cat would be safe. And maybe she did. Hard to tell with that one."

"I know she's a suspect," I said. "But it's hard to picture her as a killer, isn't it?"

"She's a master manipulator," he said, "but no, she doesn't quite fit the general killer profile. There are plenty of cases of women killing cheating boyfriends or husbands, though."

"So maybe Bernie, the good-looking ski instructor, was cheating with one of his rich students," I suggested. "But what do you think about Hugh Bingham? I guess a man killing his own father would be pretty rare, wouldn't it?"

"Not as rare as you might think," he said. "But so far Bingham has quite a few witnesses as to his whereabouts for just about the entire day in question. He's heavily involved in his mother's candy business, so he's usually right in the midst of everything that's going on over there. He studied business administration in college—has a master's degree—and she claims that she's completely satisfied with his work." I remembered his story about sometimes smelling chocolate for eight or ten hours in a single day. That's a lot of involvement.

"Have you been able to find out if Trisha can keep Bathsheba at the shelter?" I asked, still concerned about the New Hampshire–based cat's fate.

"Unfortunately, no, she can't. It's true that there's a dog there now, but it belongs to one of the supervisors," he said. "I told her we'd try to find a temporary home for Bathsheba—mostly because I know you won't rest until you're sure the cat is safe."

"You know me so well—and I think I know of a temporary foster parent for Trisha's cat."

"Not us, please." He held up his hands in mock

horror. "We already have O'Ryan and Toby, and Ella Marie will be here soon."

"Not us. Betsy. Her sweet, old tiger cat, Pixie, crossed the rainbow bridge not long ago and I'll bet she still has the cat toys and Pixie's bed at her place. She'd be happy to have a cat's company for a while."

"That would be a good solution for the time being," he agreed.

"She'll be at the Angels meeting. I can run the idea by her then."

"You've decided to go to the meeting?" he asked.

"I think those three women's minds at work, plus Michael Martell's, all concentrating on Bernie Bingham's death—after a viewing of *Midsomer Murders*—will turn up ideas no one else would possibly even think of," I told him—and I was sure of it.

"True that," he agreed. "If I get off work early enough I'll join you."

I put the salad bowls into the dishwasher, and we went out into the backyard for a quick game of Frisbee with Toby. I pointed out the wonder of Michael's garden, all lit with twinkling solar lights. "Maybe we should think about doing something special out here—besides mowing the grass."

"I've got that all figured out," he said, leveling a neatly angled Frisbee shot almost over Toby's head. The smart dog jumped and caught it. "I know exactly how it will look."

"You do?" I was surprised. While we'd discussed at length all the changes we'd make for our baby's room, we'd never talked about the yard. "What do you have in mind?"

"Why, an outdoor swing set, of course," he said. "One with a slide. Didn't you have one when you were little?"

Of course I had. "Yes," I said. "Along with permanent scraped knees."

"I know." Big smile. "And did you use waxed paper on the slide so you'd go a lot faster?"

"No. I never thought of it. But if we get a slide for Ella Marie I'm game to try it."

With the plans for the backyard decided upon, dog exercised, dishes washed, counters cleaned, and both of us showered and pajamaed, we turned on the TV and climbed into bed just in time for the nightly news. The good-looking nightly news anchor, Buck Covington, led off with a news flash. "There's been a break in the Chocolate Shop Murder," he announced in the breathless voice he'd mastered for such occasions. "Our top field reporter, Scott Palmer, is here to share with WICH-TV viewers an exclusive interview with Ms. Shirley Parker, the owner and CEO of Casa de Chocolatte. Scott is on-site at the stately Parker mansion on Salem's historic Washington Square."

The scene shifted to the room I recognized immediately as the elegant, antique-filled main-floor showroom of the Parker candy company. Shirley Parker, wearing all white and holding the black cat in her lap, sat in one of the gold fabric Louis XVI wingback chairs while Scott, holding my favorite stick mic, faced her from a simple early American ladder-back chair. *Well staged, Scott*, I thought.

Scott used what he seems to think sounds like a big network announcer voice. "Thank you for joining us,

Ms. Parker," he intoned. "I understand that there's been some excitement here at your home within the last hour. Tell us what's happened."

Pete sat bolt upright, disturbing O'Ryan's snooze. "What the hell is going on?" He reached for his phone. I knew he was calling police headquarters and that he'd had no notifications about the Parker mansion within the last hour at all.

I watched and listened to Scott's interview while at the same time hearing Pete's one-sided conversation with someone at SPD. Shirley Parker said very clearly and plainly that there had been a break-in on her property through the cellar entrance to her home and that someone may have attempted to open a large safe where company records are stored.

"Have the police already left?" Scott asked. "I didn't see a police presence outside."

"My son made the necessary calls," she said. "I believe he thought calling the media would bring quicker action." She stroked the cat. "And you got here in minutes."

Meanwhile, Pete had raised his voice. "Are you watching this? Well, turn on the TV. They have a story on the news about a break-in at the Parker place."

Scott continued. "We have a video of the person our cameraman observed leaving the Parker premises immediately after the break-in occurred. Buck, can you show the viewers the intruder? Viewers, if you recognize this man, please call the number on your screen."

"I'll meet you at the Parker place," Pete yelled into the phone, already pulling his pants on. "Cripes. What kind of moron calls a TV show instead of the cops?" he asked, yanking a hoodie over his head, then looking at me. "And what the hell did he mean by that? That calling the media would bring quicker action than calling the police? Moron!" He spat the word, then turned to me. "I'll be back as soon as I can."

The video was quite dark, obviously shot outdoors, but the figure of a tall, broad-shouldered man in light-colored clothing was plainly visible. There was some sort of mask over his face, but I recognized the clothing immediately. He wore the white one-piece jumpsuit that I'd seen on the workers in the large framed photograph of the kitchen crew downstairs. "Pete," I called to his retreating back. "He's wearing the uniform all of the candymakers there wear at work. There's a picture of them in that room she's sitting in right now."

The unusual late-night commotion had awakened the dog, who wanted to follow Pete, but dutifully obeyed my hand signal to sit—a response he'd been taught by his previous owner. He sat, confused. O'Ryan had momentarily looked up from his sleeping spot at the foot of the bed, blinked a couple of times, and gone back to sleep. I was wide awake, fascinated by the action on the screen, trying to suppress the tiny twinge of jealousy that Scott had been the recipient of the preposterous phone call instead of me. *What kind of moron calls a TV show instead of the cops?* my husband had asked. Shirley Parker had identified the guilty party: her son, Hugh Bingham.

Scott leaned toward Shirley, favoring her with one of his long, soulful looks. Without breaking eye contact, Shirley continued her story. "I was working at my desk"—she gestured toward the front of the room—

"when Blackie here"—she patted the cat's head—"Blackie alerted me to a sound coming from below."

OMG. They really named him Blackie.

"I certainly wasn't going to investigate it myself," she declared. "So I called my son. He made the call to you."

"Did your son go downstairs?" Scott asked the logical question.

"I told him not to. It could have been dangerous."

"You're right, of course," Scott agreed. "So has *any-one* gone downstairs?"

"I don't think so. Your camerapeople caught the thief outside the back cellar door. It's a good thing you all got here so quickly. Now they'll find out who he is and recover whatever he stole from me."

Scott frowned slightly, then quickly adjusted his expression. *He tries not to frown—says it makes wrinkles.* "How do you know the thief tried to open the safe?"

She did a perfect eye roll. "Because that's where the secret Penny Parker recipes are."

"You don't think he got the recipes, do you?"

"No. But he must have taken something." Shirley petted the cat in her lap. "He's wearing one of our uniforms. Maybe he even stole that. We have a whole room full of them in every possible size. Our people select a uniform when they report to work. They put it in the laundry basket when the shift is over. Chocolate can be messy."

"Let's take another look at the thief leaving the building. Buck?"

Buck Covington answered. "We'll close with that,

Scott. It's almost midnight. Stay tuned, everybody, for *Tarot Time with River North*."

The video of the man in white rolled again. I leaned closer to the TV. Was he carrying something? Perhaps he had a package of some sort tucked under his right arm. River's theme music—*Danse Macabre*—began, and the shot of her newly redecorated set filled the screen.

The camera focused on River, ethereally gorgeous in silver and royal blue with her trademark silver stars and moons woven into her long black hair. Sometimes Buck Covington stays around and makes a brief appearance on *Tarot Time*. Much of the audience has figured out that River and Buck are an item, and they seem to look forward to Buck showing up on set to shuffle the cards or read the first commercial. Buck, with his movie-star-perfect features, is a fitting companion for her. Together, they make one of those beautiful couples we never get tired of looking at, like David Beckham and Posh Spice, or Taylor Swift and Travis Kelce. If I'd been at work instead of in bed, I'd have made a sticky note right away to remind me to call River and tell her about the absence of visions since I'd become pregnant.

I'll do it first thing in the morning.

River asked Buck to draw the first card for the night's readings and announced the scary movie for the night— *Bird Box*—a totally creepy film starring Sandra Bullock. I'd seen the movie before and didn't plan to call in for a reading. *They should have stayed with the news and skipped* Tarot Time, I thought. You don't take your top news anchor off a live story and make him shuffle cards.

But I wasn't program director for the news department. Too bad.

Pete had said he'd be home as soon as he could. I hoped so. I had questions. I shut off the TV, turned on the reading lamp, and picked up the paperback novel on the nightstand, killing time until I heard his car in the driveway. Toby took off running to meet him. O'Ryan turned around three times at the foot of the bed, then lay down and went back to sleep.

"You're still awake," Pete said, smiling. "Want to hear the latest about the big candy shop heist?"

"Of course I do."

"We blew up the shot of the masked guy in white to see what he was carrying. Darndest thing." He shook his head. "You'll never guess what he'd swiped."

"Come on. It's too late for guessing games. What is it?"

"It's a box of Casa de Chocolatte candy."

Chapter Eleven

What a silly ending to a breaking news story. Some-body swiped a box of candy. Big deal. The police department wasn't about to expend much manpower on the pettiest of petty thefts. I punched the pillow and rolled over. "Good night," I said. "That was hardly worth staying up for."

"We're thinking that the original intent might have been what Ms. Parker suspected in the first place. To get the secret recipes out of the safe." Pete climbed back into bed beside me. "When that failed, the crook grabbed a box of candy on the way out the cellar door, just for the hell of it."

"You know, that actually makes sense," I said. "I'll bet that's exactly what happened. Wasn't the cellar door locked?"

"It is now." Grim cop voice. "That bulkhead opens onto the oldest part of the foundation of the house. The walls are made of big chunks of granite. No lights, dark and dirty. No wonder nobody uses it."

"Unless they don't want to be seen using the regular entrances," I guessed. "Have you guys come up with any ideas about who the crook might be?"

"Not yet. As you noticed, he was wearing a company-issued uniform, so chances are he's an employee. Anyway, we got some good footprints in the soft dirt outside the bulkhead."

"Do you think that will tell you anything useful?" I wondered aloud.

"Probably not." Just-the-facts cop voice. "The shoes are company-issued too. There's a whole room full of those as well."

"I'm sure you'll figure it out," I assured him. "Meanwhile, we have the Angels working on the case, and maybe we can ask Betsy to help get Trisha Violette's cat, Bathsheba, out of New Hampshire."

"We seem to be surrounded with cats lately," he said. "Besides O'Ryan and Frankie, I mean. Now we're involved with Bathsheba and Blackie."

"Blackie!" I scoffed. "What a dumb name for such a fine-looking cat. He should be 'Raja,' or 'Simba.'"

"Whatever you say, sweetheart. It's late. Shall we turn out the lights and grab some sleep?"

"Good idea," I said. "Busy day tomorrow. And George Washington is coming over in the morning with some paint samples for the nursery."

"Samples? How many colors of pink are there?" He laughed and reached for the light switch.

I was the first one up in the morning for a change. I didn't want George Washington to catch me in my jammies. I was showered, brushed, combed, made up, and dressed by seven thirty. I'd even loaded up Mr. Coffee and had it brewing when Pete joined me in the kitchen. George arrived at about the same time. I poured three mugs of coffee while George spread paint sample charts all over the top of the Lucite table.

Who knew there were so many shades of pink? We'd already had a dresser, crib, and changing table in blush pink stashed in the attic, along with a bright raspberry rocking chair for me. We settled on a combination of Bubble Gum paint for three walls and Sweet Pea for the contrasting one. Aunt Ibby had a baby shower planned for me, and I'd filled out a form indicating some accessories I'd like to have. "Ella Marie, I'm sure you're going to love your room," I told my swollen tummy.

I posted the chosen color chips on the kitchen bulletin board and made a date with George for the painting to begin. Pete and I shared English muffins with strawberry preserves and more coffee for breakfast, then decided we'd have lunch on our own and that he'd pick up Chinese food for dinner. "Are you planning to walk to work and back again today?" Pete asked. "Or would you like a ride one way or the other?"

"Wanda the Weather Girl says it's going to be fine all day," I told him. "No worries." I tossed on a lightweight NASCAR jacket, kissed my husband, patted Toby, picked O'Ryan up for a quick lick on my nose, and left via the front door.

I stepped out into morning sunshine shaded by Winter Street's wonderful old trees, maple and oak and elm, and headed toward the common. I'd allowed plenty of time for the walk to work and decided to take the pleasant route down Hawthorne Boulevard to Derby Street, avoiding much of Washington Square in general and the Parker mansion in particular. Walking to work in good weather offers time to do some thinking—not the hurried kind you do in the office or in school, but the leisurely kind where you can be as unfocused or rattlebrained as you want to be. I'd only gone as far as the statue of Nathaniel Hawthorne when I stopped visualizing the planned-for pink room and began thinking about cats. Random cats. Cats I'd had when I was a kid—Shadow and Blue and Mary Jane Fluffernutter. Yep. Mary Jane Fluffernutter. Then I thought about Frankie. I'd named her for Benjamin Franklin, who wrote on bedding older women, "When all candles be out, all cats be gray." Frankie used to show up occasionally at Aunt Ibby's house when the weather was bad. Her current residence with Michael is the longest I've ever seen her stay in one place. The newest cat acquaintance, Blackie, was still in my thoughts. Blackie, who may have been a witness to murder. I worried about poor Bathsheba too, threatened with animal control if she didn't get rescued pretty soon.

By the time I passed the Catholic church, my concentration was back to where it probably should have been all along: on the coming day's work at WICH-TV. Maybe even before I got to my programming duties, I'd see what Scott had to say about the previous night's bizarre late-breaking news event—starring him! I was sure he'd be delighted to talk about it. Doan would undoubtedly want me to locate more candy venues with free samples.

I climbed the marble steps to WICH-TV and walked across the black-and-white-tiled floor toward Old Clunky, trying not to step on the black squares. Rhonda waved to me through the glass door of the reception area. "Wow. What a morning," she said as soon as I stepped inside. "My phone is ringing off the hook."

"The late news?" I asked, knowing the answer.

"It hasn't stopped since . . ." She held up her hand and spoke into her headset. "WICH-TV. Please hold." She returned her attention to me. ". . . since I got here. And the night guy says it rang all night. Mostly stations all around the state wanting to talk to Scott about what happened." She pointed down to the whiteboard and returned to her phone duty. "WICH-TV. How may I direct your call?"

My whiteboard message was simple. And unwelcome. *Lee. Call Hugh Bingham.* It was followed by a number.

Chapter Twelve

I hurried along the ramp past the newsroom and unlocked the door to my glass-walled office. I looked through the window partially covered with sticky notes into the newsroom next door. Sticky notes on the wall are admittedly not a high-tech method of keeping track of important things—and, of course, the same items are stored on my phone—but I do love a paper trail. What if the grid fails? I'll still have pink and green and purple stickies to keep me on track.

I transferred Hugh Bingham's number onto a green sticky and slapped it onto the glass. Then I picked a hot pink one and wrote *Call River* and slapped that one on too. Scott, on the other side of the window, reacted to the motions and made the familiar "call me" signal. So I did.

"That whole thing was amazing, Scott," I said. "You must have been astonished when you got the call."

"It was crazy. Who would call the local TV station instead of the police when there's been a break-in?" he asked.

"Hugh Bingham would, apparently," I said.

"Do you know him?" Scott asked.

"I do," I said. I didn't bother trying to keep the annoyance out of my voice.

"He's part of your candy story, right?"

"He is," I agreed, then tried for a quick subject switch. "Did you ever find Bernie Bingham's girlfriend?"

"She found me," he said with a smile. "We did a thirty-minute interview. I'll probably air it tonight with Buck. But it'll take a while for Marty to clean it up. What a potty mouth on that one! The thing will probably get down to fifteen minutes by the time we get through bleeping it."

"She found me too, but Pete was there and he told her to keep it clean. She mostly wanted to talk about her cat."

"Oh yeah, she mentioned the cat to me too. Only it was the bleepin' cat. She showed me a picture. I suppose Trisha's a prime suspect, huh?" I knew Scott was prying to see if I'd tell him what Pete thought about it all.

"I guess anybody and everybody who had access to the candy factory within the time frame they've established is a suspect," I told him.

"Even you?" He faked a shocked look.

"Not me. He'd already been dead for a while when I found him."

"How about the wife, or the son?" he asked. "You've met them both. What do *you* think of them?

"Hey, I'm reporting on their candy business, not their lifestyle," I said. "I'm learning how they make chocolates and I've brought some nice samples back to the station. Have you checked out the break room lately?"

"Are you kidding? There's practically a line at the door." His smile was appreciative. "The chocolates are good, but I love all those old-fashioned penny candies."

"Me too. I have a red barley candy lollipop stashed in my purse for later," I admitted, smiling through the glass. It was one of those rare moments when Scott and I agreed on something. My glance lighted on the green sticky bearing Hugh Bingham's number. "Gotta go," I told him. "Duty calls."

There was no way to avoid it. I called the number.

"Good morning, Lee. It's such a pleasure to see your name pop up on my phone." He sounded as though he meant it.

"Good morning, Hugh." I returned the greeting. "I have a message that you called me."

"I did," he said. "I'm wondering when we can set up that video. Mother is so looking forward to doing it now that the police have finished with—you know. The recent unpleasantness."

And I'm so looking forward to getting it over with. And who calls his own father's murder an "unpleasantness"?

"I'll speak with one of our videographers about it today," I promised. "When I began this assignment, I didn't realize there were so many candy venues in Salem. I'll call you the minute I have a firm time."

I called Francine. "How's your availability for the chocolate factory shoot? The natives are getting restless."

"Doan wants some of the smaller ones done first," she reported. "New clients, and besides, Buffy is friends with the owner of Salem Sweetland. Maybe Old Jim can do it though."

"Good idea," I said, and thanked her. I've always enjoyed working with Old Jim. That's what everyone calls WICH-TV's backup videographer. Francine was tops in the field and she was always assigned the new mobile unit while Jim used the converted Volkswagen van, but he had an eye for details—important details—that some of the other camerapeople, including Francine, sometimes missed.

I called Old Jim. "The chocolate candy place, huh?" he said. "That sounds interesting. I'm doing a promo for the city for the Farmers' Market right now, but how's this afternoon around three?"

"I'll meet you in the parking lot," I told Jim, and—as promised—called Hugh Bingham back. "How's this afternoon at a little after three?" I asked. "Does that give you enough time to prepare?"

"That will work fine," he said, "and you'll be glad to know the production line is working today, so you'll get a good look at the actual process."

"Excellent," I said. "We'll see you then."

"I'm looking forward to seeing you again, Lee."

That sounds too friendly. No ready response came to mind, so I simply said, "Goodbye."

I thought some more about the conversation I'd had with Scott—about how everybody who had access to the place was a suspect. How many sticky notes would it take to put them all on the window wall? I decided to put them on pale yellow stickies—a color I rarely used.

I began with Hugh Bingham, printing neatly, carefully, and leaving room on the square surface for notes. Next came Shirley Parker, followed by Trisha Violette. Had Bernie told her about the back entrance? I printed the question on her sticky. I paused, then printed *Candy Box Man* on the next one. Did all of the Casa de Chocolatte employees have keys to the place? Or keypad codes like the WICH-TV staff did? If they did, there weren't enough stickies left on the pale yellow pad. I thought it was likely that they entered through the front door though, as I had. In that case, they would have been seen going down the stairs. But that unlocked bulkhead entrance in the backyard was quite another story.

I stared at the sticky with Shirley Parker's name on it. She, after all, seemed to me to have the best motive for murder. Bernie had not only been a cheating husband, but an expensive-to-maintain ex-husband as well. Then what about Hugh? He wasn't about to rock the comfortable boat he'd been riding in all his life. Trisha, on the other hand, was a first-class boat rocker. The candy box man was a true unknown component. Did he have a grudge against Bernie Bingham, as so many people did, or was he just a random sweet-snitching recipe seeker?

I sent out to McDonald's for what amounted to a

kid's Happy Meal for lunch—a six-piece nuggets and small fries—and dipped the fries into barbecue sauce while I pondered the stickies.

Of course, what I was left with was four pale yellow question marks.

Chapter Thirteen

I had time before three o'clock to pull down a couple more stickies. The reminder about a birthday gift for Wanda was first. Our Wanda is not only the most glamourous weather forecaster ever, and a top-flight meteorologist to boot—she's also a nationally acclaimed, award-winning cook. It's hard to find a cooking-related utensil she doesn't already have in her "Cooking with Wanda the Weather Girl" set at the rear of the studio. I took a chance on a Himalayan salt block cooking plate.Next I pulled down the lavender reminder to ask Aunt Ibby for a library book on candy making. I'd stuck that one up there when I'd first been assigned to the candy store hunt. Now I wondered about several new aspects of the business. I hoped to find a list of utensils used in the making of chocolates. Was there one missing from the basement of the Parker mansion?

I made a note to ask her about the book at the Angels meeting. It was much too early to call River.

I grabbed the green WICH-TV jacket from my locker and shrugged into it. I was a few minutes early for meeting Jim in the parking lot, but he was already there, the old VW freshly washed and engine purring. I climbed into the passenger seat. "It's so good to be working with you, Jim," I told him, meaning it sincerely.

"My pleasure, Lee," he said. "It's been a while. A chocolate factory tour should make a real interesting presentation."

"I think so too," I said, not adding *as long as there's no body on the floor*.

Jim must have picked up my thought. "This will be much better than your last visit there."

"I sure hope so."

Jim had figured out a way to park in a public lot behind the hotel so that on foot, with Jim carrying his Sony camcorder and my stick mic, and me with my handbag over one shoulder and an assortment of clip mics in a leather carrying case on the other, we could cut through an alley to Washington Square and the Parker mansion. Easy peasy. I pushed open the unlocked door to Casa de Chocolatte, and once again faced Shirley Parker at her desk—looking fabulous in a black three-piece business suit with a tailored white silk shirt. Her face, carefully made up, appeared youthful. Maybe she'd had work done, I thought, but if she had it was extremely well done—nothing artificial or stretched-looking about it, as sometimes is the case.

"Lee! How good to see you again." She stood, walked around the desk, and surprised me with a warm hug. "Hugh has been anxiously waiting to give your viewers a tour of our facility. Will you want to start here in this room? That's the way we usually begin the public tours. "

I hadn't realized that Hugh had planned to act as tour director, but why not? He was good-looking and articulate and certainly knew the business. "That will be fine," I told her, and introduced her to Jim.

"I'll let Hugh know that you're both here," she said, pressing a button on an intercom similar to the one on Rhonda's desk. "Darling, come on up here. Hurry."

Almost immediately, Hugh appeared at the head of the stairs. He wore an absurdly long white apron over his suit, and, even worse, an elasticized white hairnet tightly covered his forehead, ears, and hair. I struggled not to laugh. It took only seconds for him to tear away the net and apron—to magically become once again the confident young executive director of a successful company—but in my mind the visual damage could never be undone.

It cannot be easy to smile, and at the same time, glare at somebody, but Hugh Bingham achieved it. *If looks could kill . . .* I heard the old saying in my mind as the man focused on his mother. He crossed the room quickly, then, smile appropriately warm, right hand extended, greeted me. "Lee. So good to see you. You caught me at work and I must apologize for that. When Mother said to hurry I thought something might be wrong up here." Again the cold look in Shirley's direction.

"No problem." I switched my handbag to the other arm and grasped his hand. "Please meet my videographer, Jim. Jim, this is Mr. Bingham." Jim's hands were full, so he nodded the acknowledgment, said "How do you do," then, positioning the Sony on his shoulder, he handed the stick mic to me.

"If it suits you, Hugh," I began, "I've brought along some clip mics for you and Shirley. I plan to use my own mic to introduce you and to follow along while you direct the tour." I opened the leather case, removed two mics, and showed the pair how to clip on the receivers and how to hide the transmitters under their clothes. "Ready?" I asked.

"I'm ready," Hugh said. "Mother?"

When Shirley smiled I realized suddenly how very much the two looked alike—more like brother and sister than mother and son. They had what might be called classic good looks. The high forehead, strong chin, and what Aunt Ibby called an aquiline nose worked equally well for both the man and the woman. "Let's go," Shirley said.

"Okay. Let's begin with a shot of the house from outside, Jim. Then show me walking through the front door into this beautiful room. I'll introduce Shirley, and she'll introduce Hugh." I addressed Shirley. "Does that work for you?"

"Yes. Then perhaps you can follow Hugh downstairs, where he can explain the process of producing our chocolates." The proud smile again. "He does it so perfectly. He really should be on TV all the time."

"He'd be great at doing commercials for you," I suggested. "Shall I have someone from sales call you?"

A tiny frown crossed her face. "Is that terribly expensive?"

"It depends a lot on the time of day. A fifteen-second ad during the late news hour might be six hundred dollars, and the same ad early in the morning could be seventy-five," I explained. "It depends on the audience you want to reach. For instance, the Toy Trawler toy store buys the morning spots because that's when the kids shows are on, and the young moms watch the morning news and weather. Sometimes Sunday ads are cheaper than weekdays because the viewership drops—except when we have local Sunday baseball or hockey or football."

"Hmmm. It's definitely worth thinking about," she said. "But let's do this one first so Hugh can get back to his *real* job—running our business."

Hugh didn't need makeup—or perhaps he'd already had some discreetly applied. At any rate, he looked good. Jim did a quick sound check of the mics and gave me a thumbs-up signal.

"We're not live," I told Hugh, "so don't worry about any flubs."

"We'll be fine," he said. "We've actually finished work for the day, and everything is shipshape down there, but I've asked the workers to stay for a bit so that you can talk to them."

"That's great. We can reshoot any part we need to. The whole thing will be edited carefully before it's aired."

"Can we see the edited version before the station uses it?" Shirley wanted to know.

"You certainly can," I told her, hoping she wouldn't expect to make a lot of changes. It wasn't as though she was paying for it . . . except with some free candy. Actually, if she found it unacceptable, I just wouldn't run it at all—but now wasn't the time to tell her so.

That's what we did. Neither mother nor son gave any indication of the tension that had existed just moments before. From the front door introduction to meeting with the workers in the downstairs workspace, everything went exactly as we'd planned. Jim took his time walking around the immaculate room, pausing beside the bright copper bowls, the display of tools, the photos on the wall, the conveyor belt. One might think we'd rehearsed it. The chocolate makers were all hairnetted and gown-and-apron-garbed, much as Hugh had been earlier. As he moved among them, asking an occasional question, the people, without exception, gave carefully worded replies. He explained the uses of the various pieces of equipment in simple terms without sounding as though he was talking down to the audience. He gestured toward a neatly arranged pegboard. "Here are some of the tools we use daily." He gestured to some pointy, arrow-shaped gadgets, some long, narrow forks, some spoons with holes in them, an assortment of knives, and some kitchen shears in graduated sizes, giving them all names: "Dipping tool, fondue fork, drop roller, slotted spoon, fudge shears, marshmallow snippers." Even Jim looked impressed when we wrapped up the segment in record time.

To make it all even better, Shirley presented me with

a shopping bag full of boxed chocolates—"To share with your friends at the station. And be sure to take some to dear Ibby too." I assured her that I would, and thanked her again. I wished Hugh a good day and left through that magnificent door, knowing we'd done a good job and yet glad that I'd never have to deal with him again.

Chapter Fourteen

Back at the station I checked with Marty about the editing of the piece we'd just turned in. I wanted to know when we'd be able to air it so that I could get my ducks in a row—airtime-wise. While I waited for her input, I walked around the darkened studio once again, making sure that all of the shows under my charge had their sets up to my picky standards. All was in order, although the *Shopping Salem* backdrop—which is laid out like a giant cubby—was a bit overcrowded and took a while to organize. I'd almost finished when the lights on River's set suddenly blazed. It was a little early for my friend to be on-site, but there she was. I hurried to greet her.

When she's not wearing one of her glamorous *Tarot Time* outfits, River's TV fans might not recognize her. Today, without makeup, she wore fashionably ripped jeans and a too-big-for-her Boston University T-shirt, her long black hair in two pigtails over her shoulders. She greeted me with her usual enthusiastic patchouli-scented hug, ever careful of my protruding tummy.

"I'm so happy to see you," I told her. "I have a question."

Her eyes widened. "Visions?"

"Nope. Lack of visions. I realized recently that I haven't had even one since I became pregnant. Does that mean something?"

"Maybe. Your visions seem to me almost like waking dreams. I could take a look at Ariel's dream book and see what the witch aspect might be," she offered. "Do you think it might be a spell of some kind?" In addition to her card reading talent, River is also a practicing witch.

I thought about it. "It doesn't *feel* witchy," I decided.

"Okay then. Do you have time for a quick reading?" She reached for the silk bag containing her tarot deck. "I have time to do one for you. I came by early to be sure tonight's movie had arrived.

"I do," I told her. "And I also have a new acquaintance who makes me uncomfortable for no good reason."

"There may not be an *apparent* reason, but there could be a good one." She slid the beautiful cards from the bag. She bowed her head. "I dedicate this deck to serve others with spiritual growth, for wisdom, knowledge, and to bring peace to she who seeks its wisdom." River placed the card she uses to represent me—the Queen of Wands—face-up on table. This queen holds a sunflower in her left hand, and there's a black cat in front of her. She handed me the deck to shuffle. I don't do anything fancy like Buck does, but years of playing gin rummy with my aunt means I do it quite well. I handed the shuffled deck back and she began the familiar ten-card Celtic Cross layout. The first card was the Page of Swords. "I wonder who this is," River said. "Does the fellow who makes you uncomfortable have brown hair and brown eyes?"

"That could be Hugh," I said. "He has brown hair and those unreadable brown eyes that are not 'windows into the soul' at all."

"You see the flock of birds and the wild clouds around him? He's walking on rough ground. There's a feeling of trouble brewing here—even outright strife within a family. But this person has learned to be diplomatic in his dealings. He's a graceful man." She smiled. "He's probably a good dancer."

She reached for the second card and placed it across the first one. I recognized the Seven of Pentacles. "We see here a young farmer leaning on his hoe. He's quietly, intently studying the plant he's so carefully cultivated. His work is done, but will he gather a good harvest? What if all he's planted doesn't ripen? Doesn't mature as he believes it should? In other words, a significant investment can turn out to be unprofitable for him." The picture of the farmer made me think of my next-door neighbor with the amazing garden, but I was quite sure Michael had no place at all in my reading. She placed the third card, face-up directly below the center two—the Seven of Swords.

"Another seven," I said. "Only this one isn't a farmer. He looks like a bad guy. A crook." The man on the card had his arms full of swords. He'd left a couple of them behind, and he appeared to be running away from a place with a lot of tents.

"You're right," River said. "The man is taking something that isn't his. Maybe this Hugh is running away from something he's done. Something he doesn't want to pay for." She looked up from the cards. "Does that fit?"

"It could," I agreed. "But Hugh doesn't really *need* to steal anything."

She put the fourth card to the left of the center. The Nine of Pentacles showed a well-dressed woman in what looked like a vineyard. There was a house in the background and she had a bird perched on her hand. "She looks happy," I said. "She has a house and grapes and a tame bird."

"See? You're getting good at this," River told me. "Yes. She is content with the good things in life. She's widowed or single and wise about her own interests. Do you recognize her?"

"Absolutely," I said. "That's Hugh's mother. Shirley."

"Good." She placed the next face-up card above the center pile. "This card can tell us something about your future." I recognized the card right away. It's hard to miss the Fool. I'd seen it many times in River's on-screen readings for callers, but didn't recall it ever showing up for me before. The card shows a merry-looking fellow, facing forward instead of at the edge of the cliff right in front of him.

"Is it about danger?" I asked.

"It's about choices," she said. "It looks as though you'll have a choice to make soon." She reached across the table and took my hand. "This may be important, Lee. I'm telling you as a friend and not just a reader—you'll know when it shows up. The choice will be totally up to you. Take your time and be sure to choose wisely." She returned her attention to the layout on the table and tapped the card at the right side of the arrangement, completing the form of a cross. The card was the Ace of Wands. River's smile sparkled. "I could have foretold this one without the card," she exclaimed. The card showed a strong hand, emerging from floating clouds, offering a flowering wand. There's a castle in the background.

"It's beautiful," I said.

"Yes. It is." She gave a soft, silvery giggle. "This card in this position in the layout gives us a promise of what your near future holds. I'm smiling because it often foretells a birth. I think we already knew that. It's possible that the cushioning aspects of the soft clouds is what's protecting you from the visions during the pregnancy." She placed a new card to the right of the base of the cross. "This card may have to do with your concern about this Hugh person. About your negative feelings concerning him." The card was the Two of Pentacles. "Here a happy-looking young man balances two pentacles held together by a cord shaped like a numeral eight. There are a couple of ships behind him that seem to be on high seas."

"It looks as if he's doing quite a balancing act," I observed.

"Yes. He may be trying to juggle two different situations at the same time while still maintaining harmony, and keeping up the lighthearted appearance in spite of some background upheavals." She put both elbows on the table, her fists beneath her chin, and looked into my eyes. "What do you say? Does that sound like him?"

"I think Hugh could do all that and still keep everything going smoothly. He's an awfully good manager."

"But you don't like him."

"I didn't say that. I said he makes me uncomfortable."

"That's true. You did say that." She placed another face-up card above the juggler. "Let's see what your family, loved ones, and friends have to say." This was the card I always hope will show up in my readings. The Knight of Swords is the card that, for me, represents Pete. Here's a brave knight who dashes across open country on an errand of romantic chivalry. He's embarrassed whenever I tell him that. "Here comes Pete," River said. "Always courageous and protective of you—but you already know that." She chose another card and put it above the Pete card. "Another from the Pentacles suit," River pointed out. "The Page. Pentacles often indicate money and earthly possessions. The young person here standing in a field of flowers with a mountain in the background might be a woman or a man. Sometimes this card is called 'the Princess of the Echoing Hills.'"

"Echoing Hills," I said. "Like the White Mountains in New Hampshire?"

"Could be," River agreed. "What makes you say that?"

"There's a young woman involved in all this chocolate factory business who has a connection to New Hampshire," I explained, thinking of Trisha.

"Is this person kind and careful, with strong opinions?"

I smiled at the *strong opinions* part. "I don't know her very well, but she has strong opinions for sure, and doesn't mind sharing them. She loves cats," I added, "so she probably has a kind side too."

River put another card above the one I'd already decided must be Trisha Violette. This would be the tenth and last card in the familiar layout. I think the Six of Cups is one of the most pleasant cards in the deck to look at. A boy and a girl are on a green lawn in front of a cottage. The boy offers the girl a cup full of flowers, and five more flower-filled cups are neatly arranged in the foreground. "This looks like good news," I suggested. "It's such a pretty card."

"It is," she agreed. "This card may bring back happy childhood memories for you. It could mean a reunion with a childhood friend or acquaintance. There'll almost surely be a gift from an admirer."

"Aunt Ibby is planning a baby shower," I reminded her.

"I've heard rumors of one here at the station too," River said with a wink. "Gifts from admirers is an easy read."

"It's a good reading all around, isn't it?" I asked. It seemed so to me.

River gathered up the cards, returning them to the silk bag. "Yes. To sum it up, let's concentrate on the many good aspects of the layout. The Knight of Swords, your Pete, is in a position of protection for you, and the Fool will advise you against unwise choices. You've already figured out who some of the cards represent, so you're aware of both positive and negative aspects of the events coming your way. The Ace of Wands is all about the birth of your baby—a wonderful, happy experience for everyone concerned, and your own happy childhood remains a constant source of strength for you. Once the cushioning clouds of the Ace of Wands have evaporated with the birth, your gift of visions will likely return."

River always insists that the damned visions are a "gift." I don't see it that way, and she knows it. I didn't comment, but she couldn't have missed my eye roll. She continued. "You've probably noticed that a lot of this reading centers around choices. Be optimistic in spite of some dark spots. There are plenty of positive and constructive opportunities along your path. Be aware of your surroundings. Keep your ears and eyes open." She walked around to my side of the table. I stood and we shared a hug. "And call me whenever you need me. Day or night. I'm always here for you—as a tarot reader, or—if need be—as a witch."

"I know."

Chapter Fifteen

I climbed the metal staircase to the second floor, dropped off the bag of chocolate goodies in the break room, shoved the candy box intended for Aunt Ibby unceremoniously into my office, and stopped once again in front of the open door of the room where Marty wields her editing magic. I tapped on the glass. "How's it coming along?" I asked.

"Piece of cake," she said. "Chocolate cake." Her smile was broad. "Whoever that announcer is, he did a great job. We ought to use him more often."

"He's not ours," I admitted. "He's not even a professional. He's the client's son."

"Send somebody from sales over there then. Sell them some time and he can do the commercials," she said. She tapped on her computer. "I'm sending you the best clips of the guy."

"I already thought of that," I admitted. "I'll show these to Doan and see what he thinks about it."

"He'll try to get the guy to work here for free," she said.

I thought about the Page of Swords and what River had said about the brown-haired, brown-eyed man who was dealing with rough ground and a whole flock of birds, with trouble brewing all around him. *He's diplomatic in his dealings*, River had said. *He's probably a good dancer.*

"I think this one eats people like our general manager for breakfast," I told Marty. "He'll tap-dance all over poor Doan and might even wind up owning the station."

"Now, *that* would make a documentary worth watching." Marty has a great deep-down belly laugh. "Put me on camera for that one."

"This'll be the last of the candy factory videos," I told her, relief probably evident in my voice. "Just a few more of the smaller shops to go and we're done with the Halloween candy promo. On to the witch shops and ghost tours."

"I'll bet you'll be glad you don't have to go into the Parker place anymore—I mean, after you found old Bernie in there."

"That's for sure," I agreed. "I wish they'd figure out why he's dead though. It's keeping Pete pretty busy."

"It's keeping Scott busy too," she said. "Weird, wasn't it—how they called the TV station instead of the cops when there was a break-in over there?"

"Very weird," I agreed. "I'm glad I didn't have to cover it."

"You could do it if you had to. You and Old Jim do a good job together."

"WICH-TV is blessed with good camerapeople. You and Francine and Jim—all pros," I told her, meaning it sincerely. "That's most of the fun of working here."

"Are you ready to hang it up for a while yet? You must be, what—six, seven months along?" she asked. "Aren't you ready to put your feet up and take it easy for the rest of the time?"

"Seven—almost eight. I'll finish the candy thing anyway," I said. "I feel fine. So good that I could probably keep working right up to the last minute."

"Sure. And we could shoot the birth live on TV, huh? Doan would love it!"

"Not *that* good!"

I continued past the news department and returned to my office to pick up my aunt's candy. I scribbled another sticky note while I was there. *Show Doan video of Hugh Bingham.* I made a mental note at the same time.

If Doan wants me to work with Bingham, tell him it's time for me to go home, put my feet up, and wait for baby to arrive. I thought once again about the Fool card that had shown up in my reading. *Take your time*, River had said, *and be sure to choose wisely.*

I chose not to work with Hugh Bingham. Ever.

I peeked through the glass at the newsroom clock. It was earlier than I usually leave for the walk across the common, but I figured that it was also earlier than Bingham's walking time too. I tucked Aunt Ibby's chocolate box under my arm, locked my office, and started for the reception area. If Doan was available I'd

show him Marty's clip, pitch the idea of Bingham doing his own commercial, check out of work early, and
stop at Aunt Ibby's house on my way down Winter
Street to my own home.

Rhonda greeted me with a big smile and a finger
pointed to the whiteboard. *See Mr. Doan re: new assignment.*

New assignment? I mouthed silently.

She shrugged and motioned to the manager's office.
Maybe it wasn't time for putting my feet up after all. I
left Aunt Ibby's candy with Rhonda and tapped on the
partly open door. "Come in, Lee," Bruce Doan called.

I stepped onto recently installed deep purple wall-
to-wall carpet. "Yes, sir? You wanted to see me?"

"Are you up for a short field reporter stint?" he
asked.

"Maybe," I hedged. "What's it about?"

"Sit down. Make yourself comfortable," he suggested. "I'll tell you all about it."

I sat.

"It's about that woman who's trying to get her cat
out of New Hampshire, or get to New Hampshire so
she can take care of it. Ever since she told Scott about
her 'bleepin' cat,' we've had about a hundred calls
from people wanting to help her. Go figure." He threw
both hands into the air. "Out of all the people who have
problems in this city, it seems like everybody wants to
help the foul-mouthed girlfriend of a dead grifter. I'll
never figure out human nature."

"It is interesting though, isn't it?"

"Well, what do you say? If you don't want it I'll give

it to Scott." He tapped impatient fingers on the desk-top. I'd already made up my mind.

"I'll take it," I told him. "Where do you want me to start?"

"Right now the woman is over at the shelter, raising hell." He had a wry smile. "Do you know of any safe place you can stash her while you check out some of the offers of help?"

"I can't take her to my house," I said. "The spare room is being painted, and anyway Pete wouldn't stand for it. But my aunt has a couple of Airbnb apartments in her house that she rents out. Will the station pay?"

Deep, brow-furrowing scowl. "Okay. I guess so. If it doesn't take too long, and if she doesn't jack the price up."

I ignored the implied insult. "I'll check and see if she'll even consider taking Trisha in. The foul language may be a problem. Even the mildest cuss words are frowned on in her house."

"Get on it right away, then. Let me know what she says."

"I'd planned to stop by my aunt's house on my way home today."

He checked his Rolex. "Why don't you leave now and we'll get this show on the road."

"Okay," I agreed. "I'll let you know what she says."

"If I remember correctly, your aunt likes cats," he reminded me.

"That's true. And so do I."

In fact, if Bernie's death hadn't been a police matter, and if I hadn't been married to the investigating detective, I'd have offered to go up and fetch the cat myself. I was beginning to like the assignment already. "There's another thing about Bernie Bingham beside his girl-friend. It's his son, Hugh. It turns out that he has the voice and the face for TV. Marty has sent you some clips. We're thinking of sending a salesperson to see him about doing commercials for the Casa de Choco-latte . . . unless you think it might be in bad taste so soon after his father's murder."

I remembered Francine's remark. *Since when does bad taste bother Doan?*

"That's the company with the Parker family for-tune." Big smile. "They can well afford it. Sure. Send one of the top salespeople over there pronto."

I made the call to sales, picked up the candy box from Rhonda, and left for Winter Street.

Chapter Sixteen

I took the long way around the edge of the common instead of using the center pathway just in case you-know-who might be coincidentally taking a walk at the same time. I dared a quick look toward the Parker mansion every few minutes, planning to start jogging if he showed up over there. Maybe even running.

I exited from the Washington Square north gate and hurried across to the Civil War memorial on the corner. The coast was clear all the way. Aunt Ibby's house isn't far from the corner of Winter Street, but I didn't slow my pace even then. I dashed up her front steps, happy to see O'Ryan's fuzzy face in the tall side window next to the door. I rang the doorbell and used my key in the lock at the same time. I pushed the door open and tumbled into the foyer, almost bumping into my aunt and nearly tripping over the welcoming cat at the same time.

"Well, I'm happy to see you too, Maralee." She patted her still-red hair and smoothed the skirt of a gray silk shirt dress. "Why the big hurry?"

I handed her the candy box and peeked out the side window. I knew he wasn't there, yet I couldn't help myself. Aunt Ibby laid the candy box on a Sheraton side table and put a comforting arm around my waist. "Are you still afraid of that man?"

"I'm not afraid of him," I rationalized. "I just don't want to be anywhere near him."

"I think that's being afraid," she said. "Does Pete know about him scaring you this way?"

"No. He knows that I didn't like working with Hugh, but that's not because of fear. The man is perfectly polite and respectful. He just makes me feel uneasy for some reason."

"Trust your instincts," she said. "You don't have to work with him for the station anymore, do you? Isn't the candy series over with?"

"Pretty much," I said. "I just need to find a few smaller shops to visit." I realized as I spoke that I was facing the hall tree with its long, bevel-edged mirror, which had held so many frightening visions in the past—and I was facing *that* without even a bit of fear.

"So you don't have to go back to where you found . . . that man?"

"I don't."

"That's a relief. No more Binghams to deal with, right? Come on out to the kitchen with me. I'm whipping up a little dessert for the meeting."

"Almost right. I need to talk to you about Bernie

Bingham's girlfriend, Trisha Violette, though." I followed her through the living room.

"The pretty girl with the potty mouth who's lost her cat?"

I sighed. "That's her. It's about her cat. Bathsheba. Apparently, she's struck a chord with the WICH-TV viewers. Everybody wants to take her to New Hampshire to get her cat or else get the cat and bring it back here."

"Isn't that nice? I hope she gets Bathsheba back safely."

"She can't have the cat at the shelter where she's being held. I'm planning to ask Betsy to foster the cat temporarily, just to be sure she's safe, but now I need to ask you to rent one of your Airbnb rooms to Trisha. Mr. Doan has assigned me to document the return of the cat. I think we're going to call it 'Saving Bathsheba,' but in order to do it Trisha needs a secure, cop-approved, cat-friendly place to stay here in Salem."

"We're certainly cat-friendly here, aren't we, O'Ryan?" she asked the big yellow cat, who'd seated himself in one of the captain's chairs beside the round kitchen table. "Pete knows how secure this house is. Ever since that night when a madman sneaked in here and kidnapped me, I have every alarm system known to science."

"I know," I said. "I still shudder when I think how close we were to losing you." I reached for her, drawing her close for a hug. "I'm sure we can work out the security thing. I'll be back later for the Angels meeting, and Pete said he'd come along with me if he has time.

I'll touch base with Betsy about her driving up to New Hampshire and fetching Bathsheba back here."

I gave O'Ryan a goodbye pat on the head and made my way back to the front hall, daring another glance at the mirror—where, once again, nothing unusual was going on. I stepped out the door, and after a cautious look in all directions, I left my aunt's house and proceeded down Winter Street to my own.

As soon as I unlocked the front door and heard Tim McGraw singing I knew that Pete was already there. Toby ran to greet me with tail wags and doggy kisses. "I'm home," I called.

"I'm in the kitchen," he answered. "Do we have any soy sauce?"

We did. I found it, and our Chinese dinner, complete with my favorites—moo goo gai pan, crab rangoon, and snow peas—was served by candlelight and complemented with fortune cookies. Mine promised, "An exciting opportunity lies ahead of you." That gave me the opportunity to tell Pete about my new documentary assignment—"Saving Bathsheba."

He listened attentively, only asking a couple of questions about the wisdom of moving Trisha from the shelter to Aunt Ibby's house. I reminded him of the security measures already in place there and the fact that bringing her cat to Salem would assure Chief Whaley that escape artist Trisha would be much less of a flight risk once she knew her cat was safe. "I'm going to ask Betsy tonight at the meeting to speed things up by making a run up to New Hampshire to get the cat and to be its foster cat-mom for the time being."

"It might work." Hesitant cop voice. "I'm going to approve Trisha's move from the shelter to your aunt's place right away. Anyway, just having the cat away from the possibility of animal control taking over is helpful."

"It will make Trisha a little more relaxed, and the WICH-TV audience will see it as some kind of progress," I said. "I'm quite sure Betsy will agree. She misses her own cat a lot. Are you planning on coming to the meeting with me?"

"I wasn't sure, but I saw Michael in the yard and he says he's going, so, yes, I think I'll tag along."

"It should be interesting. Funny we should be talking about cats. This week's episode is named 'Claws Out.' The trailer says there's a crazy cat lady in it."

We cleared the table and began loading the dishwasher. "Shall we skip the ice cream tonight?" he asked. "I'm guessing there'll be dessert at Ibby's."

"She said she was whipping up something, so I'm sure we can count on it," I promised.

"Were you planning on walking down to her house? It's a nice evening. The moon is almost full."

If Pete hadn't agreed to come with me there was no way I would have considered walking down Winter Street alone—moonlight or not. Aunt Ibby had asked me if I'd talked to Pete about Hugh Bingham—if I'd told him the man scared me. I'd denied that he frightened me, but what else would I call it? She was right. I needed to tell Pete what I was feeling. Was it just some silly kind of discomfort? Or was it actually fear?

Chapter Seventeen

Walking on a moonlit night on one of Salem's most beautiful streets between two tall, strong, trusted men made me brave. I decided to share my concern, silly or not, with both of them—the police detective and the repentant killer.

"I need to share something with you two," I began. "I've already talked with Aunt Ibby and River about it. Maybe it's something. Maybe it's nothing."

"What's wrong?" Pete grasped my elbow. "Is it the baby? Are you feeling all right?"

"Oh dear! It's nothing like that. I'm fine. Baby is fine. I've never felt better. Honest!"

"What is it, then?" Michael's voice was calm. Steady. "How can we help?"

"It's about a person I've met recently. A man," I told them. "He makes me uncomfortable and I don't know why."

"Bingham," Pete said. "Hugh Bingham."

"That's right," I told him. "How did you know?"

"Because, my darling, I've known you for a long time. And in all that time I've never known you to be so glad to finish an assignment."

"You wanted me to be done with it too," I recalled.

Michael spoke up. "I was glad when you finished it too. Remember I told you that Bernie Bingham had made some powerful enemies? I wished from the start that you'd distance yourself from those people."

"Tell me exactly what makes you so uneasy about him," Pete demanded.

"For one thing," I confessed, "he seems to show up where I am too often. More than coincidentally, I'd say."

"A stalker," Michael proposed. "Is this guy following you?"

"I'm not sure . . . I mean, it's probably nothing," I stammered.

"I'll have a talk with him tomorrow," Pete said. Serious cop voice. "Don't worry about him anymore. I'll handle it."

The words brought me an immediate sense of relief. Pete would handle it. I thought again of the Knight of Swords protecting me, righting all wrongs. The rest of the way to my aunt's house I almost felt as if I was floating. Betsy's Mercedes was parked out front. Louisa often rode along with her, so maybe they were both inside. It was nearly time for the much-anticipated *Midsomer Murders* program to begin. We three climbed the stairs and I, happily pregnant and now worry free, rang the bell.

Aunt Ibby opened the door instantly. She must have been standing in the foyer when the chimes rang. "Come in, my dears. The girls are already here and a fresh blueberry pie is cooling in the pantry. Did I tell you we'll be seeing 'Claws Out'? Plenty of cats—and Paddy the dog is in it too." She waved us into the living room, where Betsy and Louisa were already facing the big-screen TV. "Remember Paddy? John and Sarah's little terrier?" I remembered, and Pete said he did too.

Michael one-upped us by remembering the title of the episode. "'The Village That Rose from the Dead,'" he pronounced. "A good one."

We trooped into the living room, greeted Louisa and Betsy with hugs, and took our usual seats in matching upholstered club chairs. I took the opportunity to tell Betsy of Trisha's concern about Bathsheba. "Trisha can't have a pet while she's in the shelter, so she's going to take one of Aunt Ibby's rooms," I explained, "and if she doesn't get Bathsheba out of New Hampshire this week, the animal control folks will take her. Could you make a run up to New Hampshire—it's just over the border in Brookfield—and be foster cat-mom for just a little while? I'm sure there's a cat carrier for Bathsheba."

Betsy hesitated for about a nanosecond before she said, "Yes. And I still have Pixie's carrier." Her smile told me that she welcomed the challenge. Aunt Ibby had, as usual, provided each of us with a yellow legal pad and a Salem Public Library pen for note-taking during the program. O'Ryan joined us just as the show was about to start, sitting on his haunches at Aunt Ibby's feet, ears perked up and eyes focused on the screen.

"I'm not surprised that O'Ryan is interested. We're going to learn about how the investigators use technology to find missing cats and dogs." She clicked on the TV and the credits rolled over a shot of the idyllic British village of Binwell. "Maybe we can think about how technology might be used to find the answer to our recent local killing in what the press is calling the 'Chocolate Shop Murder.'" She raised a questioning eyebrow in Pete's direction. He didn't acknowledge the look.

We weren't far into the story when pet detective Frank Bailey was killed in a parking lot. Tai turned up soon after and we learned that the always obedient, though sometimes mischievous, Paddy suddenly refused to obey familiar commands. Toss in crazy cat lady Lorna, who already had dozens of cats and also steals other people's cats to add to her collection. We were all hooked—most of us furiously scribbling notes, O'Ryan commenting with an occasional throaty yowl. By the time Detective Chief Inspector John Barnaby and Detective Sergeant Jamie Winter sorted out the trail of drugs, debts, and a dog-collar electric shock, we'd silenced the TV and Ibby had served the blueberry pie. We were finally ready to discuss both cases—the fictional one and the very real one. Michael, ever the mystery writer, posed the first question. "If Frank Bailey was never the intended victim," he said, "what if Bernie Bingham wasn't the intended target either?"

Wow. I'd never thought of that. What if Bernie had interrupted someone who shouldn't have been there at that particular time? What if the intended target was still in danger?

"On the show, Tai and Frank Bailey were men of similar height and build," Louisa pointed out. "Also, they'd both been wearing dark motorcycle jackets and full-face helmets."

"What about Bernie Bingham's clothes, Lee?" Betsy asked. "Can you remember what he was wearing?"

I closed my eyes, willing the sight I'd seen in the cold room back into focus. "A white dress shirt," I said. "It was open at the throat, and I think he was wearing a gold necklace. Tan slacks. Sort of what a businessman might wear on casual Friday." I looked at Pete. "Sometimes I've seen Pete wearing a similar outfit before he puts a jacket on."

"Me too," Michael offered. "I guess most guys have the plain white shirt/tan slacks outfit on hand. Now, what about the weapon?"

"According to the ME, it was a sharp instrument," Pete said. "The videos from WICH-TV showed several sharp tools they use in making candy."

"I saw those big shears on the video Lee made," Michael said. "It reminded me of one of my Fenton Bishop books in the *Antique Alley* series." He closed his eyes for a second. "I used sewing shears for the murder in *Cross-stitch Double-cross*."

"I'm sure the police have examined every sharp object in that entire building." I looked at Pete for verification.

"We were there immediately after Lee found Bingham's body. The entire place, except for the area around the body, was absolutely clean. There wasn't a trace of

blood anywhere else. There wouldn't have been time
for a killer to stab the victim, then clean the weapon
and return it to its usual place among the candy making
tools."

"What did the killer in the book do with the scissors,
Michael?" Betsy wanted to know.

"Oh, she just wiped them off and put them back into
her sewing basket" was the offhand reply. "She figured
she'd clean them up later."

"She?" Several of us asked the one-word question at
once.

"Yes. Of course. Say, don't any of you read my
books?" He made a face. "Sure it's a she. It doesn't always have to be a man who does the killing." My
thoughts immediately turned once again to Shirley Parker
and just as rapidly to Trisha Violette. He was right. It
doesn't always have to be a man who does the killing.

Betsy made the next observation. "There was a bag
of drugs in the show. Do we know that there aren't
drugs involved in the Parker mansion business? I
mean, you could move a lot of drugs in sealed candy
boxes."

Since there hadn't been any mention of drug use regarding the people involved that we knew about, and
none of the questions to Chief Whaley had touched on
the subject, we'd all bypassed the topic. I looked at
Peter, who didn't offer any comment. "We've heard
that Bernie had some pretty shady characters around
him," I said. "It wouldn't be too surprising if one or
more of them was involved in drugs, would it? It seems
as if he had a lot of debt. What if he owed money to
someone like that?"

Michael gave a wise nod. "I've tried to warn you, Lee. I admit that my sources aren't the most trustworthy people in the world—after all, most of them are doing time for one thing or another—but more than one of them has told me that old Bernie burned some powerful people. These are people you don't want to meet in a dark alley. Frankly, I worry about you being involved with the Binghams for any reason. Even chocolate candy."

"That part of my research is finished," I assured him. "I don't need to talk to any of them ever again."

"I've talked to Bruce Doan about it," Pete said. "There won't be any more Parker mansion assignments."

"You have?" I was happily surprised. "I mean, thank you for doing that."

"I worry about you," he said.

"I know. I'm sorry," I apologized. "But once I'm a stay-at-home mom with baby Ella Marie you won't ever have to worry anymore." My aunt wasn't the only person in the room to stifle a snicker at that remark. Louisa laughed out loud, and Pete just closed his eyes.

"You seem to have a knack for landing in the middle of trouble," Michael observed with an absolutely straight face. "It wasn't always at the TV station either. It happened when you were teaching classes at the Tabby too. Like when you took your class on a cemetery tour and you found a body? You're just one of those people things happen to. You can't help it. It's not your fault."

"It's true," Aunt Ibby said, agreeing with Michael's assessment. "When you were a little girl at scout camp, why was it always *your* tent the bear tried to get into?

And do you remember when you were in third grade and the mayor visited your class while you were reading your essay on city government and you wound up on local TV?"

"That was the day I decided on a career in television," I said. "I fell in love with the camera."

"The camera loves you too," Betsy said. "It doesn't love everybody, you know. It still likes me. How else would I still be modeling at my age?"

"It doesn't love me," Michael deadpanned. "Did you ever see my mug shot?"

"It seems to love you when you're Fenton Bishop," Louisa said. "The back cover author photo on your books looks like a movie star."

"A miracle of technology," he admitted. "Between AI and Photoshop, the publisher has created a new me. Imagine how disappointed readers must be when they come to an in-person signing event and get a look at the real Fenton Bishop."

"If you ask me," my aunt said, "and nobody has— but I think you are a very attractive man." Heads nodded all around like a room full of bobblehead dolls, and the conversation about who the camera loves—or not—was thankfully ended and we returned to the matter at hand: the murder of Bernie Bingham.

"The TV show has taken us in several directions we might not have thought about," Pete said. "But remember—the murder of Bingham is real and the television murder is the product of fiction writers. There's no indication, for instance, that drugs are involved in the Bingham matter. We do not know what sort of weapon was used in this killing. Let's not make assumptions about the 'sharp instrument' because of a weapon mentioned in one of Michael's books." Pete accepted another slice of blueberry pie. "Let's not get sidetracked."

"That reminds me," my aunt said. "Maralee, I put that book on candy making you asked about on the hall tree seat. Don't forget to take it with you when you leave."

"Thanks. I'm going to look up 'sharp, pointed candy making tools.'" I told her. "I'll try not to get sidetracked."

"Pete's right though," Louisa agreed. "Just because Tai and Frank in the show were dressed alike doesn't mean the white shirt and tan slacks prove anything at all in the *real* murder."

Betsy folded her arms. "I disagree. I think we should look for someone else, some other man, wearing a similar outfit on the same day."

"If we find someone like that," I offered, "that person might have been the intended target."

"We'd have to warn him," my aunt said, "and we'd better hurry up and find him—before the killer does."

Chapter Eighteen

Michael and Pete and I walked three abreast along the wide sidewalk toward home. I carried the candy book that I'd gotten from Aunt Ibby under one arm. We moved aside and murmured greetings to an approaching dog-walking neighbor. After the man had passed, Michael whispered, "He's wearing tan slacks."

I smothered a laugh. "Stop it. He's the pastor of the congregational church."

"I'm just sayin'," Michael insisted. "We need to be observant."

"Where do you get that *we*?" Pete wanted to know. "Studying a TV murder is one thing. Actually investigating a murder is up to the police department."

"True," I said. "But if we see something, we should say something, right? I mean, that's what the posters and buttons and T-shirts say."

"Sometimes," he admitted, "but don't believe everything you read on a button. People call us with the darndest things."

"Like what?"

"Oh, I don't know—like reporting a perfectly nice pastor because he's wearing tan slacks." We all laughed at that.

"I'm interested in what you said, Michael, about your woman killer stashing the murder weapon in the sewing basket until she could clean it," I told him. "How did that work out for her?"

"Pretty well, until she tried using the same scissors—before she'd had a chance to clean them—to stab her boyfriend, claiming self-defense." Big smile. "When the first victim's DNA showed up in the boyfriend's wound, my sleuth solved the mystery. No problem."

"The cross-stitch double-cross. I get it," I said. "It fits the title. What do you think, Pete? If Bernie's killer tries using the same weapon on somebody else, could they find Bernie's DNA in the wound?"

"It's a pretty unlikely scenario," he said, "but . . . theoretically, I suppose it's a possibility."

"That's all it has to be in a book," Michael declared. "It doesn't have to be probable—just possible."

"I like hearing you talk about writing, Michael," I told him. "It's interesting, the way you can take ordinary, everyday circumstances and figure out how to make a mystery from them."

He smiled. "I think you'll be interested in some good news about writing—I mean, I'm pretty sure it's good. I've just signed a brand-new contract for another Fenton Bishop series. This one will involve something I see and do every day—and will, of course, involve murder."

"How exciting," I said. "Congratulations. What will it be about?"

"The publisher has named the series *The Garden Club Mysteries*."

"I should have guessed," Pete said. "You've figured out how to make all that backyard work yield more than vegetables and flowers."

"It's an absolutely brilliant idea, Michael," I told him. "Have you started on the first book yet?"

A shy smile and a hushed tone of voice. "I've outlined it. The working title is *Angel's Trumpet*."

"A religious aspect?" I asked.

"Far from it," he said. "A garden is a great source of poisonous plants, as you might imagine. Poisons galore—perfect for a murder mystery series. No. Angel's trumpet is a small tree—a shrub, actually—with beautiful trumpet-shaped blossoms. The flowers are fragrant, sweet smelling, and come in many beautiful colors. But here's the fun part. Practically every bit of the plant is poisonous—full of terrible things like atropine and scopolamine. Agatha Christie used both of those, by the way—atropine in "The Cretan Bull," and scopolamine in her first play, *Black Coffee*." He exhaled a self-satisfied sigh. "I'll get a long series out of my fictitious garden club. Not just because of the poison aspect. Gardeners use tools that can easily double as weapons. Think about it. Claw rakes, hand sickles, machetes, pitchforks—a never-ending arsenal! I'm loving the idea. And I'll start with angel's trumpet. What do you think?"

"It's going to be wonderful. I'm so happy for you," I told him.

We'd reached our house and were greeted by two cats, one on each front doorstep—O'Ryan on ours and, next door, Frankie on Michael's. "Sort of like anxious parents waiting up for us, aren't they?" Pete observed. Or like guardian cats, I thought, waiting for me and Ella Marie to arrive home safely.

Pete unlocked the door and O'Ryan scooted inside ahead of us. I glanced over to Michael's house to see if Frankie would display similar behavior. She didn't go inside even though Michael paused in the doorway, beckoning to her to do so. Instead, with a wide, pink-mouthed yawn, she strolled across the sidewalk, and sat on *our* front steps, looking up at me but making no attempt to follow O'Ryan.

Cats. Go figure.

"I don't know what that was all about." Pete held the door open for me, growling "Scat" to Frankie, who obeyed and headed back to her own house. "But I'm sure it has something to do with pregnancy hormones and such. Want to watch some more TV before we turn in?"

"Sure," I agreed. "Along with maybe a nice cup of decaf and a powdered sugar doughnut?"

"I wonder if you'll still like those doughnuts after Ella Marie arrives."

"I don't know. She probably will though." We both laughed at that idea. I kicked off my shoes, put the candy book on an end table, and headed for the kitchen. "Coffee and doughnut for you too?" I asked.

"Why not? I'll do a little extra time at the gym tomorrow and work it off." Pete has to stay in shape for his job, which from time to time might require chasing somebody on foot or even getting into a physical tussle. I was still doing some doctor-prescribed routines for expectant mommies, but I'd promised myself I'd get back to a regular diet-and-exercise routine after baby Ella arrived. I popped a couple of decafs into the Keurig and put our doughnuts on a Fiestaware plate. I didn't expect the after-baby diet to include sugar doughnuts—all the more reason to savor this one!

Pete turned on the kitchen TV and we sat facing one another across the kitchen table, with O'Ryan clearly visible at my feet through the clear Lucite tabletop. I've never figured out whether or not he knows we can see him when he's down there. It was cozy there, in our warm, pretty kitchen with husband, cat, doughnuts, and a colorful commercial for a local art gallery on TV. I sipped my coffee, relaxed and happy. That feeling slipped away when the "Breaking News" banner appeared on the screen. Scott Palmer was positioned in front of the Salem police station. "The medical examiner has not yet released the body of recent murder victim Bernie Bingham to his family." Muted network announcer voice. "The investigation into Bingham's death continues." Scott segued into some of the previously recorded videos, including the one of the body being removed from the Parker estate, and some of the still shots I'd taken before I'd discovered the body.

"How come the body hasn't been released?" I asked.

"There's a lot of investigation yet to be done," he said

"I get it. Hey, look." I pointed to the screen. "There's

my picture of the candy tools. Look at those shears. And the knives. Are those wicked-looking weapons or what?"

The camera returned to the studio and Scott, wearing one of his long, soulful looks.

"Sources report some progress in the Bernie Bingham matter," Scott reported. "This station has been instrumental in bringing new information to the attention of the police." His own report of the call-in from Hugh Bingham completed the breaking news segment.

"The only thing new there was the information about the body not being released yet," I commented. "Do you know anything about the funeral arrangements?"

"Just that Shirley Parker is in charge. Hugh and an Uncle Earl will be honorary pall bearers. It looks as if it's going to be quite the dog and pony show. Shirley has always spared no expense when it came to her exhusband, and apparently his death is no exception. Chief isn't happy about any of it."

"Who's Uncle Earl?" I wondered aloud. "Did Bernie have a brother?"

"I don't know," Pete said. "Maybe he's an uncle on the Parker side of the family."

"None of my business anyway," I said. "I'm glad to be finished with all things Bingham."

"Forever." Pete put his mug down hard enough to slosh the coffee onto the table.

I handed him a paper napkin. "Forever," I agreed.

Chapter Nineteen

I arrived at work a little before nine, the candy book under my arm. Pete called and confirmed that Trisha Violette had been safely moved to Aunt Ibby's house. The first words I saw on Rhonda's whiteboard were in red capital letters. *LEE SEE DOAN*. I wasn't surprised. I figured that I was going to hear about Pete's instruction to keep me away from all things Bingham. I was right.

"Why is your husband so insistent about this particular candy story?" Bruce Doan demanded. "It didn't get any more airtime than the others, and the candy is really good. Is there something new going on with the Binghams because of Bernie's death? Something I should know about?" He was clearly upset. "If there's going to be some kind of legal trouble, police involvement, I need to be prepared for it."

"I'm sure there's no need to worry," I assured him.

"It's actually more of a personal matter. After all, my experience with Casa de Chocolatte began really badly. Pete just doesn't want me to have to be around that family. It's been frankly—well—upsetting."

"Oh sure. I should have thought of that. It's a pregnant lady thing. Right?"

It was on the tip of my tongue to deny it, but hey, maybe it was a pregnant lady thing. Hugh Bingham had been nothing but polite and respectful to me. "I guess so," I agreed. "It was a bad experience for me."

"Okay. No problem here. Scott is doing a good job on it anyway. You'd better stick to Halloween candy and leave the *real* news to him."

I don't have this red hair and Irish forebears for nothing. I felt a surge of anger, and almost bit my tongue to prevent some unladylike words from escaping. *Like I can't still do REAL news?* "Since I'm married to a detective," I said in a level tone, "I can't be involved in a matter that's under investigation anyway."

"Oh sure. Got it. No offense intended."

I know when I'm being humored. I don't like it. I took a deep breath. "None taken," I muttered. "Is Old Jim around? There are a couple more candy shops we might want to look at." I attempted a sweet smile. "For the Halloween candy story."

"I think he's doing a weather segment about hurricane preparedness with Wanda," he said. "He's around here somewhere."

"Thanks," I said.

"Don't forget to get samples."

"Sure thing." Still gritting my teeth, I nearly ran into Scott on my way out the reception room door.

"Hey, Moon," he said. "How's everything going? Still on the sugar high assignment?"

"I'm afraid so," I said. "You still chasing down Bingham's?"

"Yeah. It's getting old, you know? Nothing new has turned up. That Bernie had made so many enemies the suspect list looks like the old-time Salem yellow pages." His shoulders slumped and he fake-sighed.

"Say, on the subject of Bernie," I said, letting my too-long dormant field reporter's curiosity surface even though I'd officially forsaken all things Bingham. "Who is this Uncle Earl they've pegged for pall bearer? Is he a Bingham or a Parker?"

"Neither one. He's one of those honorary uncles that every family seems to have. He's a friend of the family, and the children had to have something to call him besides Mr. Hennesey, so he became Uncle Earl."

"Earl Hennesey, huh?" We approached Old Clunky. "Have you met him?"

"Not yet."

"A friend of which family?" I wondered.

"Shirley Parker doesn't think much of him, but he was tight with Bernie, and Hugh likes him, so she's going along with it." Scott pressed the elevator button and the brass door slid open. "You going down?"

"Yes." We entered the cage together. "Is he a Salem man?"

"Born and bred. He went to school with Bernie. Salem public schools," he offered. "They came from the same neighborhood down near Turner Street. They were both kids from Irish immigrant families and they met at the House of the Seven Gables settlement program. They got into trouble together back then."

"What kind of trouble?" Old Clunky began its rattling descent.

"I haven't had time yet to do a lot of research, but it was pretty much petty stuff. Stealing cigarettes. Toilet-papering trees. Skipping school. I've heard that Bernie once did some time at the Plummer reform school out on Winter Island."

"What for?"

"Stealing a teacher's wallet." The card showing the Seven of Swords in River's reading came to mind. Those boys were into stealing for sure. Maybe the sword stealer was Bernie. Or Uncle Earl.

"They stayed friends when they grew up?"

"So Shirley Parker claims."

"Are you planning to interview him?" I wanted to know. "I'll bet he has some good stories to tell."

"I'm trying to track him down," he said.

The door slid open onto the first-floor lobby and I stepped out onto the black-and-white tiles just as Old Jim came through the front door. "Hello, Lee," he said. "I heard you were looking for me."

"I am. We need a couple more candy shops. Can you think of any we missed?"

Scott, beside me, greeted Jim. "We were just talking about the House of the Seven Gables," he said. "Don't they still have that old-fashioned candy shop in there?"

It was a slap-yourself-on-the-forehead moment. "Hepzibah's Cent Shop," I recited, remembering the classic old story. "Trinkets and candy." I grabbed Old Jim's arm. "Let's go, Jim. Thanks Scott. I owe you one."

Scott grinned. "You can pay me in penny candy."

We didn't have much preparation time and I was sure we'd need permission to photograph inside the important National Historic Landmark property. Fortunately the Doans were senior members of The Gables Society, and that rated special privileges. Ever-efficient Rhonda had printed out a condensed history of the house for me to study on the short ride over there. The building didn't open for tours until ten, so we were given permission to film in the shop from nine thirty to nine forty-five.

While I took the stairs back up to my office to retrieve the green WICH-TV jacket—which by this time I needed to wear unbuttoned—and put the candy book on my desk, Jim picked up the shoulder-mount Sony and the keys to the VW mobile unit, and, just like old times, we were on our way.

Chapter Twenty

I'd visited the old house before, of course. I still re-membered the obligatory middle school trip, and how brave I'd felt ascending the scary secret staircase to the attic. The 1668 house inspired native son Na-thaniel Hawthorne's famous novel and is one of Salem's top tourist destinations, but for now we needed only to visit the re-created candy shop on the first floor. We were admitted by a guide through the old kitchen, with its enormous recessed fireplace, and from there to the entrance to the cent shop. Our escort explained that the shop had been added to the house in 1910 because those who'd read about Hepzibah's shop in Hawthorne's novel expected to see it there.

Jim began filming as I moved into the shop from the kitchen. I gave a bit of the history of the house and the shop, then looked around and told the viewers what they were about to see. I'd seen old postcards of the store, and it didn't look a lot different now. There were linens and glassware and teacups and souvenir plates and spoons, and plenty of candy in tall glass containers and behind curved display cases. There were even gingerbread elephants lined up on a windowsill. Salem has had a fondness for elephants since the first one ever exhibited in the United States arrived here aboard Jacob Crowninshield's vessel, the *America*, on November 2, 1795. One thing I wasn't able to share with the viewers was the wonderful smell of the place—candy and gingerbread and starched cotton, with a whiff of woodsmoke from the adjoining kitchen. We wrapped up the shoot with a close-up of a significant display of silver souvenir spoons from the original Daniel Low's. I reminded viewers that the venerable building that housed that fine old department store is now Rockafellas Restaurant.

Jim had just lowered his camera, then he tugged at my elbow. "See that guy waiting just outside the door?" he whispered, tilting his head slightly. "In the yellow shirt?"

I peered through wavy window glass and whispered back, "Yes. What about him?"

"I think it could be the Bingham's Uncle Earl. The *Salem News* ran a picture of him when he was young." One of the reasons I love working with Old Jim is because he sees things that other photographers miss. If he thought the yellow-shirted man was the aging elusive uncle, he was probably right.

"Keep rolling," I told him. "We still have a couple of

minutes. I'm going to go pick up one of those elephants and talk about it. Just include him at the edge of the frame."

We played out the charade. Jim did exactly as I'd asked. I wrapped up the shoot with a "Thank you" to the tour guide, who handed me a good-enough-sized bag of candies to please both Scott and Doan. We climbed back into the VW and, as Jim put it, "headed for the barn."

Our first stop was at Marty's editing desk to drop off the morning's work. "If it's not too much trouble, can you make a couple of still shots of the man in a yellow shirt at the very end of the candy shop footage?" I asked. I wasn't exactly sure about what I'd do with the information that "Uncle Earl" Hennessey was currently hanging around at his childhood stomping grounds. Was I too pregnant to embark on a field reporting venture? Or maybe, if not too pregnant—too *married*? There was no doubt that Pete was not going to approve any news reporter TV for me for the time being, especially a story involving a Bingham—especially one possibly involving *Hugh* Bingham. Should I simply hand the photos and the idea over to Scott along with a bag full of penny candy? If it turned out to be anything newsworthy, I figured, since it was *my* video footage, and if Scott got a spot on the late news, I'd at least rate the second-banana seat beside Buck Covington. Anyway, Jim and I had a good candy store story to add to our pre-Halloween series. Decision made. Scott would get Uncle Earl along with a good supply of Mary Janes, Bull's Eyes, and Black Crows.

Scott was, understandably, delighted with the photos, the information, and the candy. "If this turns out to be a good lead, I'll be back to owing you one, Moon," he said. "Thanks."

"Keep me up to speed on it, will you?" I asked. "I had no idea my simple little chocolate story would take so many twists and turns."

"Will do," he said. "Francine and I are heading over to Turner Street right now. Maybe I can corner Earl Hennesey and see what he has to say about his old buddy's murder. If you'll pardon a cliché—if anybody knows where all the bodies are buried in Bernie Bingham's world, it's Uncle Earl."

I could picture Scott, with camera rolling, shoving a mic in a cornered Earl's face, barraging him with questions. Somehow I couldn't quite picture me doing anything similar right now. I realized that, at the moment, I was a lot more comfortable with concentrating on getting Bernie Bingham's girlfriend's cat safely back from New Hampshire. I wished Scott a good interview and didn't bother to tell him that he had a Sugar Daddy pop sticking out of his breast pocket.

My immediate concern was Bathsheba. Betsy hadn't yet let me know when she planned to head north to New Hampshire, and I was sure she wouldn't mind if I called to check. The sooner Trisha Violette could rest easy about her cat, the easier it would be for the police to question her about Bernie Bingham. Betsy answered right away. "I'm just gassing up the Mercedes and I'll be on my way today." There was excitement in her voice. "It's a beautiful day for a drive and there's nothing that would give me more pleasure than rescuing a lost kitty. Thanks for thinking of me for this good deed, Lee."

I wished her a pleasant journey and thanked her again for making the trip, then took the metal staircase back to Marty's territory for a final look at the Gable's shop footage. It was good. The shop looked perfect, and I looked pretty good too. Marty, with her excellent instincts, had not included the part with the man in the yellow shirt, but had managed to include my little spiel about the gingerbread elephants. My next stop was at my glass cubicle, where I sat in my comfortable desk chair and stared at the variety of colored stickies nearly obscuring the window facing the newsroom. I was clearly not at a loss for things to do.

I pulled down a random pink one. *Ask Jim for photo prints of candy making utensils.* Random or not, I couldn't have picked anything more timely. Aunt Ibby's book on candy making, with photos and descriptions of methods and—more important—tools was already on my desk. Jim's photos would provide a photographic reminder of the tools they used at Casa de Chocolatte without necessitating another visit to the forbidden territory across the common.

I left a message on Jim's phone and pulled down a baby blue sticky. *Make appointment for Toby's bath and clip.* That was an easy one. Toby enjoys his spa days with the groomer. I'd just completed that task when Jim returned my call.

"I've got those photos ready for you," Jim said, "and I looked up the video footage we ran of that guy doing the tour of the candy factory showing the same area."

Long pause. "Something doesn't add up. Have you got time to go over them with me?"

"I sure do. Come on down," I told him. "I brought in the book with descriptions of all the proper tools and what they do. Maybe that will help." I flipped the book open to the tools section, which I'd marked with a Salem Public Library bookmark. I'd just reached for a yellow sticky when a smiling Scott appeared behind the glass. I reached for the phone. "How'd it go?" I asked.

"A home run," he said. "An exclusive interview with the elusive Uncle Earl. The reason he's back in the old hood is because he's broke. Trying to mooch a place to sleep from old pals." He gave me one of those long, sad Scott Palmer looks. "He'd tried to put the touch on Shirley but she said no. He thinks Hugh will slip him a few bucks behind her back though. Anyway, it looks like he might have been the last person to see old Bernie alive. Francine got the whole thing on video." Another big grin. "Marty's editing it now. Earl has a mouth on him like Trisha Violette's. Besides that, I need to run it by the cops first in case there's something there they need to know."

"Did you contact Pete?" I asked.

"Of course I did. Who else would I call? He's on his way over here."

"So this Earl person may have been the last person to see Bernie Bingham alive? What makes him think that?"

"He claims that he and Bernie walked together to the Parker place that afternoon to see about Bernie picking up his alimony money instead of having it sent to New Hampshire. He saw Bernie go in through the front door. You probably arrived there pretty soon after he did."

I didn't want to think about anything Bingham anymore. Ever. I was very glad to hear that Pete was on his way—my Knight of Swords, coming to protect me.

Chapter Twenty-one

Pete and Old Jim arrived at almost the same time. Pete texted that he'd check what Scott had going on first, then see me. Jim came straight to my office. He didn't waste any time on conversation, just pulled two eight-by-ten color photos from a manila envelope and spread them out on the top of my desk. "See if you see what I see," he demanded. He tapped the first photo with an impatient forefinger. "This is one of the pictures you snapped with your phone right before you found the dead guy." I leaned forward and confirmed what he'd said.

He tapped the other photo. "Here's one from the last trip you and I made over there when Hugh Bingham gave the tour." At first glance the two photos looked almost identical, one with a bit sharper focus than the other. I guessed that one must have been taken with Jim's Sony.

"Look carefully," he said.

I saw it. I took a quick inward breath. "Ohmigod, Jim! There are five knives in my photo. There are six in yours."

"The murder weapon," he said. "I have no doubt."

"Somebody cleaned it up and put it back where it belonged," I reasoned. "It wasn't missed because no one was working on the day he died. Then the kitchen was closed down while the investigation went on, and by the time the whole crew was back, the knife was back too."

"That's the way I see it," Jim said.

"Pete's in the building," I told him. "He needs to see these."

"He sure does."

"Wait here with me, okay?"

"Yep."

I put the manila envelope on top of the pictures just in case prying field reporter eyes peeked through the glass walls of my office. There was no more conversation between Jim and me as we waited for Pete. There was no need of any. We'd been friends so long that a companionable silence was comfortable for us. We saw Pete through the glass wall. He stood beside Scott, both of them focused on a small screen. I knew they were viewing the unedited version of the surprising interview with Earl Hennessey. That information would help pinpoint the time of Bernie's death. What Jim and I were about to show him might pinpoint the murder weapon.

Once Pete saw what we had he lost no time in immediately ordering the downstairs portion of Casa de Chocolatte closed for more investigation. Then he called Shirley Parker and informed her that they'd make the shutdown as brief as possible and that he'd appreciate her help in identifying each of the knives used in the candy making process. I couldn't hear her reply, but I knew it must be positive, because he told her he'd be there with his team within fifteen minutes.

"Come along, you two," he said. "Bring your pictures."

Jim and I looked at each other. "Us?"

"Firsthand evidence," he said. "Her cooperation in corroborating yours will help speed things along. My forensic specialists will meet us there too. I need to know who uses the knives and what they're used for. How often are they sharpened? Who takes charge of keeping them in good condition?"

We joined Pete in the cruiser, Jim with the Sony and a couple of clip-on mics in a carrying case. "Just in case we need them," he said. Pete parked behind the mansion—no sense in advertising the fact that the police were there again. We three walked around to the front steps. The sign with instructions to walk right in had been replaced with one that said "Please Ring." That made perfect sense since it was in fact a crime scene. I pushed the doorbell and a cute young woman in what resembled one of those French maid costumes answered immediately. We identified ourselves, which wasn't really necessary, since Shirley, impeccably dressed in a navy blue Giorgio Armani number, could see us clearly from where she sat. Gracious as always, she reached across the desk and shook hands with all three of us. "The other members of your team are downstairs with Hugh," she said. "I asked him to wait for you. Go right along down and join them."

Pete, Jim, and I descended the curvy staircase. Hugh Bingham acknowledged us with a nod. He stood in front of the tool display, facing the agents, beginning the delivery of what sounded like a well-rehearsed spiel for a Girl Scout candy factory tour. One of the forensics guys held a small video recorder. Jim tried to be unintrusive with his.

"Some of our tools are custom-made for us, while others are readily available in any confectioner's supply house," Hugh began. He motioned toward the assortment of cutting devices. "Our knives all have special sanitary handles." He pointed to a long knife with a slanted blunt end. "This is a fudge knife, with a twelve-inch blade. It's designed to cut big, thick slices of our delicious fudge. The knife next to it is actually the same size as a regular butcher knife. It also has a twelve-inch blade and is used for cutting our caramels or nougats into uniform squares. The shorter knife beside that one has just an eight-inch blade, but it has what we call a 'rounded belly.'" He laughed and pointed to his own waistline. "Not like mine. No. This rounded part gives it a rocking motion to make it easier to cut through things like peanut brittle or almond bark. Now, see this tiny little guy with a curvy blade? It looks almost dainty, and it's only a bit under nine inches long. But this one, handmade in Tuscany, is called a chocolate knife. It's the most expensive knife we have, but it cuts as easily through a large piece of hard chocolate as if it was butter. Here's a serrated knife. You probably have one just like it at home. We use it for chopping high-quality chocolate into chips instead of relying on the more expensive bagged ones." He pointed to the selection of shears. "These candy shears help us speed up our hard candy production. We make our own hard candy mix for flavor and color, boil it to high heat, then pour it into a pan. When it sets up we cut it into uniform pieces with the proper-sized candy shears, encase it, and box it." He moved on to the dipping tools and the fondue forks. One of the forensics detectives held up a hand. "Thank you, Mr. Bingham. That's all we'll need for now. We appreciate your time."

They said their polite goodbyes and headed back upstairs. Jim returned his camera equipment to the case. Shirley, still at her desk, turned to us, all smiles and motherly pride. "Doesn't Hugh do a marvelous job telling our story?"

Ignoring the question, and using his best professional cop voice, Pete got down to business. "We have a pair of photos, Ms. Parker. Lee took one of them on the day she discovered the body. It has a time stamp on it. Could you check your visitors list or your security cameras to be sure the times coincide? The second one is from the Halloween advertising video showing the same area and is also time-stamped. Your cameras will probably agree within a few minutes of that one. Can you check? Then we'd also like a little more detail from you about the care and handling of the knives and shears your son just so aptly described for us."

"Certainly. That will be no problem at all." Another proud mom smile. "Hugh tried to give each of your charming forensics associates an eighteen-piece assortment of our cream centers and truffles." She made a pretty pout. "But they said they couldn't accept them."

"I'm sorry. We don't ordinarily accept gifts," Pete said. I was embarrassed. Here I was, actively hustling all the candy stores in town for free goodies, and Pete felt duty-bound to turn down a few dozen pieces of chocolate.

"Maybe we could buy them for the guys, Pete," I suggested.

"Good idea." Pete pulled a credit card from his wallet and successfully masked his astonishment at the price of a couple of boxes of teensy boutique handmade chocolates, while Shirley pushed a card reader in his direction and smilingly accepted payment.

"I've had one of the secretaries check the time stamps of your pictures against ours," she said, "and they do line up almost exactly. What was the other thing you wanted to know? Something about our knives?"

"Yes. Lee's aunt gave her a book about candy making that stressed the importance of always keeping the tools sanitary and sharp. May I ask who is in charge of making sure all of yours are in top shape every day?"

"I'll have to check that with Hugh," she said. "He's in charge of details like cleaning and polishing, along with all his other duties. Hold on. I'll ask him." She touched a buzzer. "Darling? Lee and Pete are here and they want to know who keeps our knives sharp and clean. Why? I don't know. Police stuff, I guess." Short pause. "Okay, I'll tell them." She faced us. "We have a professional company that does it on a regular basis. They come here to do it. We don't have to send them out. Hugh says that they're professionally cleaned and sharpened at least once a week." She scribbled a name on a notepad and handed it to Pete. "They're right here in Salem. You can call them."

"Thank you." Pete stuffed the note into his pocket. "I appreciate your cooperation. However, we will need to remove all of your knives from the premises immediately for closer examination."

She gave a slight inclination of her head. "I'm not surprised. I suppose it's possible that one of our knives killed Bernie." She waved a smiling dismissal.

"One more question," he said. "We have a witness who says that he saw Bernie go into your front door shortly before he was killed. He told the witness that, as long as he was in Salem anyway, he intended to ask you to give him a check for the alimony payment. Did he ask you that?"

She gave a confused shake of her head. "No. I believe the money was sent in the usual manner. A direct deposit to his account. Anyway, I haven't seen Bernie in months."

Chapter Twenty-two

I was surprised by her statement that she hadn't seen her ex-husband in months. If Pete was surprised, he didn't show it. Since she'd always continued to bail Bernie out financially whenever he needed it, enough so that Chief Whaley was annoyed by her generosity, and they shared a son, I would have thought that they kept in closer touch.

"Your contact with Mr. Bingham was by phone? E-mail?" Pete wanted to know.

"My contact with Bernie was financial. I felt sorry for him. We no longer had anything in common." Her eyes were downcast. "We certainly moved in different—um—different social circles."

"He didn't make a habit of visiting you here in your home?" Pete asked.

"Good heavens, no!" The horrified look seemed genuine.

"I understand you have agreed to make his—final arrangements?" Kindly cop voice.

"Of course. I'll proceed as soon as his body is released." She looked up again. "Can you give me some idea of when that might be?"

"That's entirely up to Dr. Egan, the medical examiner. It was a fairly clean in-and-out stabbing. He's examined the wound to try to figure out what kind of weapon was used," Pete explained in his most patient cop voice. "It's possible to know whether a blade was single- or double-edged or serrated. So far it looks like it could have been your nine-inch chocolate knife."

"Knives are knives." She sounded impatient. "It could have come from anywhere, couldn't it? None of our knives are unusual for candymakers. "

"You're right. He couldn't say for sure it was exactly *your* knife. Just that one of yours is similar to the one that killed Bernie."

"I suppose you'll look for fingerprints," she said, "even though our people all wear latex gloves and all of our knives are perfectly clean. As you know, they're cleaned by professionals."

"I understand. Obviously, a killer would clean the knife. Sometimes though, a little blood might seep into the space where the hand guard and the blade are joined. If the ME can locate it there, he could create a DNA profile of the blood. If it matches the victim's DNA profile, why then, we'd know that this particular knife was the murder weapon."

"Really?" Shirley inspected her manicured fingernails. "Interesting."

"Yes," Pete said. "Besides that, sometimes an attacker

might suffer minor hand or finger cuts as the knife slips in his hand. A sample of his blood on or around the victim would require some explaining."

Shirley focused on me, frowning slightly. "But dear Lee, all this talk of blood and guts must be upsetting to you. I know when I was carrying Hugh I got queasy over any little thing."

I smiled at the thoughtfulness. I'd been lucky enough to avoid the dreaded morning sickness. "I'm okay," I said, "even though I'd rather talk about chocolates."

"Me too," she said. "Did you notice that each chocolate is encased in its own tiny brown fluted paper cup? Then they are each, one by one, packed by hand into the appropriate box."

"They look like miniature cupcake baking cups," I said. "I noticed them beside the conveyor belt."

"Correct. The workers pick up the candy from the belt, put it into a brown paper cup, and place it into the appropriately sized box. They have to know how many of each variety go in each box, and they must do it fast. It takes special hand-eye coordination, as you can well imagine." She smiled. "I'm quite good at it myself."

I stood close enough to Pete that I heard his phone buzz. "Excuse me," he said, turning his back, inspecting the screen. He returned the phone to his pocket. "It appears that you can go ahead with the funeral arrangements, Ms. Parker. Dr. Egan has completed his examinations."

"I'm glad to hear it, and Hugh will be too. I'll contact the funeral director about a very modest, low-key ceremony, and Hugh can get in touch with the other person involved." She wrinkled her nose. "One of Bernie's disreputable childhood friends." She cast a ladylike glare in Pete's direction. "I presume we can get back to business now. Hugh has already managed to obtain a duplicate set of knives to replace the ones your people . . . appropriated." I sensed the implied *stole* in her tone.

"Of course," Pete assured her.

"I'll reassemble our workforce right away, then. They are, after all, the best confectioners in the business." Another frosty glare at Pete. "I only hope none of them have found jobs with a competitor after all this delay."

"Thank you for your cooperation," Pete said. "We'll be on our way." He held my elbow firmly, steering me toward the lovely front door. "That's that," he whispered as we descended the steps and headed for his car. "I'm taking you home now. I may be working late for a while. There's still a lot of narrowing down to do among the suspects—and boy, do we have too many suspects. And with all the open doors at the Parker estate, a lot of them had access to the chocolate knife. Old Bernie must have burned everybody in town at one time or another. No more Binghams for you though, I promise."

I hoped it was true.

As soon as we turned onto Winter Street I saw Betsy's Mercedes parked in front of Aunt Ibby's house. "Look. Betsy's back with Bathsheba." I was excited. "Let's stop. I need to get pictures of Trisha being reunited with her cat. I'd better call and get Jim or

Francine over here in a hurry." Rhonda answered immediately and I knew there'd be a mobile unit on Winter Street within minutes.

It was a happy reunion scene for sure. Bruce Doan couldn't ask for anything better. Cat and mistress were obviously both delighted to be together. Bathsheba turned out to be a gorgeous, truly photogenic white Siberian. She was everything Trisha had said she was and more. There was hugging and patting and kitty kisses and so many real tears of happiness from Trisha that the top of Bathsheba's head was wet.

There was another surprise when Betsy displayed a second cat carrier. I recognized Pixie's name in gold script on the carrying handle. "Bathsheba made a friend when she was at the animal control place," Betsy announced. She held the carrier at an angle so that we could look inside at a small tabby cat whose bright green eyes peered out shyly. "This is Mercy. I couldn't leave her behind. She's coming home with me." It was Trisha's story, after all, and we didn't film Betsy and Mercy for WICH-TV's viewers, but I used my own camera and recorded the moment anyway. I hoped we'd be seeing little Mercy for some years to come.

The station posted the "Bernie's girlfriend and her cat" story as soon as Marty was able to bleep out Trisha's more colorful welcomes to Bathsheba. It was hailed by viewers with loving words and more than a few offers of money for bus fare back to New Hampshire for them. Doan was really happy. "Maybe we should do more pet stories," he said. "Since you've got the candy shop thing pretty much wrapped up, why not look around for some cute animal subjects? You've still got a month or so to go before you do the maternity leave thing, right?"

"I've got about six weeks before the baby is due," I explained. "I guess I could check out one or two of the pet shelters around Salem," I offered.

"Try for three," he said. "You've got plenty of time."

I was so relieved by being finished with all things Bingham—feline or human—that I agreed to the three cute animal stories. Anyway, maybe publicizing some of the animals residing at the shelters would result in finding forever homes for the pets. That gave me a warm feeling. Our Toby was a rescue pet, and I couldn't imagine our family without him. Anyway, after all the awful Bingham involvement, cute pets should be easy peasy.

Chapter Twenty-three

As soon as we got home, Pete made himself a cup of coffee and relaxed on the couch—taking a well-earned break before heading back to the station—while I changed into a loose muumuu and slippers and began a search for pet shelters in or near Salem. I put my stack of index cards and a pen beside me on the desk. I still like that low-tech, strictly private means of keeping track of information. I was glad to find several likely shelters. Pals was an all-volunteer no-kill rescue group for cats and kittens. The Northeast Animal Shelter on Highland Avenue pledged to protect animals from cruelty and neglect and had recently rescued pets from a testing lab and from a massive out-of-state hurricane. One Tail at a Time in nearby Haverhill placed at-risk dogs from overcrowded shelters into good homes. It was a great start, and enough information to share with Doan so that he'd know I was taking the assignment seriously. I leaned back in my chair and reached for the nearby box of Casa de Chocolatte assorted truffles. I popped a dark chocolate one into my mouth and studied the attractive box. It was the middle-sized box, the five-by-eleven-inch one that held eighteen of the paper-cupped pieces.

I hadn't even finished chewing my truffle before I realized what I was looking at. "Pete!" I yelled.

He literally jumped from the couch. "Are you okay?"

"The Chocolate Box Man," I stuttered. "The knife would fit in this box!" I pointed.

He got it right away. "The killer stashed the knife in a candy box, hid it, then came back later to retrieve it."

"Then, after he'd cleaned it, he put it back—sometime between my first photo and Jim's video," I finished, knowing we were right.

Pete strapped on his holster and shrugged into his jacket. "I'll get right back onto everything we have so far on Chocolate Box Man," he promised. "Photo, footprints, mask, and white uniform. Maybe there's something else there—something we might have missed in the first analysis. Don't worry about dinner. I'll do DoorDash."

"I'm going back to work too. I'll study my photos again, and I'll go over the videos, both mine and Scott's, edited and unedited, with Marty. We could very well have missed something too," I acknowledged. "After all, we were just looking for candy treats, not a murderer."

I walked with Pete to the back door, let the station know I was on my way and why, then dashed, as much as an almost-eight-months-pregnant lady can dash—

waddled is more like it—up the stairs, changing from comfortable muumuu back into presentable work clothes. On the way out to the Jeep I grabbed the index cards, just in case I might run into Doan, who always appreciates multitasking employees, deciding on the fly that I'd start my latest assignment with the no-kill cat and kitten shelter. "Kittens are always adorable, and something involving no killing seems like a good idea right about now," I told Toby, who'd followed me up and down the stairs. "And the minute I get back I'll take you for a nice, long walk. I promise." Ever alert, Marty had rounded up Jim and Scott, so the three of us were on the same page in no time flat. There were indeed a couple of things we'd all missed back when we were just tracking down lollipops and gingerbread elephants. We watched, frame by frame, Scott's unplanned video that the WICH-TV night-shift cameraman had caught, showing the dim, shadowy form of Chocolate Box Man. "I was as amazed as anyone when Hugh handed me this gem," Scott admitted.

"It helps to be in the right place at the right time," Marty observed. "You lucked out. Too bad the guy is wearing a face mask."

"Not unusual," I told her. "They all wear hairnets and latex gloves and even face masks if they have a cold. The place is immaculately clean."

We all leaned closer. "Can you bring him up a little nearer? Is that a standard-issue uniform at the candy factory?"

She did.

"He must be one of the chocolate workers." Jim

pointed at the screen. "See? The company name is embroidered on the breast pocket."

"Pete may want to do another screening of the night-shift workers—although Chocolate Box Man isn't *necessarily* one of them, is he? I mean, maybe he doesn't even work there at all. When I was alone down there by myself I could have swiped a uniform easily."

"The chocolate pot thickens," Marty offered. Jim, Scott, and I groaned in unison at the terrible pun.

"I still find it hard to believe that someone would call a TV station instead of the police when a murder is involved," I said.

"Me too," Scott agreed, "but I'm glad it was me who got the call. My ratings have been up ever since. It's kind of a weird commentary on human nature, I guess, but people really like to hear about murders."

It's a lot more exciting than kitties and puppies, I admitted to myself.

I got home before Pete did. There were a few envelopes on the floor of the front hall, where they'd landed from the mail slot in the front door. I riffled through a few bills, a couple of ads, and a pink envelope bearing Aunt Ibby's return address. I opened that one first, guessing correctly that it was the invitation to my promised baby shower. I already knew the date, but I'd asked for an invitation so I could save it for Ella Marie's planned scrapbook. I put the invitation on the little table along with the other mail, then leashed an expectant Toby for his promised walk.

Toby likes the small park area behind the Civil War memorial, so we went there first. He also likes the common, but I was still leery about running into Hugh Bingham there, so we walked along the sidewalk across Winter Street from our house. I looked over at Aunt Ibby's house. There were some lights on in one of the third-floor apartments. Trisha Violette's space. I smiled, thinking of the happy reunion she and Bathsheba must be having. We arrived back at our own house, where O'Ryan and Frankie waited for us on the front step. Toby greeted the two with cautious sniffs. Of course neither cat showed any sign of dog-fear. "Hello you guys," I said, stooping carefully to give them each a pat. "It won't be long now before we get our baby and you can stop guarding me—although I must admit I love the extra attention."

Once inside I fixed a little snack to share with Pete—nothing fancy, just some cheese and crackers and Pepsi. Enough to keep him awake for a while. He'd been working some extra-long shifts, and I wanted to hear whatever he had to share about Chocolate Box Man. After all, I'd shared what I'd learned about the murder-knife-in-the-candy-box with him.

By then O'Ryan had come indoors and taken his perch on the front windowsill, Toby snoozing on the floor beneath him. It was a lovely picture of domestic tranquility. Mom-to-be and pets awaiting the homecoming of daddy-to-be. A sudden growl from O'Ryan broke the spell. O'Ryan rarely growls. What had he seen from his special vantage point? I moved faster than I'd thought I could and ducked behind him, focusing on the dimming light outside. There was nothing unusual in front of our house. O'Ryan growled again, this time deep in his throat. He actually clawed at the window. I moved closer. The man was all the way across the street, walking slowly, studying a piece of paper in his hand. I recognized that confident walk. I recognized him.

Why was Hugh Bingham taking an evening stroll on my street? And perhaps more importantly, why was the folded paper he held bright pink? I knew in my heart that it was a baby shower invitation, one with the directions to the site of the happy event: Aunt Ibby's house, barely a block away on Winter Street. "I'm damned sure *he* wasn't invited," I told the cat and dog, "but I wouldn't be surprised if Shirley was."

O'Ryan abandoned the windowsill and made a dash for the sunroom. Toby and I followed the cat. Thankfully, Pete was home and we were all safe.

Chapter Twenty-four

I waited at least long enough for him to take off his jacket, stash his gun, and sit down at the table before I began to bombard him with questions.

"So did Chocolate Box Man kill Bernie? Or is he covering up for someone else?" I asked.

"I don't know."

"Okay. Something else has turned up you need to know about. It's not even about Bernie. At least, I don't think it's about Bernie." I told him about seeing Hugh Bingham across from our house, and about the pink folded paper he held in his hands. "I think it could be an invitation to the baby shower. What if he's trying to figure out when I won't be home for some reason? The shower is the day after tomorrow. I guess Aunt Ibby may have invited Shirley Parker, and he may have grabbed her invitation. I'll ask her. But anyway, I don't like it."

"I don't like it either," Pete said. "Of course, it could be some kind of advertising flyer that just happens to be pink, but if it *is* actually the invitation, he'll know where you are and what time you'll be there." His brow furrowed. "I think I'll break precedent and go to a baby shower. O'Ryan and I will sit in the kitchen while you girls oooh and ahhh over baby stuff."

"I'll feel better with you there," I told him. O'Ryan gave a muffled meow. "I'll feel better if you're there too, big boy," I said. A little while later when all three of us were in the big bed together I felt totally fine and went to sleep like the proverbial baby myself—barely thinking about the next day's busy schedule of visiting cats and dogs.

Boom! I sat upright in bed—wide awake and terrified. What had happened? The room was quiet. O'Ryan blinked sleepy eyes from his usual spot at the foot of the bed. Pete rolled over and mumbled, "Babe? Are you okay?" Then he sat up too. "Is it time?"

"No. Not yet." I knew that my suitcase was packed and ready for the short trip to the hospital. This was not the time. "I guess it was just a nightmare." His arms were around me, holding me, comforting, soothing the terror. Troubling thoughts, pictures, and realizations tumbled into consciousness.

"Do you want to tell me about it?"

"It was . . . I was . . . We were . . ." I struggled to make sense of the dream. It had been one of those starkly realistic ones, the kind that seem to be in Technicolor and surround sound—almost like watching a movie, except you're the unwilling star. "I was in a place I've never seen before," I told him. "A house—or at least a room in a house." It was an old house; I could tell because of the wallpaper—nobody uses that flowery wallpaper anymore—and lace curtains. There was a man sitting in a big wingback chair with a white kitten in his lap. "There was a kitten. A white kitten," I told him.

"That doesn't sound too scary so far."

"There was an alligator under the man's chair." I suppressed a shudder. "When I lived in Florida we always worried about alligators coming out of the water and eating small pets. I wanted to pick up the kitten, to hold it so the alligator couldn't get to it, but I couldn't move." *Is this kitten Tricia's white cat?* "In the dream I close my eyes. I don't want to see what I'm afraid is going to happen. But when I open my eyes the cat and the gator are both gone. The man is still there."

"Do you know who the man is?" Pete's voice was gentle.

"I don't think so. Maybe. He's sort of familiar though—he looks almost like my high school history teacher, Mr. Connors."

"Sorry, babe. I don't know anything about dreams. Maybe River could help."

"Of course. River can figure it out. She has Ariel's dream book. You're so smart. Thank you." I rolled over, gave him a kiss on the forehead, snuggled into the pillow, and, with the dream question answered, dozed off again. The next time I awoke, it was to the familiar sound of a good old Patsy Cline somebody-done-somebody-wrong song and the smell of morning coffee.

As I showered and dressed for work, I forced myself to concentrate on my current WICH-TV assignment—

pets. Preferably cute pets. I'd already decided to start with a visit to Pals—the no-kill cat and kittens shelter. I shook away disturbing thoughts of the white dream cat, and Pete and I shared a couple of Eggo blueberry pancakes with real maple syrup. It was Pete's turn to take Toby for his morning walk, so I was the first to head out to the yard via the sunroom. O'Ryan walked ahead of me, waited until I was safely buckled into the Jeep, then climbed up onto the fence that belonged to the neighbor behind our property and started on his shortcut route toward Aunt Ibby's house.

I checked in with Rhonda early. The whiteboard was blank, so apparently Bruce Doan hadn't yet thought up another hat for me to wear before I began my maternity leave. I said as much to Rhonda. "Oh," she said. "He hasn't talked to you yet about sending Francine over to the hospital to film the delivery? Discreetly, of course." She managed to keep a straight face. "By the way, he's wondering if you're planning on breastfeeding. Discreetly, of course."

"No, he certainly hasn't mentioned either possibility—even discreetly." I almost laughed aloud at the very idea. "Shall I tell him now to forget it, or let him dream on?"

"Let him dream."

Dreams. I need to talk to River. Soon.

"I'm planning to go over to Pals this morning," I told her. "Is either Francine or Old Jim around? We'll be getting pictures of cute kitties."

"Francine will probably be up for that. Cute kitties, huh? Yesterday she had to go with Scott to prowl around in some musty old cellar looking for a secret passage.

She came back with scraped knees and cobwebs in her hair and no secret passage." Rhonda giggled. "Kitties would be a welcome change. I'll buzz her."

A musty old cellar, huh? That could only be the old granite-walled part of the underbelly of the Parker mansion. I love working with Francine anytime, and hearing about what she might have seen among the cobwebs might be interesting—not that I planned to be involved in any way with any Parkers—or Binghams.

The idea of filming rescue cats and kitties was indeed a welcome change for Francine. She texted me immediately that she'd have the motor running in the new mobile unit by ten. That gave me a good hour to fill. I headed down to my office to pick up the way-too-tight WICH-TV jacket. Besides that, there might be time to attend to another sticky or two.

I pulled the jacket from the locker, wiggled into the office chair, and wheeled it as close to the desk as I could. As soon as I reached for a sticky—a light blue one—Scott's face appeared in the glass. He pointed to my phone and I complied. "Hey, Moon, what's up? Looks like Doan's going to keep you working right up until the last minute. Are you doing okay?"

"Thanks for asking, Scott. Yes, I'm still feeling good. I've got a couple of easy ones—visiting a few local animal shelters. Cute puppies and kitties. You know." I held up the jacket. "The only problem is fitting into the uniform."

"I see what you mean. Hey, wait a minute." He snapped his fingers. "I'm bigger than you and I have at least three of those jackets. Take one of mine and roll up the sleeves. That might be more comfortable for you."

I knew he was right. "That would be great, Scott, if you can spare one. Francine and I are going over to take pictures at Pals at around ten. I can return it to you as soon as we get back."

"No hurry," he said. "Keep it as long as you like. If you're feeling okay Doan will keep you working. That paid maternity leave thing must be killing him. I'll be right over with the jacket." He stood up and hurried away out of my sight.

Within a few minutes he knocked on my office door, green jacket on a hanger over his shoulder. "Come on in," I called. "It's not locked."

"Here you go, kid," he said, extending the jacket toward me.

Gratefully, I accepted it. "This is a lifesaver. I owe you one." I repeated the promise, so often stated between us throughout the many years we'd worked at WICH-TV.

"You bet." Big, goofy smile and the long look. "I'll be waiting to collect."

"Rhonda says that you and Francine did some recent cellar crawling. Did you turn up anything new?" I doubted that I'd get a straight answer.

"Turn on the late news tonight. You'll see what we found." Another big grin. "I'll be right beside Buck Covington."

I resisted the strong temptation to stick my tongue out at him. *Francine will tell me all about it anyway.*

Chapter Twenty-five

A few minutes before ten I shrugged into the new-to-me green jacket and rolled the sleeves up a few inches. I couldn't exactly button it over my belly, and there was no mirror in my office, but my reflection in the glass door looked pretty good. I thought the much bigger shoulder pads in Scott's jacket gave me kind of a military posture, and I stood a little straighter to accent that. I set out to meet Francine, using the ramp past the newsroom and the metal door to the parking lot. As promised, she was there with the new mobile unit. I navigated the high step carefully, took my accustomed seat, and fastened the seat belt. "This seems like old times," I told her.

"It sure does." She handed me my favorite stick mic. "Some of my best stories have been the ones we've shared over the years."

"I know," I said. "Mine too. We were there when a mom talked her son out of jumping to his death."

"And we were there when they brought a dead guy out of the library where your aunt works," she recalled.

"Yep." I nodded, remembering. "And speaking of dead guys, we were right on the spot when they pulled that old Mustang out of a granite quarry, along with what was in it. Tell me about the cellar under the Parker place. I thought I'd crawled over every inch of that house, but from what Rhonda said about your adventure over there, I must have missed a chunk of it."

"Believe me, you don't want to go there. If you didn't know it was there you wouldn't notice it. It's in the old, unused part of the cellar. There's a heavy door behind an old coal chute. Scott opened it. Dirty, damp, and disgusting doesn't begin to cover it." Francine gripped the steering wheel tightly and we rolled out onto Derby Street. She looked from right to left, dropping her voice. "You know about the tunnels under Salem, don't you?"

"Of course I do. Back when I was teaching at the Tabby we spent a whole semester once trying to figure out what was going on down there." We passed the Friendly Tavern on the opposite side of Derby Street. I pointed. "There's supposed to be a tunnel under there— with a pirate ghost in it."

"Right," she agreed. "There's one under Rocafella's too. Their ghost is a lady in a blue dress who they say was murdered and buried down there. She was first sighted right after the restaurant opened in the old Daniel Low building in 2003. She about scared a bartender to death! Since then a lot of people have claimed to see her. Anyway, back in the seventeen hundreds, when the old ship captains used to try to avoid paying taxes, they built a lot of tunnels around the common where their mansions were so they could smuggle their illegal cargo ashore without paying the duty on any of it. Scott and I found out yesterday that there's one under the Parker mansion."

"Is there a ghost in that one?" I asked.

"Not that I know of." Her tone was serious. "But in Salem, you can never be sure."

"That's true. Pete and I had our wedding reception at Rockafellas and never saw the blue lady ghost. But do you know where the tunnel under the Parker place leads?"

"No. Not yet. It was caved in after we went in a few yards. We're guessing it's probably connected to some of the other old houses along Washington Street," she explained.

"Even if the old houses are gone," I suggested, "I'll bet the tunnels are still connected down there."

"Sure they are." She pointed to a popular steakhouse. "That place uses a piece of a tunnel for their wine cellar. I've heard that during the Cold War some folks made bomb shelters out of them. I did a feature about it once with Phil Archer before you were a field reporter." Phil was the daytime news chief at the station.

"O'Ryan and I had a bit of an adventure in one of those bomb shelters way back before I even met you," I told her. "Someday I'll tell you all about it."

"Was it connected to a tunnel? Like the one under the Parker's house?" she wanted to know.

"It was connected to a tunnel for sure." I shivered at the memory.

"Want to take a look at the Parker tunnel? We can take a camera down there."

"I promised Pete I'd stay away from the Parkers and the Binghams," I said. "Anyway, I'm not in shape for tunnel crawling. But keep me up to speed on what you find out down there, will you?"

"Of course I will. Scott's real interested because of the Chocolate Shop Murder."

"So am I," I admitted. "I hate that name though."

"I know. It sounds a little Nancy Drew-ish, doesn't it?"

"Nah. Nancy would know better."

"But back to the tunnel crawling." Francine's eyes sparkled with excitement. "Scott's been keeping in touch with that Uncle Earl character, and he knew about the tunnel under the house. Earl said that he and Bernie used to use it like a secret clubhouse when they were kids. They used to talk about it all the time even when they grew up. Earl says that after Bernie got married to Shirley and they had the kid—Hugh—one day when Hugh was around four years old they took him down there, just so he could have the experience, you know?"

"Wow. Did Shirley know about it?"

"Yep. The kid told her. She exploded, naturally. What mother wouldn't? It was dangerous. She forbade Bernie to have anything to do with Earl ever again."

"That would account for her feelings about Bernie's old pal, wouldn't it?" I said.

"Even so, she's agreed to have him in the funeral because Bernie would have wanted him there." We pulled into the small lot behind Pals. "She must have really loved him."

I couldn't see it and I told her so. "He was a good-looking, lying, cheating SOB," I insisted. "I can't imagine why a classy lady like Shirley even gave him the time of day." I sighed. "But as my aunt Ibby often says, 'There's no accounting for taste, said the old lady as she kissed the cow.'"

"That's funny," Francine said. "My grandmother said almost exactly the same thing. There must be a grandmother's handbook somewhere that they all read." We climbed out of the mobile, Francine with the camera and sound equipment and me with my mic and a bag of various clip-ons. We were welcomed at the door by a volunteer with two kittens hugged to her chest and another on her shoulder. I was glad to hear Francine's camera whirring gently behind me. What an opening shot! The facility itself was simple, with pale green walls and a white tile floor. A marmalade-colored cat viewed us suspiciously from the top of a carpet-covered scratching post.

"That's Adonis," the smiling volunteer told us. "He thinks he owns the place." There were a dozen or so pens lined up all around the big room, and sunshine filtered through a wide window onto playful, tumbling kittens, mama cats nursing little ones, and grown cats wearing the dreaded Elizabethan collars to prevent them from licking wounds. "We're so glad to see you," the young woman announced. "The publicity on your station will mean a lot for our adoption program. We take as many cats and kittens as we can accommodate here, and the more we can place in good homes, the more we'll have room for."

The visit was a satisfying one for both Francine and me, and I was sure the viewers of WICH-TV would be tempted to visit and to offer one or more of these lovelies a home. I was sorely tempted myself by a gorgeous tuxedo boy named Oscar, but resisted. Bruce Doan likes stories like this one—considered an "evergreen"—because they can be used anytime during the year.

It was shortly after noon when we delivered our morning's footage to Marty for editing. I would have liked to talk to Francine a little more about the previous day's tunnel exploration, but she needed to rush right out again, this time with Phil for a piece about Salem's open-air art museum featuring eighty large-scale murals by global and New England artists in the area known as The Point. I took advantage of the break, picked up a sandwich and iced tea from the Friendly Tavern, and retired to my office, where I could put my feet up and take a little rest. I looked into the next-door newsroom over my row of varicolored sticky notes. The place was darned near empty. Was everybody here busy except me? The momentary "poor me" lasted only a few seconds. I was happy to still be working at a job I loved, and I was pretty sure I was going to miss it after Baby Ella Marie arrived—and that was going to be very soon.

The morning's conversations about tunnels and ghosts brought me back to the previous night's disturbing dream. Cat, alligator, mysterious man. *Maybe River could help,*

Pete had suggested. It was nearly two o'clock. Was it too early to call River?

I killed a little time by pulling down a few of the stickies. One pink, one green, and one yellow. The pink one informed me that the Jeep was due for an oil change next month. I decided to do it this week and get it over with. The green sticky said, *Learn as if you were to live forever. Gandhi.* Sometimes I put up inspirational quotes or sound advice. This was a favorite, and right now I planned to learn as much as I could about local underground tunnels, about Bernie's death, and—as soon as possible—about what my dream meant. I left the yellow one face down on the desk and tapped in River's phone number.

She answered on the first ring. That was good. I hadn't wakened her. "Hi, River," I said. "It's me with a question."

"I know it's you and of course you have a question. Have the visions come back? What's going on? Is everything okay?" There was loving concern in her voice.

"Yes. I mean, everything is good with baby and Pete and me. Nope. No visions. It's about a strange dream I had. You still have Ariel's dream book, don't you?"

"I do, but it's on my set at the station. It's on the little shelf under my table. Tell me about the dream and I can tell you what words to look up," she advised. "It'll be kind of a do-it-yourself dream analysis."

"Okay. I'll run down there now and get back to you." I didn't run, but I made my way down to the studio, fooled around with the electrical panel until I got River's set lighted, found the dream book, sat in her big wicker fanback chair, and called her. "Got it," I reported, and proceeded once again to repeat the details of the nightmare.

"No wonder you were upset. Lots of symbols there for sure." She made a shuddering sound. "Brrrr. Alligators, cats, and a wingback chair. Oh my! I took notes while you were talking. Let's start with that wing chair. I remember reading about chairs before. Something about 'staying put,' I think. Look under *chair* in the book."

I looked. "It says 'taking time out to contemplate a situation,' " I told her, "and 'staying put with a decision.' And the wing chair means 'a feeling of protection.' "

"Does that make sense?" River asked.

"Sure does. I'm about to become a stay-at-home mom."

"You're off to a good start. Let's see what the alligator means."

I flipped over to the *A*s. "Oh boy. 'Lurking danger. Hidden threats.' And listen to this. 'A situation or person you don't fully trust.' "

"That would be the man named Hugh, I guess," she said. "The Seven of Swords. Remember, he still has two swords left in the ground. His plan, whatever it is, may fail. Try the *C*s again. For the chocolate."

I flipped ahead. " 'Chocolate. A self-reward. Not minding taking off work.' That's a perfect one—and as long as I'm in the *C*s, I'll look at *cat*." I found it right away. "I remember this," I said. "We've looked up cat before. A dream of a cat means behavior that is protective of itself. It also can mean appearing confident but being scared away when challenged."

"Yes. You need to be protective of yourself." River

sounded serious. "You said the man looked like a teacher you once had. Look at the word *teacher*."

I looked. "It means an answer to a problem. 'Taking action will solve the problem.' What action? I don't get it."

"You said he was a history teacher. Try looking under *history*."

"'History represents reexamining the past,'" I read aloud. "'You may be trying to gain insight into past events.'" I thought about that. "It's true," I admitted. "But the past events might go back a long, long way."

Maybe all the way back to the days of the underground tunnels.

"Think it all over," River advised. "Sometimes it takes a while for the mind to process the information a dream has given to you. Sort of like your visions. Remember?"

I remembered. I thanked her for her help, told her I love her, reminded her of the upcoming shower, replaced the book where I'd found it, and made my way back to my office. Arranging my newly acquired WICH-TV jacket carefully on a hanger, I put it into my locker, kicked off my shoes, and sat gratefully in my comfortable leather chair. The yellow sticky note was still face down on my desk. I flipped it over.

Put your feet up and relax, it commanded. More sound advice.

"Done." I followed the directions, crumpled up the yellow square, and tossed it into the trash.

Chapter Twenty-six

I gave some serious thought to seeing if Old Jim wanted to drive me to the second destination on my cute animal list, the one with the rescue pets. I decided against it. No need to rush into this thing. Tomorrow would do. I'd make one more trip up to the reception desk and see if Rhonda had anything new for me on the whiteboard. If there was nothing, I would—as Old Jim liked to say—"head for the barn."

All she had for me was a requisition slip from the host of *Shopping Salem*. He needed somebody to go to the gift shop at the Peabody Essex Museum to pick up a few of the Salem Historic Houses blocks. I knew what he meant. Paintings of a good many of my city's historic buildings had been reproduced on small, decorative, flat wooden blocks. Visitors and residents alike seem to enjoy displaying them. Aunt Ibby uses them as spacers between book categories in her home library.

Perfect. A trip to the museum gave me a good reason to leave early, and it kept me on the clock.

"That'll be good," Rhonda pronounced. "It should keep you busy until five. You'll get credit for a whole day's work."

"Whatever you say," I agreed. Prowling around in the museum was one of my favorite things to do, and I don't do it often enough. I rode Old Clunky down to the lobby, wished Chester, the parking lot attendant, a good evening, and started my Jeep. Parking isn't easy anywhere in Salem, but I lucked out on one of the two-hour meters not too far from the entrance of the museum and went straight to the gift shop. The blocks with house views were displayed right up front. I recognized one of the little houses right away. It was dressed up with Christmas decorations in the little windows, and there was one in Aunt Ibby's collection. The message on the back of the block told me it was the Andrew-Safford House. I recognized it because I'd recently driven past it—just a few houses beyond the Parker mansion.

A question immediately popped into my consciousness. *I wonder if it's connected to the other houses on Washington Square by the tunnels?*

History represents reexamining the past, the dream book had told me. *You may be trying to gain insight into past events.*

My own past events surely didn't go back to the days of underground passageways under opulent mansions. My *recent* history went back to a body in a cellar under *one* particular mansion. That was where my concentration needed to be. Never mind the miscellaneous information cluttering up my mind. *Poof!* I willed away the tunnel ghosts and the cobwebs in Francine's hair and Salem's bomb shelters and wine cellars.

I'd already filled out a WICH-TV requisition slip for a dozen block houses. I gathered together twelve of what I considered the prettiest ones with a variety of appearances—some Georgian, some Federal, some brick, some painted, including the Safford house. The woman behind the counter put them into an attractive canvas bag, and a young man carried them out to the Jeep for me. There was time to drive back to the station and unload my haul of houses before five o'clock—or I could go straight home and deliver them to *Shopping Salem* in the morning.

Dilemma. I decided to get it over with and go back to WICH-TV. I called Pete to tell him not to worry if I was a little late coming home. He said he'd wait for me and that he'd take me to dinner at Greene's Tavern— one of our all-time favorite pub grub places since back in our early dating days. This was turning out to be a pretty nice day. Cute kitties, a trip to the museum, and a dinner date. I pulled into my regular parking space, waved to Chester for help with the bag of houses, and took Old Clunky upstairs once again. Rhonda was still at her desk and promised to see that the *Shopping Salem* host got the expected merchandise in the morning. I wished her a good night. She pointed down to the whiteboard. "Another note for you from Doan."

Lee, call this guy. It was followed by a number. I recognized it. Hugh Bingham.

"Do you know what it's about?" I struggled to keep my voice steady.

"Something about trying to hire him as an announcer,
I think. Apparently, Buffy Doan really likes his voice.
You know how it is with the Doans. What Buffy wants,
Buffy gets."

I knew the truth of that statement. I hadn't forgotten
how Buffy's nephew Howie Templeton had been
handed *my* field reporter spot as soon as he graduated
from broadcasting school, resulting in my "promotion"
to program director—along with my current position
as producer of documentaries. Not that it had turned
out badly for me. It hadn't. But still, none of it had
been *my* decision. Maybe it was time to heed the advice from Ariel's dream book. *Taking time out to contemplate a situation.*

I did not want to speak with Hugh Bingham no matter what his call was about. Anyway, Pete didn't want
me to have anything further to do with the Bingham
family. I contemplated the situation.

"I don't think so." My voice sounded hesitant, even
to me. I tried again. "Message received," I declared.
"But, no."

Rhonda raised a perfectly arched eyebrow. "No?"

"No," I repeated. "I'm not going to return that call,
or any call from that number. Ever."

"Gotcha," she said. "Loud and clear. I'll let manage-
ment know."

"Thanks," I said. "He'll probably chalk it up to a
'pregnancy thing' anyway. Besides that, I'm going to
be a stay-at-home mom pretty soon anyway, and I don't
care who he hires for an announcer."

She covered her mouth but couldn't quite mask a
snicker. "Sure. Nobody here believes that, you know.

You've been in the business too long to walk away from it now. There are plenty of moms working on TV. Even the maternity leave time away from us will drive you nuts. You love this place and you know it."

"Baby Ella Marie needs me," I insisted. "I've been reading up on it. You should see my bookcase. I have more than a dozen books on child raising. I've been studying. I'm not going to have time for anything else."

She made a silly face. "Baloney. That child will have people lining up to babysit." She counted on her fingers. "Your Aunt Ibby and all those girlfriends of hers. Pete's sister. Pete's mother. Even me sometimes. And what about Wanda? And Marty? We'll all want a turn." She glanced around, then whispered, "It's possible that Doan might want you to do a piece now and then about being a mom. That wouldn't take much time, and your regular audience would love it."

She had a point, no doubt. I wasn't going to admit it though. "You'll see," I told her. "I'm going to love staying home. Anyway, I'm planning on breastfeeding. Every day would have to be Take Your Kid to Work Day."

She stood. "Okay. Whatever you say. I'll go tell the boss you're not going to call that guy." She walked toward the door marked "Manager," then turned toward me. "You'll be back."

"Good night," I told her again. "I have a hot date for dinner with a cute cop. I'll see you tomorrow."

Still smiling, I rode downstairs on Old Clunky, exited onto Derby Street, and rounded the building to the parking lot. Chester, wearing his lot man T-shirt, walked with me to my parking space. "Listen, Lee," he said when we were next to my Jeep. "I don't want to alarm you, and it's probably nothing. I mean, this is a great-looking Jeep—all tricked-out like it is. I've seen a lot of people stop and take a look at it. I try to discourage the ones that want to leave a rubber duck on it. But there's this one guy . . ." He paused. "He doesn't drive onto the lot at all. He just walks by almost every day and he stops and looks over at your space. It's almost like he wants to make sure you're here."

"I'm sure it's nothing too, Chester," I said, trying to sound convincing. "Probably a Jeep fan. But if you can, just for the heck of it, if he's not looking, could you use your phone and take a picture of him?"

"I already did." He pulled a phone from his back pocket. "Know him?"

I knew him. I didn't reply right away.

"Is he somebody that you know? Is he okay?"

"He's a guy Doan is thinking about hiring as an announcer," I said truthfully. But was he okay? I still didn't know the answer to that.

Chapter Twenty-seven

With nothing specific in mind for dinner, we had decided that an impromptu date night at Greene's Tavern was a good idea. We've been customers there for a long time. Kelly Greene, the owner's daughter, had been one of my first students at the Tabby. The place had barely changed a bit during the five years since we'd first discovered it. It's one of those wonderful little bars where "everybody knows your name." The wide, comfortable booths, the big TV screens, the stone fireplace, the retro jukebox complete with bubble lights were like reliable old friends. Aspiring actress Kelly took our orders—hot dogs and Pepsi for each of us—and we briefly caught up with each other's lives.

"Baby due pretty soon, I'm guessing." Kelly gave my tummy a gentle pat. "Am I still on the list as an honorary aunt?"

"Absolutely," I assured her. "I read that you have a role in the new play over at the Gloucester Stage theater."

She beamed. "I'm playing Diana in *Wish You Were Here*. The career is looking up."

"We're so proud of you," I told her.

"A lot of it is due to the encouragement you've always given me. I'd still like a career in television though," she said. "If I keep learning, maybe someday you'll see me on the Hallmark Channel."

"Gandhi once said, 'Learn as if you were to live forever,'" I told her.

"Wow." Her eyes widened. "Gandhi. You are so smart." I accepted the compliment graciously and didn't bother to tell her I was quoting a green sticky note.

I knew I'd learned something from Chester that I needed to share with Pete. Should I do it now, or wait until we got home? It was an easy decision. As soon as Kelly left to fill our orders, I began. "I don't know what this means," I said, "but I'm sure you'll want to know about it." I related what the lot man had told me. "It was definitely Hugh," I told him. "He could be there about an announcer's job. It seems that Buffy Doan likes his voice." I told him too about the message from Doan himself, telling me to call Hugh's number, and that I'd refused to do it.

"You've handled it right," he told me. "I thought Doan understood me when I told him I didn't want you involved with anyone in that chocolate business."

"Maybe he didn't recognize the phone number," I said. "And it's Buffy who wants Hugh to be an announcer. You know how that goes."

"I know. And I know how much you enjoy your job," he said. "But if it means he's going to be around you— upsetting you—I'll have to ask you to start your maternity leave early."

"You're right," I agreed. "I'll finish up the animal thing tomorrow and start practicing staying home."

He reached for my hand and squeezed it. "I love you," he said.

Kelly appeared with our orders on the familiar round Budweiser tray. "I heard that," she said. "And look. you're still holding hands. Still in love." She rolled her eyes upward and gave a dramatic sigh. "I hope I can have a marriage like yours someday."

"I hope that for you too," I told her, meaning it.

"Tell me about the animals," Pete encouraged as we dug in to our hotdogs. "I'll bet that's an assignment you're enjoying."

"I am. We visited cats and kittens today, and tomorrow I'll get to see dogs and puppies and all kinds of rescue pets," I reported. "I love encouraging people to give these animals a chance to be part of a family. As the Pals manager told me, the more cats and kitties they can place, the more room they have for others. The other rescue places have the same message. The more animals they can rehome, the more room they have for others—and the more happy animals with new families to love and to love them."

"Like Toby."

"Exactly. And even Bathsheba is sort of a rescue cat. Betsy rescued her from who-knows-what kind of a future."

"Having her cat back has made a change in Trisha, that's for sure," Pete said. "She's being downright co-operative."

"About Bernie Bingham?"

"About Bernie and Shirley and Hugh and the Parker mansion and even the cellar underneath the place," he said. "The woman has a remarkable memory for detail. If everything she's telling us is true, Bernie shared a lot of information with her."

I could feel my field reporter brain kick in. "Off the record?" I recited.

He frowned. "What record? You're writing about pets now, remember?"

I knew my face had colored. "Sorry," I said. "Old habits die hard."

The frown deepened. "I hope you're going to enjoy your new position as Mom as much as you've enjoyed being on TV."

"I will," I assured him. "I'm sure of it. I've been reading books about it all. I have so much to learn—and as Gandhi said, 'Learn as if you were to live forever.'"

He smiled, the frown gone. "It seems to me I've heard that quote before—quite recently."

"You have," I agreed. "Tomorrow I'm going to learn some more about rescue pets."

"That's a good choice."

"Reporting on pets is such an easy assignment. No rush. No stress," I explained. "It's possible that Doan might like me to do something similar from time to time," I said, remembering that Rhonda had hinted at such an assignment. "Maybe even something to do with being a first-time mom."

"Do you think you'll have time? Or that you'll even want to do such a thing?"

"I don't know," I admitted. "I'd be pretty picky about it for sure. I mean, if I didn't feel like it, or if I wasn't comfortable about the topic, I wouldn't do it." I waited to see what his thoughts on the idea might be. No response. "What do *you* think about it? Would *you* be comfortable with me doing the occasional mommy shot?"

"Same as you," he said. "I don't know." He reached for the menu. "Do you feel like ordering dessert?"

"There's always room for ice cream," I said. Kelly, good waitress that she is, saw the motion and appeared tableside. "Dessert?" she asked, pencil poised over her pad. We ordered. Vanilla ice cream for Pete. Chocolate for me.

"Your aunt sent me an invitation to the shower tomorrow night," she said. "Do you like all pink stuff for the baby or do you want to change it up—like maybe some green or blue or purple?"

Aunt Ibby had invited Kelly? Had she invited *all* of my old students? How huge was this shower going to be? I answered the question. "I think a variety of colors is a good idea, Kelly. Ella Marie might get tired of wearing pink all the time. I know I would. Thanks for thinking of it."

"Kelly has a point there," Pete said. "Maybe we've overdone it with all the pink paint and furniture."

"Great minds," I said. "I just had the very same thought. Let's call George Washington and maybe repaint a few things." Kelly delivered the ice cream and I dipped my spoon into the sweet coldness, then paused with it halfway to my mouth. "Maybe that's a topic for one of those no-stress shoots for Doan."

Pete gave a fake eye roll. "Repainting baby furniture?"

"I haven't had a chance to process it yet," I alibied. "Just a thought." I had to admit to myself though, producing a little video every now and then would be kind of fun.

We finished our meals, said our goodbyes to Kelly and her dad, Joe, and stepped out into the still fairly early Salem night. "Shall we take a little ride around town?" Pete suggested.

"Good idea," I agreed. Greene's is in one of the older parts of Salem, established neighborhoods where it seems as if generations of families have lived in the houses lining the narrow, sometimes one-way streets of Salem's waterfront district. We drove past a yard full of metal sculptures, not far from the historic Custom House, moved along on the very familiar Derby Street, passed the TV station, and soon found our way to the Salem Willows.

"Look," I said, "There's the saltwater taffy place. I should include that in the candy series."

"Do you want to stop now and grab a picture or two?"

"Good idea," I said. "I remember watching that taffy-pulling machine when I was a kid. Fascinating."

"I did too. I wonder if we were ever at the Willows at the same time when we were kids, both watching the taffy stretching and changing shape."

"I wonder about things like that too," I agreed. "Like were we both in the same movie theater at the same time. Or at the same high school football game?"

"It's more likely than not." We pulled over as close to E.W. Hobbs section of the boardwalk as we could. It looked just as it had for as long as I could remember. Pete walked around to open the door for me. "Wait," I said, pointing as a Range Rover passed us and parked across the street. "That looks like Hugh Bingham's car. Could he be . . . following us? I mean, like tracking me somehow?"

As I watched, another car approached the parked Range Rover from behind, darned near sideswiping it. It was unmistakably a Bentley. Was Shirley trying to frighten her own son? "What was that all about?" I asked Pete. "Did she just try to hit him?"

"You never can tell with those two, can you? We'll find out. Stay here." Pete closed my door. "Lock it," he said and walked across to where the Range Rover had stopped and turned off the lights. Pete approached the driver's side. I watched from the side window, wishing I could hear what was being said. It seemed as if a lot of time had passed, but the clock on the dash told me it had only been a little more than five minutes when Pete walked back across the street.

He climbed into the cruiser. "It wasn't Hugh at all," he reported. "It's his mother, Shirley. She said she had a sudden craving for a chop suey sandwich and borrowed his car. She says they each have keys to the other's vehicle."

"So do we," I recalled. "I mean you have the extra

fob to the Jeep. I can't drive *any* of yours, of course. The chief wouldn't like it. But was Hugh driving *her* car? Trying to scare her? And do you believe her about the chop suey sandwich craving??"

"I would have," he said, "if I hadn't spotted Uncle Earl ducking around the side of the gaming arcade. This is his old neighborhood, remember? His and Bernie Bingham's."

"Shirley always claims that she has no use for Earl," I reasoned. "That she's only including him in the funeral because Bernie would have wanted him there."

"It's not against the law to change your mind," he said. "Let's get that picture of the taffy and go home."

"Are you sure Shirley is all right? Maybe she doesn't even know Earl is here," I pointed out. "Maybe we should hang around until she leaves."

"Pregnant lady's instinct?" he asked.

"Maybe."

"Okay. Take your time getting the picture. Maybe buy a pound of it." Sly smile. "I like the vanilla ones."

"They have great popcorn too," I reminded him. "Hot and buttered."

"Let's get a bag of that too."

"Earl was the last person to see Bernie alive," I reminded him. "Shirley's connection with him is all mixed up, isn't it?"

"While you're taking the picture and buying out the store I'll keep an eye on the situation here."

I made my way to the counter, where a smiling teenage boy took my order. I told him who I was and handed him one of my old WICH-TV business cards, the one that said I was "Historical Documentary Executive Director." I asked for permission to take a picture of the taffy puller. He called his manager over to the counter and I explained my mission again. The idea that the store would be featured for Halloween struck the desired chord, and I took several pictures of the taffy process and included, at the manager's request, some shots of the significant popcorn production in progress. That hot, buttered popcorn smelled awfully good. I'd been watching my weight carefully throughout the pregnancy. "I only have a few weeks left," I told myself as I popped a few of the buttery kernels into my mouth.

"Smells good here, doesn't it, Ms. Mondello?" I hadn't seen or heard Earl Hennesey walk up behind me.

"Yes," I said, turning to see if Pete was watching. I didn't see him at all.

"I used to love this place when I was a kid," Earl said. "The owner back then used to feel sorry for me and sneak little cups of popcorn to me. Sometimes that was all I had to eat in a day."

Was this one of those situations where you're supposed to say *Indeed*? I settled for "Oh?"

"Yep. But I still love the stuff." He put a five-dollar bill on the counter. "Now I can afford to pay for it."

I remembered my recent conversation with Scott about Earl's fortunes. Scott had said the man was broke. That he was hanging around the old neighborhood trying to mooch a place to sleep from old buddies. That he'd put the touch on Shirley Parker for money and that she'd turned him down flat. I glanced around, still looking for Pete, sure he wouldn't be far off, leaving me in the company of shady Uncle Earl.

I saw Pete. He was, once again, at the driver's side of Hugh Bingham's car, in conversation, I presumed, with Shirley. Was that where Earl's newfound wealth had come from? And if it was, had he exchanged something of value for popcorn money?

Chapter Twenty-eight

I could hardly wait for Pete to come back and tell me—if he would—just what was going on between Earl Hennesey and the Bingham family. The idea that Shirley's sudden desire for a chop suey sandwich had amazingly coincided with Earl's craving for popcorn was darned hard to believe. Was she using Hugh's classy Range Rover instead of her own high-end Bentley because she was a bit of a snob about where she might be seen, or because she was afraid of someone in particular knowing where she was?

While Earl waited for his popcorn, he continued to maintain eye contact. He seemed to expect further comment from me. Was I supposed to engage in small talk about the relative merits of the regular hot, buttered variety as opposed to the pink-sugared kind? Or could I come right out and ask him how his financial bonanza had come about?

Nothing ventured, nothing gained, my aunt was fond of saying. Would Earl be offended by a personal question? I decided to take the risk.

"Have you accepted a position somewhere locally, Mr. Hennessey?" I queried with all the polite interviewing technique I'd accumulated over years of quizzing sometimes reluctant subjects.

"A position?" He spoke the words with such near disdain that I almost laughed aloud. "Not exactly. I'm more of an odd-jobs man." He smiled, exposing teeth that would have benefited from significant childhood dental work. "Yep, that's it. A couple of odd jobs have come my way lately."

Was it time for a sincere *Indeed*? I settled for "Glad to hear it," searching the parking lot once again for Pete to come back and bail me out of this conversation. I was happy to see him approaching and, at the same time, to see the Range Rover take off in a hurry with a squeal of tires. I couldn't help wondering if there might be a traffic cop nearby.

"Well, good to see you, Ms. Mondello. Enjoy that popcorn." Earl Hennesey wasn't about to hang around to see Pete. One could assume that his contacts with the law over the years had not always been pleasant.

"Sure thing," I said, giving him a little wave with my still-warm red-and-white popcorn box. "Good night." He disappeared into the shadows of the arcade building just as Pete reached my side.

I extended the box toward him and he reached into it. "Best popcorn in Salem," he declared.

"Uncle Earl thinks so too," I told him. "What did Shirley have to say for herself?"

"About popcorn?" he teased. I didn't dignify that with an answer. "She was here to meet up with Hennessey," he said. "She told me so right up front. She says he called to tell her he'd be in the funeral all right, but that he didn't have a proper suit to wear and if she wanted him to look decent, she'd have to buy him the clothes. Shoes, shirt, tie, and all. She gave him five hundred dollars in cash."

"No wonder he was going for the five-dollar popcorn bag. Five hundred dollars? She's probably used to buying Hugh's wardrobe and figures that's the going price for funeral wear," I offered.

"If I have Earl figured out right," Pete mused, "he'll go to one of the church thrift stores in a wealthy neighborhood and get almost-new clothes and shoes—the whole works—for twenty bucks and pocket the rest and not a soul at Bernie's funeral will know the difference."

I thought—with somewhat mixed emotions—about the piles of previous seasons' designer clothes I'd bagged up and carted to Aunt Ibby's church. Actually, there was a partially filled bag on the attic steps awaiting my pregnancy wardrobe, once I was finished with muumuus and stretch pants and spandex tops. I knew too that as soon as my after-baby figure emerged, I'd buy another closetful of new fashions.

We returned to Pete's car and headed back across the Beverly Bridge, a short distance down Essex Street, and onto Winter Street and home. Pete backed into his accustomed spot behind our house. When the headlights illuminated our rear door, neither of us expressed any surprise at seeing two cats—O'Ryan and Frankie—waiting expectantly for us on the doorstep.

"There's your escort service." Pete turned off the car, then held my door open and offered a supporting hand as I pulled myself upright—one hand holding his and the other still clutching my popcorn. Once we were inside the sunroom I peered outside, wondering if O'Ryan would follow us through the cat door, or if he'd choose to spend the night at Aunt Ibby's house or perhaps share guard duty there on the back steps with Frankie.

From next door I heard the falsetto-voiced warbling of "Here, kittykittykitty" as Michael Martell summoned a reluctant Frankie home.

"Are you okay if I go out and speak to Michael for a minute?" Pete asked. "I want to talk to him about what to do if I have to be away and you need help."

"Of course." I knew that as time for the baby's arrival grew closer, Pete was getting more nervous about it all. I was too. I was alone in the sunroom while Pete went outside to talk to Michael, but I knew that O'Ryan was still on the back step and that Pete was just a few feet away. The idea of being alone when labor started was scary. I'd been thinking of what River said about how the clouds on the Ace of Wands card cushioned the baby and that once they'd completely evaporated the visions would return. Was the dream I'd had similar enough to a vision that the cushion was going away and the birth was getting really close? It would be a good idea to have a next-door neighbor standing by just in case!

I heard their voices, but not distinctly enough to understand what they saying. I caught a word here and there—"Jeep" and "keys" and "horn." Why were they talking about cars? If I needed a ride to the hospital in a hurry it was unlikely that I'd be driving myself there in my Jeep.

Pete and O'Ryan entered the sunroom together. "Well, that'll work out just fine," he said. "Do you have the key fob to the Jeep in your purse?"

"Of course." I lifted the purse. "Right here."

"Okay. So you have it with you all the time. Here's the spare fob we got for me." He pulled it from his pocket and handed it to me. "I want you to keep this one on the bedside table on your side of the bed." Big smile. "Then if I'm not here and you're in the house alone and you need help—like if the baby is coming—all you have to do is just hit the panic button on either one of them. Between working on his book and keeping the garden growing, Michael is here almost all the time—day and night. You hit the button and the horn will blow and the lights will flash and Michael will come a-runnin'! I gave him a key to the back door. Pretty good, huh?"

"Darn good," I agreed. "I like it. Between Michael and the two guardian cats I'll be perfectly safe."

"Funny about those cats though," Pete said. "I mean, how they knew about the baby before we did."

"Cats are all kinds of magical, aren't they?" I agreed. "Reconnecting with Bathsheba has made such a difference in Trisha's life, and I'm so happy that Betsy has found little Mercy."

"Well, cats are pretty self-sufficient," Pete said, reaching for Toby's leash on its peg beside the door to the living room, while the lab pranced expectantly in a little circle. "But this guy needs people. C'mon, big guy." He gave me a quick kiss and the two headed outside. "I'll be right back."

"See you upstairs," I said. I thought some more about cats while I washed and moisturized and changed into a loose cotton nightgown. O'Ryan had stayed downstairs and I was quite sure that by then Frankie had sneaked out of his cat door to stand guard. I wondered for a long moment about Blackie. Was he napping on an Edwardian sofa or a Queen Anne chair—or was he once again relegated to the cold downstairs back room of the chocolate factory?

Chapter Twenty-nine

In the morning, Pete had a welcome suggestion. "Let's skip the Pop-Tarts and Eggos today," he said, "and treat ourselves to breakfast at the place."

"The place" is an out-of-the-way, two-story clapboard house on a side street, identified only by a neon "OPEN" sign in one window, and is our favorite early-morning breakfast spot. We hadn't been there for a while and I liked the idea. Any weekday morning there'd be a variety of vocations represented at the assorted mismatched tables, booths, and counters—all likely yard sale and thrift store finds—in the long, warm, good-smelling room. Pete and I have been going there long enough to be regarded as regulars and have a passing acquaintance with many of the other repeat patrons—commercial fishermen, nurses leaving the late shift, a kid's hockey team fresh off an early ice-time practice, cab drivers, off-duty cops—a cross section of Salem's morning people.

We each drove our own cars and were lucky enough to find side-by-side parking spaces. We headed for our favorite table in the back of the room. Two white ironstone mugs of steaming coffee appeared as if by magic along with a plastic-covered menu. "I'll be right back for your order, kids," our waitress, Dolores, said. "Today's special is Spinach quiche. It's super healthy and wicked good."

We took the suggestion and each of us ordered the special. Our very first bites proved Dolores right. Wicked good. I glanced around the rapidly filling room. "Look, there's Old Jim just coming through the door!" I waved to get his attention. Jim is a regular at the place too. In fact, he was the one who introduced us to it. "I need to book him for a trip to the Willows today to cover the saltwater taffy for the candy series," I told Pete.

"Well, okay." Pete's reply was hesitant.

"Is something wrong?" I wondered. Jim was already crossing the room toward us.

"Will you be in the mobile unit?"

"Sure. Maybe even the new one."

"And Jim will be with you the whole time?" Concern sounded in his voice.

"Every minute," I promised. "I'll do a quick standup, interview whoever is manning the taffy machine, grab the video of the process, and beat it back to the station."

"Okay then. But keep an eye out for either of the

cars from the Bingham household," he said, "and call me right away if either of them shows up. Promise?"

"Of course."

Jim joined us tableside. "Good morning, folks," he said. "Lee, I've been watching the series on cats and dogs you and Francine are doing. Good job. If I can help you out with it, I'm pretty good with animals, you know."

I knew. Jim had been with me on a number of assignments involving animals. Treed cats. Lost cats. He'd photographed me with dogs before too, including Toby—and once, even with a bear.

"No animals this time, Jim," I told him. "I'm still chasing candy stories. Can you find time today to do a shoot at the Salem Willows? It'd be a short stand-up at the saltwater taffy place."

"Glad to," he agreed. "Let's set it up with Doan and I'll grab the VW whenever you say."

Pete reminded me once again to let him know if either Bingham vehicle showed up, and I headed for the Jeep while he left in his cruiser. It didn't take long before I spotted the Bentley in my rearview mirror. Coincidentally, I was only a block away from one of those ten-minute oil change and car wash places. I couldn't help grinning as I pulled into the line, mentally checking off a sticky reminder note and at the same time forcing whoever was tailing me in the Bentley into getting a wash too. I alerted Pete to what I was doing and informed him that Shirley was right behind me.

A short time later I parked my shiny, clean Jeep in the usual space, said good morning to Chester, checked in with Rhonda, found nothing on the whiteboard, told Bruce Doan about the saltwater taffy idea, and got the assignment, with the caveat to be sure to pick up a box of the grape taffy for Buffy—because it's purple. I doubled back and checked with Jim and arranged for him to pick me up at Ariel's bench at noon.

Everything went smoothly and as planned right up until Jim and I, in the VW, pulled into a metered space within walking distance of the popular taffy and popcorn destination. I'd no sooner shimmied my way down from my elevated seat in the van to the curb when the now-familiar Range Rover hove into sight. The darned-near illegal dark-tinted side windows shielded the driver from sight. I hand-signaled Jim to wait before miking me, but there was no way for me to avoid being seen by whoever the driver was. The front windows of the oncoming car were un-tinted though, and Hugh Bingham's smile was unmistakable. Heeding Pete's advice to report any Bingham vehicles showing up, I pulled the phone from the pocket of my commodious green jacket and speed dialed Pete. "Hugh here," I texted.

"No hurry," I whispered to Jim, suggesting that he take his time with the mic and the furry windjammer on a long pole for overhead recording (the unfortunately named "dead cat").

We didn't have to stall for very long. I recognized the unmarked police car—a not-too-recent but well-maintained Chevy—when it blocked Hugh's access to the parking area. A uniformed officer climbed out and approached the Range Rover.

"Okay, Jim," I said. "Let's get this show on the road."
Jim, old pro that he is, had everything organized in a
couple of canvas bags within what seemed like seconds. Together we hurried across the pavement to the
colorful candy stand. Several members of the staff, each
wearing a neon-bright E.W. Hobbs T-shirt, peered across
the counter at us with undisguised curiosity—undoubtedly wondering by now about what was going on.
Maybe they hadn't been told about their free advertise-
ment in the WICH-TV Halloween candy promotion series. (Almost free. It was definitely going to cost them
something in grape-flavored saltwater taffy.)

I knew that the Range Rover would be tied up for a
while by the "random traffic stop" requiring a careful
examination of driver's license, Massachusetts auto
registration, insurance information, and more. With luck,
it would give me enough time to tell the staff members
that they were about to be on television and do an interview with the manager along with a few comments
from the others. I watched the taffy-puller do its magic
again—the thing never loses its fascination for me. My
questions produced an interesting little rundown about
the age of the business and its long-term relationship
with the Salem Willows. I tried hard not to let myself
get distracted by the presence of the Range Rover. But
exactly what was Hugh Bingham doing here anyway? I
didn't have the time or the opportunity to find out, but
Hugh showing up at darn near everyplace I'd been
lately had to be more than coincidence.

I was happy with the way the interview went. The
very knowledgeable manager shared that the confec-

tion was invented in an Atlantic City postcard shop back in the late 1880s. The proprietor of the shop had brought in a fellow named Bradley who sold taffy. One night an ocean swell flooded the store and the taffy was soaked in seafoam. In the morning someone asked if he still had taffy and Bradley joked that he had saltwater taffy. The name stuck, even though saltwater taffy doesn't contain saltwater—at least not from the ocean. (Although there is both salt and water in the recipe!) The saltwater taffy has been featured at the Salem Willows location for almost as long as it's been in Atlantic City—ever since 1897! The manager also shared a good-sized sample of the tasty product, including the desired purple variety. Win-win for me and the station.

By the time we'd finished our shoot, the Chevy had pulled away but the Range Rover still lingered. I guessed Hugh would probably waste some more gas in that 606 horsepower V8 engine by following the VW back to the TV station. Oh well, Mommy would pay the bill. I wondered if the traffic stop officer had learned anything of interest, and hoped Pete would let me know soon.

My tummy told me that it was past lunchtime. I looked around but didn't see any more Bingham cars. We arrived just in time for me to join Rhonda and Wanda, who were about to cross Derby street to grab a bite at the Friendly Tavern. The bartender greeted me as soon as we walked in. We sat at the bar, where service was always quicker than in a booth. "Hey, Lee. We haven't seen you much lately. Is Doan cutting back on your hours?"

"Not really, Leo. I've been working mostly on candy

stores, not taverns. It's for a Halloween trick-or-treat story." I ordered an egg salad sandwich and a sweet tea.

"Halloween, huh?" He grinned. "That reminds me. There was a lady in here asking about you a while back. She was dressed up so fancy I thought she had on a costume—honest to God. She was sporting one of those fancy hats like women wear to the Kentucky Derby and a long shiny dress and a ring with a diamond that would knock your eye out. Way too much for the room, you know?"

"She was asking about *me*?"

"Yeah. She knew your name and that you work for the TV station." He refilled my tea, leaning closer, dropping his voice. "She was pretty nosy. I didn't like her attitude. I told her I didn't know anything about you. I asked her why she wanted to know." He looked up and down the bar. "Want to know what she said?" Rhonda and Wanda each leaned forward in listening postures.

"Of course I do. Shoot."

"She wanted to know if I'd ever seen you in here with a man. She showed me a picture. Older guy. Gray hair. Mustache. I told her the truth. No. I hadn't." He spread his hands apart in a helpless gesture. "She laughed. Like she didn't believe me."

Chapter Thirty

The overdressed-for-the-room woman the bartender had mentioned had to be Shirley Parker. The older, gray-haired, mustached man in the photo was more than likely Bernie Bingham. I knew that Leo had been tending bar at the Friendly for a long time. Surely he'd run into Bernie, who was known to be a drinker, at some time over the years. I asked him, "You recognized the man in the picture she showed you though, right?"

He smiled and tapped his forehead. "Smart lady. I knew who it was right away. He used to come in here a lot back in the day, but he'd cheated so many of my regulars he was afraid to come in here anymore. He was older in the picture than I remember him, but sure. It was Bernie Bingham."

Rhonda and Wanda were familiar with my history involving Bernie. They'd both been caring, comforting

friends after I'd discovered his body, and they knew too
that Pete had told Bruce Doan I'd not be doing any reporting involving any of the Binghams. Plus, Rhonda
knew that I'd refused to answer Hugh Bingham's tele-
phone messages.

A couple of the technical guys from the station
joined us at the bar, halting the conversation involving
the Shirley-Bernie connection, but not doing away with
questions about the so-called Chocolate Shop Murder.
They both knew Pete, having met him at various station events, but I dodged their thinly veiled quizzing
about what I might know about the investigation. "I'm
not field reporting at all anymore," I said, "and Pete
and I don't discuss police business. Anyway, I'm just
doing a little part-time stuff—candy stores and puppies
and kitties."

"Women's stuff, huh?" one of them huffed. "Kind of
dull for you?"

"Yeah," the other one agreed. "You'll be back doing
the regular things—robberies and accidents and kill-
ings and all—after the baby comes, right?"

"She says she's going to be a stay-at-home mom."
Wanda's voice was firm, but her broad wink belied the
words.

Rhonda nodded vigorously. "I believe her," she said.
"I think she's really going to retire and concentrate on
being a mother—at least until baby starts school."

"Yes," I said, agreeing with Rhonda's assessment,
trying to shake away the reminders of my all-too-
recent encounters with most of those associated with
the infamous Chocolate Shop Murder—the victim, of
course; then the son, the ex-wife, the girlfriend, the

childhood buddy, even the cat. A cast of characters like that can break anyone's concentration. I made a silent vow to myself that never would I allow a TV assignment to intrude on my home life.

What *TV assignment? There won't be any more of them at least until—as Rhonda suggested—Ella Marie starts school.*

I was sure of it. Well, maybe a harmless little shoot—like candy shops or homeless kittens. Wait a minute. I was on a harmless little candy shop shoot when I found Bernie Bingham's body, and a cat needing a home had brought Tricia Violette and Bathsheba into our lives—and into my aunt's upstairs apartment.

Maybe I should just swear off TV altogether. Is there an AA for displaced television personalities? There should be. Maybe there's a prayer. Something like *Grant me the ability to be helpful where I'm needed, the instinct to mind my own business, and enough smarts to know the difference.*

Yeah, right. At least until she's in school. Kindergarten maybe. How old are they when they're in nursery school? Like around four? Could I do four years at home? Of course. Easy peasy. I adored my husband and this baby girl I carried was already loved and wanted and welcome beyond words. There'd be long walks with baby in the carriage and me walking off baby weight. We'd join some play groups so she'd socialize easily. There was story time at the library every week. Aunt Ibby said it was always well attended and the babies and mothers all loved it. Good. That would begin a reading habit for Ella Marie. There would be plenty of baby-centered activities to keep me occupied every day—and, from what friends with children told me, lots of nights too. I wouldn't even miss WICH-TV. Naturally, I'd still stay in touch with my friends there, but my requisite many hats would stay hung up for the foreseeable future.

We moved from the bar to a booth after we'd ordered our food. I didn't want to face any more questions, so with Wanda and Rhonda on one side and pregnant me along with all of our handbags on the other, we filled the booth nicely without room for anybody else.

"You know, Buffy's trying hard to get Doan to hire that guy who did the chocolate factory tour spiel as an announcer," Wanda said. "He does have a good voice, and perfect enunciation. Almost as good as Buck Covington."

"He's not as good-looking as Buck, though," Rhonda offered. "Not bad, but not great, you know?"

"Maybe he could do voice-overs," I suggested, realizing that if Doan hired him, Hugh would have less time to show up wherever I happened to be.

"That's a good idea, Lee," Wanda said. "We could use a good male voice-over. I'll mention it at the next staff meeting."

"He has a really good voice, and he knows how to sell a product," I said, encouraging the thought process.

"So you really like him, huh?" Rhonda asked.

I answered that one in a hurry. "Oh, I wouldn't say that," I announced. "I barely know the man. But I've seen his work. Completely professional." *Except for what some might consider stalking.*

"Well. Buffy likes him and that's what counts around here," Wanda stated. "If he's not an ax murderer or something he's as good as hired already."

Nobody had mentioned axes, but some other sharp objects had been discussed—and he was, after all, a Bingham.

The techies had eaten and run by this time, and I'd seen Rhonda sneaking a peek at her watch a couple of times. Realizing that I was the only one here who wasn't on the clock, I babbled a quick apology and signaled for the check. "My treat," I insisted. "I miss you guys so much. I hope we can do this again soon—real soon."

"Well, I guess you won't be surprised to see both of us tonight at the shower at your aunt's house."

"I won't be surprised at anybody I see there. It seems as if she's invited all of Salem!"

"I wouldn't be surprised if the next time we meet after tonight you'll be pushing a baby carriage," Rhonda said, "with a beautiful little girl in it."

"Actually, it wouldn't surprise me either," I admitted. "I can hardly wait to meet her in person."

We walked together across the street. Then, with goodbye hugs all around, Rhonda and Wanda went inside the building, Rhonda with a promise to call me if anything turned up for me on the whiteboard, and I unlocked the Jeep, wiggled myself in behind the wheel, and turned out onto Derby Street. I took a good, long look up and down the street and felt a tangible sense of relief when I realized that no Bingham vehicles were in sight. Even so, all the way to Washington Square I couldn't help taking a look up every side street as I passed. "Stop it," I scolded myself silently. "Those people are making you crazy." Even so, I couldn't put the desired mental blinders on, even though I tried.

I felt a sweet sense of relief when I steered the Jeep into our driveway. I felt almost as if I'd been holding my breath for a long time and at last had expelled it. "These people are making you crazy." This time I said it aloud—and believed it.

Chapter Thirty-one

M y cat reception committee greeted me on my back step. O'Ryan and Frankie, both in fully alert posture, stepped aside as I inserted my key, then—instead of using the cat door—followed me into the sunroom. "You know you two can come in and out anytime you want to," I reminded them. O'Ryan gave me a questioning look. I knew what he was thinking. *We do, silly woman. Anytime we want to.*

I wasn't quite accustomed to being at home so early in the day. It would be several hours before Pete would be home. I realized that with the baby expected soon, the chief had thoughtfully arranged for Pete to be here most nights, and I appreciated that. So did Pete. Even so, those several hours were incredibly long ones.

From his windowsill perch, O'Ryan alerted me to Pete's arrival. Together, we hurried to the sunroom, where Frankie had remained on duty at the door. I knew from Pete's expression of concern when he opened the door that something was wrong. We spoke in unison. "Are you okay?" Then we both laughed, because saying the same words at the same time is funny even when the words are not.

I put one hand on Pete's arm. "What is it?" I asked.

"I'm not sure," he said. "Maybe something. Maybe nothing." I waited for him to say more, not questioning, just waiting. After what seemed like a long pause, he continued. "It's Hugh Bingham's car. The nice Range Rover." Another pause. "It's parked in the driveway of the mansion across the common there. It looks as if it's been in an accident. Dented front fender. Broken side mirror. But no one has made an accident report."

"He may have run into a fence or something," I said. "No law against that, I guess."

"Unless it's somebody else's fence," he pointed out.

"True. Are you going to ask him about it?"

"I have. He says it's okay. No problem at all. Nothing to report and he's taking it in for repairs today."

"Did you ask Shirley about it?" I wondered.

"No. Why would I?"

"Because she often drives it," I said, "and he sometimes drives the Bentley."

"Do you think maybe she drove into something by accident and he doesn't want his mother to get in trouble?" he asked.

"Maybe. Or maybe she drove into something on purpose," I admitted. "I've seen some indications of . . .

well, a kind of unpleasantness between them." I thought about the look that had passed between them when Hugh had appeared in the apron and hairnet. *If looks could kill . . .*

I remembered too the near sideswiping we'd witnessed when the Bentley had come awfully close to creaming the Range Rover. I reminded Pete of how we'd tried to sort out who was driving what and had concluded that it looked as though Hugh, driving his mother's car, had tried to throw a good scare into her—maybe for driving *his* fancy wheels. "Maybe we should check out the Bentley and see if by some coincidence it has damage too."

"There'll be no *we* checking into dented cars," he reminded me. "You aren't a field reporter anymore," he said in his best cop voice, then smiled. "But I'll certainly see if she's filed an accident report lately." Pete made the necessary inquiry call and waited for the requested information.

We didn't have to wait long to find out if the Bentley had been involved in an accident. We didn't even have to wait for the requested accident report. It hadn't. The luxury car, in all its shining glory, drove slowly past our front window with a smiling Hugh at the wheel.

"It looks as if Hugh has borrowed Mom's car while his is in the repair shop," I observed.

"That answers that question." Pete concluded his call. "Maybe one or the other of them simply ran into a boulder or something."

"Maybe," I agreed, "but hardly anything Bingham-related turns out to be simple."

"Like, why is he still driving by our house?" Pete wondered aloud. "There's no law against it, but what is he looking for? Why was he walking across the street with what looked like a shower invitation?"

"Well, the shower is tonight and we'll see which, if any, Bingham shows up for it."

I hadn't been sure whether or not Pete had been serious when he'd said he wanted to come to the baby shower with me, but he was. "I won't get in the way," he promised. "I'll stash myself in Ibby's office and play with all her techy toys. I'm sure she has all the newest games too."

We decided to walk to the shower rather than add a car to the parking spaces in my aunt's big backyard on the Oliver Street side of her house. I was sure there'd be quite a few there, as well as wherever it was legal to park on Winter Street too.

As soon as we climbed Aunt Ibby's front stairs and pushed the doorbell, I knew she'd gone all-out for her first grand-niece's shower. The bell chimed "Thank Heaven for Little Girls" instead of her regular tune, "The Impossible Dream." She looked lovely in a softly draped midi in a dusty rose color. She greeted us both with hugs. Inside, everywhere we looked there was pink. The hall tree was festooned with pink ribbons, and the hat hooks each held a pink hat, each one sillier than the next. All of the couch cushions were now in various shades of the rosy hue, and I could see into the dining room where a pink lace tablecloth replaced the usual white linen one. Gifts were already piled up there.

"Did you see Ray outside?" my aunt asked. "He

came all the way from Boston to help with the parking situation." Ray Templeton is one of Aunt Ibby's gentleman friends, and he and his twin brother, Roger, are retired from the city of Boston police force. "He's keeping busy. Several of the neighbors have offered space in their yards." Girlish giggle. "Of course, I had to invite them too!"

"I'll go out and say hi to him," I promised. "How many people did you invite, anyway?"

"Oh, everybody." Her tone was enthusiastic and matter-of-fact at the same time. "Remember your eighth-grade English teacher, Miss Claffey?" She pointed across the room. Miss Claffey gave me a dainty pinkie-wave and a big smile. "She hasn't changed much, has she?" She hadn't. It occurred to me that if the guests included people from as far back as middle school, maybe she *had* invited "everybody," and I'd be opening presents far into the night—and writing thank-you notes far into the foreseeable future.

"Is it okay if I hang out in your office, Ibby?" Pete asked. "I'll stay out of the way of the festivities."

"I'll sneak some cake and ice cream in to you later," she promised. "All pink, of course." He gave me a quick peck on the cheek and headed into the nearby office, leaving the door a tiny bit ajar.

The new doorbell chimed about little girls again and my aunt opened the door to admit Shirley Parker— gorgeous in what I recognized from a Macy's TV commercial as a pricey, beaded Johnny Was creation. She stood in front of the pink-draped hall tree, then moved to one side to accept my handshake.

It was just after my aunt's mention of ice cream and cake and just before the beginning of the flashing lights and whirling colors in the mirror behind Shirley that I felt the first contraction.

Great. I was about to have both a vision—and a baby.

Chapter Thirty-two

"Excuse me," I said to Shirley. I walked as quickly as I could toward the office. The door swung open before I was halfway across the living room. Pete had obviously been watching.

"What's wrong, sweetheart?" He reached for me, grasping both of my hands. "Did she say something to upset you?"

"Say something? Shirley? No. I'm pretty sure I felt a contraction. A kind of medium one. I think maybe Baby Ella could be coming tonight." I tried to smile. "What should we do?"

"We should get you to the hospital" was his logical solution. "Shall I call an ambulance or run home and get the car and your bag?"

I looked at my watch. "Let's wait. Maybe these are those Braxton Hicks contractions we heard about. False labor contractions," I reasoned, trying to remember all we'd learned in our Lamaze sessions. "We need to time them anyway."

"Take some slow, deep breaths," he advised. "How long was the contraction?"

"I'm not sure. Maybe about thirty seconds."

"Then we really need to time them, then," he murmured, as if talking to himself, "and time how far apart they are too." He pulled the ever-present notebook and pen from his breast pocket. "I'm ready."

"Pete, please see if River is here. I need to tell her something."

"River? Right now? We're having a baby!"

"Please."

"Okay." He stepped into the pinkness to look for River. I kept my eyes on the mirror, where a picture was beginning to take shape. I was sure the cushioning clouds of the Ace of Wands had evaporated and the visions were back. I needed my tarot reader, and quite possibly my witch.

Thinking of what Pete had just said about timing, I took slow, deep breaths, tried to keep my eyes focused on the picture taking shape in the beveled mirror of the hall tree, and at the same time, sneaked little peeks at my watch. That first contraction had taken place at exactly six fifteen. If all the books I'd read were correct, we had plenty of time—like several hours—before we needed to think about making a run to Beverly Hospital. We'd made several test runs from our house across the Beverly Bridge to the hospital and usually made it within ten minutes.

The scene in the mirror was a familiar one. It showed the photo Jim had taken of the candy knives—the one with one knife missing. I'd barely had time to process what I was seeing when Aunt Ibby motioned for me to follow her to the kitchen. "I want to show you the cake," she whispered. At the same moment, River appeared with Pete. I could tell that she was dressed for the *Tarot Time with River North* show, which was a few hours away and, by its dark nature, never featured pink. She wore a purple velvet one-shouldered number with a long, ruby-eyed rhinestone snake emerging from the neckline, curving around one breast and then encircling her waist. She reached for a pink witch hat hanging from a hall tree hook and plopped it onto her head. "You need me?" She reached for me with both hands. "What's going on?"

The next contraction was harder than the first. I looked at my watch. This one was only fifteen minutes from the one before. Baby Ella was on the way. I squeezed River's hands. "I think the clouds have fallen away," I said. I described the vision.

"Can you tell which knife is missing?"

"The chocolate knife," I said.

"If the visions are back, you'd better get to the hospital," she advised.

"That's what I said," Pete interrupted, putting his arm around my shoulders. "Sorry, Ibby." He turned to my aunt, who stood looking back and forth between River and me. "We'll have to wait on that cake. You two stay right here with Lee. I'm going to run home and get my cruiser." He pulled the front door open and dashed outside.

Within minutes I heard the squeal of brakes. "He's here," River said. "Come on." With her on one side and

my aunt on the other, we made our way down the steps.
Pete held the passenger door open for me, helped me
into the seat, reached over, and fastened my seat belt. I
saw my packed going-to-the-hospital bag on the floor.
We were on our way.

"I didn't even get to open my presents," I protested,
then gasped as another contraction hit.

"I've called the hospital," Pete said. "They're expecting us. Hang on." The siren screamed, the red, white,
and blue lights flashing as we tore out of Winter Street
onto Bridge Street and sped toward Beverly.

Too bad Old Jim isn't here to record this, I thought.
*Doan would have loved this scene: WICH-TV staff
member in a dramatic arrival at Beverly Hospital prior
to delivering her first child.*

"Don't look now," Pete said, glancing up at the rearview mirror, "but we're sort of being tailed."

"Sort of?"

"We just passed Hugh Bingham's Range Rover. The
dents have been all hammered out and it looks like he
planned to be there ahead of us. It's kind of a reverse
tail."

"Shirley can't be driving it this time." I strained to
look at the side-view mirror. It was Hugh's car all right.
"She'd just arrived at the shower when all this started.
She must be driving the Bentley."

Two nurses with a wheelchair between them greeted
us at the emergency entrance. One took my overnight
bag, and Pete was prepared with my photo ID and insurance information. I was whisked away to my third-
floor private room, with Pete hurrying to catch up with
us. We'd taken all of the childbirth classes together, so

none of the activity came as a surprise. We'd brought along some favorite music, and I'd already told my ob-gyn that I planned to have as natural a birth as I could, opting to have a sniff of nitrous oxide available if I needed it.

Although I'd read the prescribed books and Pete and I had all those classes under our belts, I learned quickly that the actual labor and delivery required absolutely total concentration on my part. Breathe in—blow it out—push—no, don't push—breathe—breathe . . . There was no room for random thoughts of falling clouds or red lollipops or past dreams and recent visions or the Range Rover or the Bentley or Hugh Bingham following, following . . .

Pete in mask and gown spoke encouraging words and squeezed my hand. The doctor gave brief instructions from behind the tented stirrups. Masked and gowned nurses stood at either side of the foot of the bed. Then, baby Ella cried. First it was a tentative mewling sound, then a full-throated yowl. I smiled and laughed aloud as she was placed on my chest, warm and wet and sort of wiggly. A wave of love such as I'd never known before swept over me. I held her close. The tiny body seemed to fit against mine perfectly. One nurse put a warm blanket over us. "Six pounds, eight ounces, twenty inches long," the doctor pronounced. "You've got a nice little baby there, Mama."

"Look," Pete said. "I think she has reddish hair."

I looked down at the pinkish fuzz on her round little head. "Maybe," I said.

"Not a lot of babies are born with red hair," one of

the nurses observed. "Are either of you Irish, or maybe Scottish?"

"Irish and Scottish both on my mother's side," I said. "My dad was Polish."

"Irish on my mother's side too," Pete said. "All the rest of the family is Italian."

"You can try introducing her to the breast," the doctor said. "It'll give her the idea. She may not latch on right away, but she'll catch on soon enough."

The learning curve on being a mom speeds along at a rapid pace—and fortunately a lot of it seems to come quite naturally. I figured out how to hold baby Ella quite casually, after initially being afraid I'd drop her. I'd done enough babysitting during my teen years that I knew how to change a diaper and wipe a tiny bottom. I learned to pump breast milk and bottle-feed her, and she figured out how to latch on to the breast by the second day. By the time I walked out of the hospital to the waiting car I'd found that I could position her quite comfortably on my left hip. The jeans I'd chosen to wear home had an elastic waist and the Boston University sweatshirt pulled down over my still-a-bit-swollen tummy felt comfortable. I thought my newly enlarged boobs looked really good.

Pete, it turned out, took to being a daddy instantly. He could hold, burp, and cuddle Ella Marie like a pro. He'd been an uncle to two boys for quite a while and hadn't forgotten any of the skills he'd learned along the way. He'd even strapped the baby carrier into the back seat of the Jeep in record time, then slid the sleeping girl into it without waking her.

It was so good to be home. O'Ryan and Frankie welcomed us at the back door. As soon as we were inside, I smelled something wonderful cooking. Aunt Ibby had undoubtedly provided dinner. Some good fairies had brought the shower gifts home for me, and they were piled onto the coffee table in the living room, with some on the floor beside it. "Everyone wanted to help," Pete explained, "but they've all promised to wait a few days before coming over to visit—unless you need them, of course. Your aunt and her girlfriends and Wanda and Rhonda from the station, and even Buffy Doan, have offered to come over and help you anytime you need them."

We delivered the sweetly sleeping Ella Marie to her new pink first-floor digs, right next to our newly relocated master bedroom and took about a hundred pictures of her in her brand-new pink crib.

Chapter Thirty-three

Adding a small human with limited communication skills to a household requires a new learning curve for the adult humans involved. It seemed to me that in just a couple of weeks, Pete and I had adapted quite nicely. The animals did even better. The cats were ever watchful, sometimes alerting me with soft meows that Ella Marie was about to wake up. If Toby saw me preparing the baby carriage, he immediately fetched his leash so that we could multitask the walk. Mr. Doan would approve.

With some significant assistance in the form of many tasty casseroles from Aunt Ibby, the convenience of DoorDash deliveries, take-out orders from our favorite restaurants, and my slowly improving kitchen skills, nobody went hungry.

I kept up with the laundry pretty well, adding wet (or worse) baby clothes to the pile and being ever grate-

ful to whoever invented disposable diapers. I sent the
two green WICH-TV jackets—mine and Scott's—to
the dry cleaner's, with an unspoken wish that I'd get to
use mine on camera once again, at least once in a
while.

George Washington made a house call to repaint
some of the overly pink décor we'd chosen for Ella's
room. Some soft turquoise, with pops of bright yellow
here and there, broke it up nicely. I'd opened all of
those stacked-up shower gifts and had written sincere—
if brief—thank-you notes to all concerned. Ella would
be a well-dressed, properly accessorized, and toy-
entertained child for the foreseeable future. There'd still
been no date, time, or place designated for the previously planned shower the WICH-TV crowd still wanted
to host, so we had that to look forward to.

Some mornings I joined the other moms at the play-
ground on the common—the ones I'd watch enviously
when I was expecting Ella Marie. The always pleasant
walk along the convenient paths between the grass and
flowers was doubly delightful while pushing my pretty—
and definitely red-haired—little one. Only once on
those walks did I meet Hugh Bingham face-to-face.
We were each on one of the longer, impossible to side-
step paths. He paused briefly, remarked on the fine
weather and the lovely baby, and moved on. The drive-
bys on Winter Street by Range Rover and/or Bentley
had decreased too—or perhaps I wasn't looking out the
window as often as I used to.

Although the radio and TV stations and the local
newspapers still gave airtime and linage to the Choco-

late Shop Murder, public interest was clearly waning. I hadn't lost interest though, and of course my policeman husband hadn't either. I felt more confident in asking him questions about progress in the case than I had when I was working full-time at the station. One morning after feeding Ella, I'd made bacon and eggs and toast for breakfast—surely a nutritional improvement over Pop-Tarts—and Pete, as usual, had brewed the coffee. We sat at the Lucite table listening to Hank Williams bemoaning a cheatin' heart. I flat-out asked the question. "Are you actually any closer to figuring out which member of the Bernie-hater club killed him?"

He nodded, a slow, measured, cop-like nod. "Maybe," he said. "We've eliminated a lot of the people he cheated in crooked deals and unpaid debts. For most of them, those losses are a cost of doing business with the kind of people they deal with. Not worth killing over." He sipped his coffee and paused "It looks more and more like an inside job."

"Inside what?"

"Inside the immediate family" was the surprising reply.

"You mean family like Shirley and Hugh and Tricia?"

"That's about it." He nodded that scary cop-nod again. "Family."

"I don't like to think that about anybody's family," I admitted. "Even the doggone Binghams." I dared to press the question even further. "Which one is the most likely?"

"They all had about the same access to him," he

said. Long pause, which I didn't interrupt. "It seems to me that Tricia is the least likely as a killer." He said it with a half smile.

I agreed with that assessment, but didn't say so. "What does the chief think?" I asked.

"He'd like to believe it was Shirley, I'm pretty sure, although of course he doesn't say so," he said. "He's still fuming over all the times she paid those high-priced lawyers to get Bernie out of trouble, even after they were divorced."

"She's still paying his bills," I said, and mentioned Earl Hennesey's five-hundred-dollar clothing allowance for Bernie's funeral.

"And I suppose she's bought the coffin and the grave site and a nice outfit for Bernie to wear to—wherever he's going," he added. "Funerals, even small ones, don't come cheap these days."

"Do you think there'll be dishes of chocolates along with coffee and tea at the funeral home for the mourners?" I halfway joked.

He smiled at that. "I wouldn't be a bit surprised, and I don't expect that there'll be an awful lot of mourning going on."

Pete said that he'd send out for lunch and that he'd bring home take-out for dinner. "I'll surprise you!" he promised. After he left for work, as I washed the breakfast dishes, I thought some more about what he'd said concerning someone in Bernie's family being guilty of his death. When I'd discovered deceased Bernie downstairs in the mansion, Shirley and Hugh were both upstairs and each one had vouched for the other, saying neither had been down below. On the other hand,

Tricia, the one whom Pete found to be the least likely killer, had access to the old cellar door and could easily have come into the area and gone out again without anyone seeing her. Go figure. I tried to think about something else.

Once again, unbidden thoughts of WICH-TV drifted across my brain like those falling clouds in the tarot deck. I saw myself in the green jacket, stick mic in my hand, smile on my perfectly made-up face, looking into Francine's camera. Where were we? What was I covering? It didn't matter at all. I was working. The vision I'd seen just before the baby was born—the old photo of the candy tools—came back to me, the image with the chocolate knife missing floated into my consciousness again. What did it mean? I tried to shake the thought away. I needed to stop thinking about WICH-TV—about working. "No," I told myself. "Not until Ella Marie is in nursery school. You are a happy, well-provided-for stay-at-home mom. There is no *need* for you to have a job."

As though he agreed with that idea, O'Ryan squeaked out a tiny mew, followed by Ella Marie's plaintive sob from the nearby room. I tossed the dish towel onto the counter and answered the call. "Don't cry, sweetheart. Mama's coming."

Still shuffling random thoughts around like tasty buttered kernels of popcorn, I picked up my hungry baby, burped, wiped, lotioned, and rediapered her, then, sitting in my newly repainted turquoise rocker, I offered my "feed-on-demand" child some additional nourishment. Rocking and nursing makes for some quiet almost-alone time—so relaxing I nearly dozed off. The buzzing of my always nearby phone interrupted my near meditative zone. Without bothering to check caller ID I snatched it up, lapsing into WICH-TV mode—answering with my name.

"Lee Barrett."

"Ms. Barrett? I represent Casa de Chocolatte's publicity agency. Ms. Parker is interested in buying some advertising time on your station. Mr. Bingham would be available to perform in the thirty-second and sixty-second commercials."

"Thank you for calling," I interrupted. "But you need to contact the sales department." I recited the number.

"Of course. Thank you, Ms. Barrett. Sorry to bother you. This is the number Mr. Bingham gave me."

"No problem," I told her, even though it *was* a problem. I was sure that giving that woman my name was deliberate. Hugh Bingham had the station manager's name as well as the station's main number. He probably had Bruce Doan's private number as well. So what was the point of giving the publicity agency *my* name and number? Or was I looking for trouble where there wasn't any? Buying time on WICH-TV *was* a good idea. Hugh Bingham *was* a capable announcer. Maybe I was purposely putting myself into reporter mode even while I rocked my baby, fulfilling my new chosen role as Mommy.

You can wear more than one hat, you know. You've been doing it at the station for years, said a still, small voice in my head. It wasn't as though I'd be going to the station every day. "Punching the old time clock," as Jim liked to say. I'd be more like a freelance broadcaster, dreaming up topics like the candy store series—

maybe some one-hour evergreen subjects that could run anytime.

Evergreen! That's an idea by itself!

Evergreen. Christmas trees. I could easily do a whole documentary or maybe a series on that one. Next-door neighbor Michael with his garden expertise and current *Garden Club Mysteries* series would surely be a helpful source of information—excluding poison bushes and murderous garden tools, of course. But seriously, how many kinds of Christmas trees are there? Where do they come from? What's the most popular kind? How about artificial trees? Vintage artificial trees? Price ranges? What about tree decorations? Old ones? New ones? Bubble lights? Pre-lighted trees? My mind raced. I rocked faster as the ideas kept coming. I should propose this to Doan. Right away. Christmas was just around the corner.

Chapter Thirty-four

Before I could seriously consider embarking on a new venture, no matter how part-time and freelance it might be, I needed to talk with Pete about it. He and Marie had been raised by a traditional, full-time stay-at-home mom. I, on the other hand, had been raised for the most part by a working mother and a multitasking aunt who'd managed to serve as a part-time head research librarian at Salem's main library with much of the rest of her time devoted to me. She'd solved part of the problem—not, she insists, that she ever regarded me as a problem—by instituting multiple story hours at the library, where local moms brought their kids of all ages. I was in attendance at all of them, from the ones with the talking hand puppets to the ones with the interactive puzzle games. I could read by the time I was three.

"Strike while the iron is hot," Old Jim often reminded me from his wealth of platitudes and proverbs. I needed to get this idea in motion immediately if we were going to make it work. That meant I couldn't dilly-dally around with it. I needed to talk to Pete right away. Fortunately, at two weeks old, Ella Marie and her current food supply were completely portable. I could pause anytime she was hungry and repair to the break room—or maybe, since I could pump, bottle, and refrigerate as necessary, I could entrust my baby for a little while to one of the many willing babysitters who'd offered their help. It all depended on how well Pete might subscribe to the idea. He'd be home for dinner and that's when I'd have to spring it on him with no preliminary warning. He'd promised he'd surprise me that evening. It appeared that the surprise would be on him. For all the years I'd known him, Pete had been the most understanding man I'd ever met. I had a good feeling that he'd understand me this time too. Pete, after all, was a darned good multitasker himself. He managed to head up the investigation of Bernie's murder, keep track of the somewhat elusive Tricia Violette, and be at the same time an attentive model daddy to Ella Marie and a great husband in every way.

The dinner surprise was perfectly grilled haddock, with mixed steamed vegetables and sour cream–topped baked potatoes from one of our favorite restaurants, Brodie's Seaport. Dessert was hot apple pie. The vanilla ice cream topping came from our freezer. I waited until dinner was over, the dishes washed, and the baby put to bed before I broached *my* surprise.

I gave him the condensed version of what I proposed to do, leaving out the many details about Christmas trees, hoping it didn't sound as though I'd rehearsed it—which I had. He wore his thoughtful face, and there was what seemed to me to be a long pause before he spoke.

"I know you have extra time on your hands. I can see it. Whenever I come home at lunchtime I'm amazed by how everything is already done. Dishes washed. Laundry washed, dried, folded, and put away. Floors gleaming. Baby all sweet-smelling and happy. Wife all neat and pretty." He grinned. "My mother always complained how there was never enough time to get all her work done. She'd be up after dark scrubbing floors or cleaning closets or whatever. Of course," he alibied, "she had two kids."

"'Work expands to fill the time available,'" I quoted.

"Gandhi?"

"Aunt Ibby."

"Maybe after we have the second kid, little Peter Donald, you won't have time for a part-time job," he said, "but for now I think we can make it work."

"I knew you'd understand." I hugged him. "Peter Donald?"

"Sure. We'll name him for me and my brother-in-law, Donnie."

"Well, fine, but what if child number two turns out to be Carrie Isabel, for my mother and my aunt?" I wanted to know.

"Peter Donald," he insisted.

"Okay." I might as well agree, I reasoned, since that event would be some years away as far as I was concerned. "Peter Donald it is."

Much more immediately than naming a second child, I knew I had to get the proposal for the Christmas tree series on Doan's desk by morning. Not that there was any doubt about his enthusiastic acceptance of the idea—it was a sure moneymaker, advertising wise, and it should attract viewers aplenty too. He liked to maintain the niceties of program scheduling though, so a proper proposal would be filed first thing in the morning. I put my laptop on the kitchen table and got to work.

Google offered some things I hadn't even thought of. There were a couple of chop-it-down-yourself Christmas tree farms nearby—one in Topsfield and one in Beverly. You could also buy a potted tree and plant it for future Christmases. Antique stores sold the kind of gorgeous, delicate vintage tree balls I'd grown up with at Aunt Ibby's, along with bubble lights. There were at least two year-round Christmas shops within easy driving distance—Partridge in a Bear Tree shops in both Salem and Newburyport sold Christmas merchandise year-round. Some vintage shops and even thrift stores specialized in the old silver aluminum trees of the 1950s. This was going to be fun. By the time I climbed into bed beside husband and cat, I had a proposal for Doan that would run right up until Christmas Eve.

"Don't forget the mistletoe," Pete said, pulling me close for a kiss.

"You're right," I said. "I'll add that in the morning."

"Here comes Buck now." Pete pointed to the screen. "It looks like Scott has scored the second-banana seat again. I wonder what he's got. We don't have anything new. Chief didn't even have to do a presser today."

"If it's about the Chocolate Shop Murder, I don't envy him the seat. I'm glad that's something I don't have to cover."

"So am I," Pete said. "Even if they wanted you to, I'd have to play the 'ongoing investigation' card and say it would be inappropriate for you to be involved."

I thought again about what Pete had told me about "family involvement" in the matter of Bernie's death— 'family' as in Shirley, Hugh, and Tricia. "More like 'ongoing Bingham,'" I said. "Let's see what he's got."

Buck began with his perfect teleprompter delivery of some Salem City Hall matters involving sign ordinances and zoning, smoothly transitioning into some new parking regulations effective during "Halloween Happenings." After an auto dealership commercial, he introduced Scott. "Here's Scott Palmer with some breaking news about the Chocolate Shop Murder." The camera zoomed in on one of Scott's trademark long, silent looks before he began to speak.

"This morning I had the opportunity to speak with longtime Salem resident and well-known businesswoman Shirley Parker. Ms. Parker's Washington Square home was recently the scene of the mysterious death of Ms. Parker's ex-husband, Bernard 'Bernie' Bingham. Although the two have been divorced for some time, Ms. Parker has, over the years, maintained a more or less cordial relationship with Bingham. They have an adult son, Hugh Bingham, who now acts as CEO of Casa de Chocolatte. I have Ms. Parker's permission to share that interview with the viewers of WICH-TV."

The scene shifted to the now-familiar-to-me parlor/ office where Shirley Parker presided over her chocolate empire. Scott, seated in a chair I recognized as the Louis XVI wingback one I'd admired when I'd first visited the mansion, sat opposite Shirley. She wore white again, a simple but elegant three-piece suit— probably Oscar de la Renta. This time Blackie wasn't on her lap for contrast. (If I had that suit I wouldn't want cat hair on it either.)

Scott began his interview by asking her a good question. "Ms. Parker, the police have apparently not made much progress in finding the killer of your late ex-husband. Surely as his wife, and as co-parent of your son, you know many of his acquaintances—of both a business and a personal nature. Is that true?"

She gave a cool nod. "Yes, indeed."

"So perhaps you have some opinions about who might have wanted him dead, some things you might not have felt comfortable sharing with the police," he suggested.

"That's exactly right. I would never want to cause trouble for anyone who was innocent of wrongdoing— innocent of *murder*, for heaven's sake—by suggesting his or her name to the police." A vehement headshake. "I would *never* do that. I know how it feels to be interrogated for hours when you've done absolutely nothing wrong!"

"So you're saying that you suspect someone who perhaps the police have never questioned?" Scott was in his full, totally focused, leaning forward posture. "Is that correct?"

Another "Yes, indeed."

"Without naming anyone," he cautioned, "can you give us an idea of who that might be?"

Shirley leaned toward Scott, lowering her voice. "Bernie was a terrible philanderer," she confided. "Always was. Women loved him. He was so handsome, you know. He liked good-looking rich women. They *had* to be rich, you know, *and* good-looking too, because of his ego."

"Are you suggesting that one of his rich, good-looking lady friends killed him?"

"More than suggesting it, I'd say." Artfully made-up eyes widened. "I'm sure of it."

"Have you told the police?"

A soft smile played across her face. "Not yet. I'm collecting—what do you call it? Evidence." She leaned back in her chair. "I *might* be wrong—and I don't want to make a false accusation—but I don't think so."

"Thank you for talking with me, Ms. Parker." Scott leaned back in the wingback chair. "Do you have anything else you want to add?"

"No. That's enough." Again, the enigmatic smile. "For now."

At that point, Buck took over, thanking Scott and suggesting that everyone stay tuned for *Tarot Time with River North*.

Chapter Thirty-five

"Wow," I said. "What do you think about that?"

"I don't like it," Pete said. "I'll have to have another talk with Ms. Parker. If there's anything we don't need, it's an amateur 'collecting evidence.' She could get herself killed. Bernie had some tough cookies for playmates who don't want any of the rocks they hide under overturned."

"Have you questioned any of Bernie's rich, good-looking girlfriends?"

"Of course we have. Most of the ones we've talked to aren't sorry he's gone, but none have made the serious suspect list so far."

"Want to watch River?" I asked. "It looks like Buck will be shuffling the cards."

"Sure, if you want to." He propped the pillows higher. Ella Marie called from the next room. Loudly.

"Uh-oh. Feeding time again." I climbed out of bed. "She's awfully hungry lately. Your sister suggested that I talk to the doctor about getting a supplemental formula to add to her diet."

"That sounds logical," he agreed. "Marie is pretty well experienced in that sort of thing."

When I returned to the bed, Buck had already shuffled the cards. River was showing Halloween-themed movies as that holiday grew closer. The night's offering was *Trick 'r Treat*. A scary one. I'd seen it before.

"Never blow out the candle in a jack-o'-lantern before midnight," I told Pete.

"I don't think that's Gandhi," he said. "Old Jim?"

"Neither one. It's just a bit of advice from the *Trick 'r Treat* movie. I remember it because it was one of those quotes Aunt Ibby and Mr. Pennington mentioned in that movie game they play."

"Oh. Good to know. Let's watch it."

River was gorgeous in an all-black velvet high-necked gown with thigh-high side slits. It was one of her basic outfits that could be dressed up in a variety of ways. This time she'd adopted an Egyptian theme with gold—lots of gold. Her headdress, reminiscent of Nefertiti's classic look, was rendered in black and gold. Her shiny black hair in a single braid with gold stars woven through it hung over her right shoulder, while the left side was dominated by a sprawling gold representation of Bastet the cat goddess seeming to be peacefully asleep on her breast.

It was Pete's turn to say "Wow."

"She's amazing," I said. "If her fans see her walking

down Essex Street tomorrow in ripped jeans and a baggy shirt, they'll walk right past her."

"Interesting." Thoughtful cop voice. "I wonder if some of Bernie Bingham's rich, good-looking women friends are dressing down and forgoing the glamour makeup these days."

"That's quite likely. If I was one of them," I admitted, "I sure wouldn't want to call attention to myself, especially after the airing of Scott's interview with Shirley."

The movie had barely begun when Ella summoned me to her room once again—and once again, I fed, rocked, and changed her and put her back to bed. The scenario was replayed a few times during the movie and even throughout some of the breaks between commercials, when River took calls from viewers, answering questions and offering tarot readings. I sat upright in bed when River turned over the card bearing the Seven of Swords. I remembered it from my own reading. A man carrying five swords appears to be running away from something he's done. "He's a crook," I muttered, "like Bernie. He's stolen those swords and he's running away."

"The sword guy?" Pete questioned.

"Yes."

"It's interesting about the swords," he said. "Sharp steel instruments. You know, like the chocolate factory knives and scissors. Or even like in Michael's new books—machetes and pitchforks."

"You're right," I said. "That reading I had was a while back. We didn't make that connection. But you're right," I repeated. "Sharp steel instruments. And there are still two of them stuck in the ground. Let's see what River tells the caller."

We both leaned closer to the TV set. Even O'Ryan, from the foot of the bed, looked up at the screen with what seemed to be renewed interest. "The two upright swords," River explained, "signify the theft of the weapons. This thief lacks remorse. I suggest that you be on the lookout for manipulative behavior that may be employed in either a personal relationship or professional endeavors. Be aware."

"That sounds like good advice," Pete said. "Is that what she told you?"

"Nope. We concentrated on the five swords he carried. The cards don't mean exactly the same thing in every reading or for every client. Man or woman? Old or young? How does the reader view the person she's reading for? It varies a lot."

"Sounds like police work," Pete said. "Every case is different in one way or another."

"I'm going to ask River for another reading," I declared.

"I'm going to look for another reason why Bernie is dead," Pete announced.

Making even those small decisions seemed to help us both feel better. We snuggled into our pillows, and I dozed off before the movie ended. When I awoke to Ella's demanding cry, the set had been turned off and Pete was sound asleep beside me. I hurried to the baby's room, hoping the sound wouldn't wake him. As soon as I picked her up she nuzzled up against me, soon quietly contented, however briefly. I decided that I might as well spend the rest of the night in the rocking chair. It was comfortable enough to allow me to snooze, and I'd be able to reach Ella before her cries awoke Pete. The idea of supplementing her diet with a commercial formula had a lot of appeal. I'd call our pediatrician in the morning about it for sure.

Chapter Thirty-six

I tucked stray strands of unruly bed-head hair behind my ears, muttering, "I'm coming. Hold your horses," as I stumbled, bleary-eyed, through the living room. A glance at the banjo clock on the mantel told me that I'd had exactly thirty-five minutes of sleep since Ella had finally dozed into baby dreamland and I'd fallen asleep in the rocking chair beside the crib. Pete apparently hadn't had the heart to wake me before he left for work. The door chime sounded again. "For God's sake, stop ringing the damned bell." I yanked at the door-knob. *This had better be important.*

I pulled the door open just as Ella, awakened by the chimes—merrily clanging "Bless This House"—one room away from the nursery, resumed crying. Shirley Parker, all smiles, spike heels, and designer labels, bearing a large, pink-beribboned, professionally wrapped gift package, greeted me. "It's so handy—us living just across the common from each other. I could have walked over instead of driving." She pointed to the Bentley, parked beside the curb. "But carrying this thing is awkward. I can hardly wait for you to open it! May I come in?"

"Of course. Where are my manners?" I stammered. "Please do come in." Fortunately, the living room was presentable. "Won't you sit down for a minute?" I gestured toward the most comfortable chair. "As you can hear, Baby Ella is calling me. I'll be right back."

I dashed into the nursery and picked up my beautiful, fussy, wet baby. I wiped her, changed her diaper, dressed her in a cute yellow onesie, tossed a pink crib blanket over my shoulder, and presented her breast milk breakfast. The sobbing stopped. All was calm. I returned to the living room, still looking a hot mess, but by then not much caring what Shirley Parker thought about anything. She'd put the package on the coffee table, so I sat on the couch facing it.

"May I take a peek at the baby?" she whispered, leaning forward—reaching for the pink blanket.

"Sure." I moved the blanket aside enough to display Ella's sweet profile while still maintaining some modesty. I was getting pretty good at it.

"She's cute," Shirley pronounced. "Do you think she favors her father?"

"I think so, but he thinks she looks like me," I said honestly.

"It was that way with Hugh when he was little too." She sighed. "He turned out to look just like me. I'm sure he wishes he'd taken after his father. So handsome."

Again, the situation called for *Indeed.* Having seen the senior Bingham's photo, I believed that her assessment was probably correct. This time I let the opportunity to comment pass. She picked up the conversation. "Anyway, she's adorable. 'Sugar and spice and everything nice. That's what little girls are made of.'" She pushed the package toward me. "Here. Open it, please." Big smile. "It's really two separate presents, but I had them customized to match so it looks like one."

"You've already given me a shower gift," I protested as I pulled aside the ribbons, trying to remove the embossed and gold-highlighted pink wrapping paper carefully. It was a hard-to-break habit. Aunt Ibby had always been thrifty about saving really nice wrappings to reuse "someday." Lifting the cover of a bright pink box, I found layers of pink tissue paper. Shirley barely suppressed a giggle. "I couldn't resist it. It gets even pinker. George Washington told me about all the pink paint and pink furniture you have. George does some work around my house too," she explained.

By this time I'd exposed the first gift—I recognized it as a baby monitor. "We really need one of these," I told her honestly. "And I've never seen a pink one before."

"That's part of the surprise," she said. "The nightlight and sound machine are pink too. I had George paint them with nontoxic paint that's safe for babies. The sound machine plays lullabies or nature sounds or playtime tunes." She pointed to the gadget. "I wish I'd had one of these when Hugh was a baby. It's supposed to be very calming for the little ones."

"We'll surely enjoy using them both, Shirley," I told her. "It's a very thoughtful gift. Thank you so much." I stood, transferring Ella Marie to one shoulder, alternately rubbing and patting her back until the expected burp sounded. "I'm afraid I have to put this child back into her crib now. Maybe we can have a proper visit sometime soon. Thank you again for coming and for the presents." She took the hint and headed for the entryway.

"I'll let myself out," she said. "You get some rest now. You look tired.'"

That's what I was trying to do before you woke me up was my uncharitable thought. I gave her a brief wave of one hand to say "Bye-bye" and headed back through the living room toward the bedroom and—hopefully—some peace and quiet. I'd ask Pete to install the new pink baby appliances when he got home tonight. Even though the nursery was next to us, the video baby monitor was a good idea and I was glad to have it. The musical night-light sounded like a good idea too. I returned the sleeping baby to her pretty pink room, settled her in the crib, and tiptoed back to the living room. I looked at the Kit-Cat Klock over the kitchen table. Was it too early to call the doctor about the formula supplement? I called anyway and left a pleading message on his voicemail.

By then O'Ryan had strolled into the room and settled himself on my carefully folded fancy wrappings. As I watched, he turned around a couple of times, then scratched the embossed and gold-sparkled paper so enthusiastically that bits and pieces of it flew apart. "What are you doing? Making a nest?" I asked him. He looked up at me—the picture of innocence—except for the length of wet and bedraggled pink silk ribbon hanging from his mouth. "Well, so much for recycling any of that," I told myself as the cat stood, stretched, and wandered toward the sunroom. I went to the kitchen, picked up a dust pan and brush, and returned to clean up the shredded and sodden mess.

"You're a naughty boy," I told his retreating backside. His tail stood straight up in a gesture I took to mean just what it looked like. "Just wait 'til your father gets home," I mumbled, then, arms folded and still feeling grouchy, I stared out the window facing the street. The Bentley was still there, Shirley at the wheel. I couldn't tell if the engine was running. She had her phone in her hand, so at least she wasn't texting while driving. Even so, there was something about her being parked in front of my house that made me uneasy. That feeling increased big-time when Hugh Bingham's Range Rover edged into view on the opposite side of the street, moving slowly, heading toward Bridge Street.

What was going on out there? Was Hugh following Shirley? Was Shirley calling Hugh? Was Hugh watching me? Was he watching *me* watching his mother? Toby joined me at the window, putting his paws on the windowsill, watching the scene outside. Sort of like Scooby-Doo. He uttered a low growl—something he didn't do often. I stroked his silky head. "I know, boy," I told him. "I don't like them either."

Couldn't they see me standing there in the window, the draperies pulled back? With a sudden burst of bravery, I decided that I didn't care what either of them thought. I reached for my phone and snapped a quick picture, capturing both vehicles, and sent it to Pete.

The plainly marked SPD patrol car must have been right around the corner on Washington Square. It rolled along Winter Street—almost majestically, I thought, pausing briefly, but pointedly, alongside each of their cars.

Chapter Thirty-seven

A text from Pete: "You OK?"
"OK," I returned.

I was sure without even asking that he'd come home for lunch and we'd talk. Meanwhile, I took stock of the way I must look, and thoughts of going back to sleep evaporated. A cold shower was what I needed, and a fresh change of clothes.

The cold needles of water felt wonderful. I washed my hair, sponged my body with my favorite scented soap, toweled off, and stepped onto the bathroom scale, noting with satisfaction that I was another pound closer to my pre-baby weight. I peeked into the nursery, where baby Ella Marie slept sweetly, soundly, with one thumb in her mouth. It was turning out to be a pretty good day, despite the annoying beginning. I pulled on soft, comfy, cotton blend navy pants and a matching T-shirt, combed my wayward curls into some sort of order, and even dabbed on a bit of lip gloss.

This being a stay-at-home mom wasn't going to be bad at all. Our house was small enough to be fairly easy to keep tidy, and all of the appliances were new enough to clean, cook, light, push, pull, heat, or cool as directed. With a burst of coffee- and Pop-Tart-fueled energy, I became a whirlwind of activity. I made the bed, cleaned the bathroom, swept and Swiffered, dusted and polished, did a load of laundry, and folded and hung it. Popping a second Keurig cup into the coffee maker, I sat at the kitchen counter admiring my handiwork. It was only eleven thirty. *What am I supposed to do now?*

My phone, which was on the windowsill, buzzed. Thankfully, the doctor had returned my call. He suggested a brand-name formula I'd heard about from the moms on the common. I called Pete and asked him to pick some up on his way home for lunch.

My phone buzzed again. The caller ID announced WICH-TV. I snatched up the phone. "Rhonda?"

"It's me," came the familiar friendly voice of the station receptionist. "How're you doing?"

"I'm doing fine. The baby is a little doll. Pete's a perfect dad," I recited. "How's everybody over there? I miss you all." I realized as I spoke the words how true they were.

"Well, as you might remember, Wanda and Marty and I and some of the other girls here at the station were planning a shower for you when you decided to speed up the birthing process."

"Not on purpose—" I began to protest.

"It's okay. But we still have presents for you and Baby Ella," she said. "We know you're happy staying home, but if we bring all the food and drinks and everything, can we come over to your place and have the party sometime soon? You wouldn't have to do anything."

I didn't have to think it over. "I'd love that," I said, not admitting that staying home wasn't as easy as I'd thought it was going to be. "I'm ready whenever you all are."

"Okay. I hope you mean that, because we're ready. We can all be at your place tomorrow afternoon. Two-ish. You don't have to do anything. We'll bring it all. Okay?"

How could I refuse? "Okay," I said. "I'll see you all tomorrow afternoon. Two-ish."

"Great. Oh, by the way, Scott wants to know if you've got any new skinny on the Chocolate Shop Murder— the Bernie Bingham thing. We all know you were interested in it. Do you?"

"I'm sure I don't know anything that Scott doesn't know," I told her. *Except the part about Bernie's son and his ex-wife having a recent strange interest in* me.

"Well, if anything turns up, will you call him please? He's getting obsessive about it. Oh, and also, everybody here is curious about the cat girl with the potty mouth. Is she happy now that she has the cat? Does she still want to go back to New Hampshire? She's apparently not doing interviews. Doan really likes that story. Have you got any pull with her? Can you get pictures we can use? Are you going to keep

working on the candy story or are you retired altogether?"

"Whoa! One thing at a time. Trisha is at my aunt's
house right down the street, and I'm sure I can grab a
video of her with Bathsheba if that would be helpful," I
offered. "As for the candy stores, I think I've done all I
can do on that."

My mind was already whirring with the idea of
putting Ella into her new baby carriage and wheeling
her past the four houses between our home and Aunt
Ibby's to make the desired video. The fresh air would
be good for us and my aunt would love the visit. As
soon as Pete came home for lunch I'd share my plan. I
looked at the Kit-Cat Klock over the kitchen table.
Oops. Time was flying. He'd brought sandwiches and I
had made sweet iced tea. I'd made the tea the day
before—Southern style, the way Betsy had taught me
years ago. All I needed to do was fill the glasses with
ice and add a wedge of lemon to each one.

I put plates and chilled glasses on the Lucite table,
then Toby, O'Ryan, and I all watched from the living
room window for Pete's car to turn into the driveway.
All three of us hurried together to the sunroom to welcome him home. He hugged me, patted the animals,
and whispered, "Is she sleeping?"

"She is," I said.

"I couldn't bear to wake you this morning. You must
be exhausted."

"Nope. Second wind, I guess. I'm fine," I told him.
"Quick recovery must come with motherhood. I'm
wide awake. 'Rarin' to go,' as Old Jim says."

"You look wonderful." He pulled me close again with a warm kiss. He handed me two paper bags. "Here you go. Baby formula and Kelly's steak and cheese sandwiches. Get 'em while they're hot. Now, tell me about your morning visitor. What was that all about?"

"Formula first," I decided, then read the directions on the can and prepared Ella's first bottle of the stuff with high hopes that she'd be happily contented with it, pretty sure that her next call for food wouldn't be far off.

"I guess Shirley just couldn't wait to give me the gifts she'd bought for Ella Marie," I said. "They're really nice and useful. A baby monitor and a sound machine for lullabies. She even had them painted pink. Maybe you can hook them up tonight. I like the idea of the baby monitor even though she's in the next rom." I poured iced tea into the glasses.

"I do too," he agreed. "Pink, huh?" He put the hot sandwiches onto the green Fiestaware plates. "There. Lunch fit for royalty."

"Absolutely." I bit into the warm, juicy sandwich. "Rhonda called me this morning. The girls from the station are planning to bring a delayed baby shower over here tomorrow afternoon."

"As long as you feel up to it."

"I feel perfect," I insisted. "As a matter of fact, Mr. Doan would like me to go over to Aunt Ibby's and grab a fast video of Trisha and her cat. Her WICH-TV fans are anxious to know they're all right."

"Hmmm." Long pause. "What was Hugh doing? Did Shirley say anything about him being outside while she was in here bearing baby gifts?" He sipped his tea. "This is good."

"She didn't. He didn't show up until after she'd gone back to her car. What about the rescued cat video?" I pressed for an answer. "I'm dying to give Ella her first carriage ride. Just down the block."

"As long as you feel up to it," he said again. He put his dishes in the sink and picked up Toby's leash. "I'll take this big boy for a nice run before I go back to work," he said, "and I'll take a look around the neighborhood just in case there are any Binghams around."

He and Toby went out the back door, and once again, O'Ryan sat on the windowsill overlooking the street. Man and dog returned in about fifteen minutes. Toby headed for his water bowl and then curled up on the rug beneath the window, ignoring the cat peering down at him.

"I didn't see any of the Bingham vehicles," Pete said, "but if any show up there'll be a patrol car following you down to your aunt's house."

"That would be fine with me," I said. "I think they seem to be following each other around and somehow they wind up here. That patrol car driving by before didn't seem to bother either one of them. The whole thing is nutty. Like, do I really need police protection for walking down Winter Street past four houses on the way to the house where I was raised?"

"It is nutty," he agreed. "And it all started when you found Bernie's body in the cellar of the chocolate factory. Well, his funeral will be happening soon, and maybe that will be the end of it."

"I hope so. I don't expect there'll be many mourners at that event. Earl will be there, and I'm sure Trisha will want to go. She really was very fond of him," I remembered. "Will she be allowed to go?"

"It can be arranged," he said. "There'll be news media there too, I suppose."

"Count on it," I agreed. "Scott's still looking for an exclusive break in the Chocolate Shop Murder case. Is there anything new on that front that you can share? Any new likely suspects?"

"The man had so many enemies. We need to check his family members, who had no use for him either."

"Hugh and Shirley," I filled in.

"Shirley has continued to bail him out of trouble for all these years though—which is why the chief is so hot on solving this one."

"I know. And now she's even paying for his funeral," I reminded him, "besides buying new clothes—suit, shirt, tie, and shoes—for Uncle Earl to wear to the service."

"I guess she never got over loving him," Pete sighed. "Sad, isn't it?"

"He must have had *some* redeeming qualities, I suppose," I said, "besides being good-looking."

"Trisha liked him too," Pete reminded me.

"Well, between his alimony payments from Shirley and the money he hustled with the tennis and ski lessons, he was her means of support. That, and the fact that he gave her that gorgeous cat," I said. "Which reminds me, I guess I should call Aunt Ibby and ask her to tell Tricia I'll be coming over to do a new video for her fans at WICH-TV."

"I wonder if spending time with your aunt has cleaned up Tricia's potty mouth at all."

"I wouldn't be a bit surprised if it had," I said.

O'Ryan made a sputtering noise from under the table. We'd heard him do that many times before. It seems to be a cat way of expressing extreme doubt. Pete said that he agreed with O'Ryan, slipped the cat a bit of leftover roast beef, kissed me goodbye, and went back to work. It was only one thirty, and the whole afternoon loomed ahead of me.

Chapter Thirty-eight

I took my time dressing Ella Marie for her visit to Aunt Ibby's house. The new formula, combined with a breastfeeding, seemed to settle well with her, and she took the bottle greedily. The baby, contentedly drowsy, looked absolutely adorable in her pink ruffled dress and bonnet (a shower gift from Miss Claffey), topped with a hand-crocheted white sweater from Rhonda, who continues to surprise everybody with her many and varied talents. Crocheting. Who knew? As long as I had the camera handy, I took about a dozen still shots of her, then made a short video when she kicked her feet and waved her hands and gave me what I was sure was a real smile—not gas. I tucked her into the carriage, covered her with a super-soft pink blanket with teddy bears on it, placed a tiny stuffed white lamb beside her, and wheeled the carriage into the entrance hall, fol-

lowed by O'Ryan. However, this time Toby looked up
with disinterest, and returned to his nap.

I opened the front door a crack and peeked outside—
not wanting to admit to myself what I was looking for.
I didn't see anything I didn't want to see out there, so I
pushed the door open wide and carefully trundled the
carriage down the one step to the brick sidewalk.

It was a really pretty day on Winter Street. Some of
the houses had already decorated their front entrances
for Halloween, with pumpkins and brooms and even
skeletons and ghosts. Pete and I hadn't yet made a collection of holiday trimmings of our own. I had some
things I'd used indoors for Christmas and Halloween
and Valentine's Day and such when I'd had my apartment, and I'd already arranged some ceramic pumpkins,
fall leaves, and orange candles on our mantelpiece and
some bouncy bats hanging from the light pulls, and
there was a black-cat-face-shaped bowl of candy corn
on the coffee table, but Aunt Ibby had always been in
charge of the outdoor displays.

I looked at the doorway next door, the mirror image
of ours. Michael had an attractive dried flower wreath
in seasonal colors on his door. I guessed that one of the
art groups at the Tabby must have provided it, or it was
even possible that he'd made it himself. Michael had
turned out to be a better-than-average backyard gardener. The space behind his half of the house was
abloom with neat rows of herbs, perennial flowers, and
low green bushes. It wasn't unusual to see him working
outside in overalls, wielding a shovel, rake, or hoe. It
made my few pots of wilting geraniums look quite

pitiful. I made a mental note to order something decent-looking for our door. "See that?" I pointed to Michael's door décor and addressed Ella Marie. "We're going to start our own collection of holiday ornaments so you will always remember them when you are growing up in our family."

She seemed to be interested in my words and focused her eyes on my face as I spoke. That was a source of wonder to me. Some say we record everything we experience in the wonderful computer that is our brain—so I continued the conversation. "I hope you like your room." That brought a foot kick, which I took as a positive. "Okay. Listen. Shirley Parker brought over a baby monitor for your room. That's a machine that lets Mommy and Daddy watch you even when you're asleep. Cool, huh? Anyway. She had it painted pink. If you don't like it we'll have George change the color of that too." She opened her eyes wide. "Who? Shirley is the lady who woke us up early this morning." That brought a frowny face. "I know," I said. "I'm not crazy about her either."

We'd reached Aunt Ibby's front steps. She'd added some new touches to the usual Halloween decor. Real pumpkins, without faces carved into the plump flesh; a few brooms made from birch branches with natural ash wood handles; and a door wreath that seemed to be made from real fall leaves and acorns and small ears of Indian corn. "Look, Ella," I told her. "These are very special Halloween decorations. When you're a big girl I'm sure Aunt Ibby will let you help to make these things. You'll probably love the holiday even more than most Salem people do because it's so close to your birthday."

Pushing the carriage up the front steps made for a bumpy, jiggly ride for her, but she didn't seem to mind at all. I pushed the doorbell, listening for the familiar chimes. I knew the "Thank Heaven for Little Girls" tune had been a one-time thing. Again, the wondering, wide eyes. "'The Impossible Dream,' from *Man of La Mancha*. That's a story about Don Quixote," I informed her, and even sang a couple of bars from the song. She didn't frown. She must even like the way I sing, I marveled.

Aunt Ibby appeared behind the glass panel and pulled the door open. O'Ryan dashed inside while my aunt oohed and aahed over how cute the baby looked. Once inside I picked her up, holding her forward. "Do you want to hold her?" I didn't have to ask twice. I handed her over. "That man isn't still following you, is he?" She spoke in a whisper over Ella Marie's pink-bonneted head, as though she couldn't hear the words.

"No. Not today. I think Pete may have discouraged him. But I had an early-morning visit from his mother."

One shocked eyebrow shot up. "I wasn't going to mention it because I didn't want to upset you, but so did I."

"She came here too?"

"She said she saw the lights on so she knew I was up baking. Trisha and I were having breakfast in the kitchen." I must have looked surprised. "We have breakfast together every morning. This *is* a B and B, you know. Anyway, Shirley just barged right in and headed for the kitchen and sat down without being invited." My aunt, who is all about good manners, was clearly outraged at the transgression. "I know she was raised better than that! I excused myself and went into my office for a few minutes, then came out and said I'd had a phone call and pretended that we were expecting another guest and ushered her out as quickly as I could." She snuggled Ella close. "I know that *you* will be raised properly, young lady."

"We'll do our best," I promised, pulling the phone from my purse. "Shall we go up and record Tricia and Bathsheba for all her fans at WICH-TV?"

"She's ready for you—all dressed in white to match Bathsheba's coat, and both of them have orange and black ribbons in their hair—or fur—as the case may be."

"That sounds perfect," I said. "Do you think Tricia would be interested in meeting Ella, or should I leave her here with you while I take pictures?"

"Of course I'll be happy to babysit this little princess," she said, "but yes, I think Tricia would like to meet her. It isn't as though Ella's old enough to pick up naughty words."

I didn't try to explain that I've decided to talk to Ella in plain English, and anyway, quite a few old Anglo-Saxon cuss words are part of the language. I'd explain to her after she'd met Trisha that there were some words we never use in polite company. We climbed the stairs to the small apartment and knocked. "Come on in," came the call from inside. Bathsheba met us at the door. She looked proud of her beribboned self and posed nicely for a solo portrait.

Tricia, in a cat-matching white pinwale corduroy jumpsuit with a provocative neckline and orange and black ribbons braided into her hair and another blend of the two formed into a boutonniere pinned to one shoulder, welcomed us with an un-bleeped "Nice to see you again."

"Good to see you too," I told her. "I thought you might like to meet our almost-brand-new baby. This is Ella Marie." Then I spoke to the baby. "Ella Marie, please meet our friend Tricia."

"Hey, Lee, I'm glad you don't talk to the kid in that bleepin' baby talk." She used a particularly objectionable adjective, extended a friendly hand, and shook Ella's tiny fingers. I was almost tempted to put my hands over Ella's ears, but remembered my recent decision to accept *all* of the words at our disposal. "Don't worry," she said. "I just sprayed on some hand sanitizer. Hi, kid. Welcome to my bleeped-up, pile of bleep world." I was clearly going to have some serious naughty-word-explaining to do after this visit. I handed the baby back to my aunt, who held Ella's hand in a cute bye-bye wave and headed back downstairs. I got to work with the camera right away. I had Tricia hold the very willing Bathsheba while I asked some standard short interview questions, hoping the answers wouldn't be *too* obscenity-laced. "Our viewers are so interested in how you and this handsome cat are doing these days. I know you're awaiting questioning about the Bernie Bingham death, but I won't be asking you about that. You both seem to be comfortable here in this pretty apartment."

"Yes," she said. "The food is great here and Bathsheba loves sitting in the sunshine in that big dormer window over there. She gets the nice fresh cat food that she really likes. This place sure as bleep beats sitting in a jail cell. I guess the cops know I didn't off Bernie.

I loved that old bleep. He took good care of me and my cat." She stroked Bathsheba's fluffy coat, and the cat responded by giving her a pink-tongued lick on the cheek. Great TV! The audience would love seeing this side of Tricia, and Marty could clean up the language easily, with AI substituting some of the words with more appropriate ones to make it all flow nicely. I asked if she had anything she'd like to say to the many people who cared about her and Bathsheba, and she answered quite sincerely that she wanted to thank all of the folks who were praying for her. No cuss words at all in that thought. More great TV! The rest of the interview, with my softball questions and her no-nonsense answers, couldn't have been better. My thanks were sincere when I signed off.

"That was just about perfect, Tricia," I told her. "Your fans will be so happy that you and this gorgeous girl cat are doing so well here."

"I love this place. It sure beats that women's shelter they had me in before. All those babies crying and women complaining—not that I blame them. They mostly had some rotten men in their lives." She leaned forward. "Listen. It's none of my business, but after your aunt left the kitchen to go to her office, something that crazy lady said this morning made me wonder. You haven't been fooling around on your old man, have you?"

"WHAT?" I almost let a bleep-word fly myself. "What on earth are you talking about? Of course I haven't. What did the crazy lady—Shirley—say about me?"

Tricia spread her hands in a don't-blame-me attitude. "Hey, I don't believe a word she said, but she's absolutely convinced that you and Bernie had a thing going. She said she spotted you as soon as you showed up to take pictures of her chocolate shop. 'Just exactly his type,' she told me. You're a good-looking rich woman who can pay for tennis and golf and ski lessons. She thinks he talked you into bed and took pictures to blackmail you. I guess that's how he made most of his money." She shook her head in an "I don't believe it" motion. "She thinks your kid is Bernie's baby and she's kind of pissed that she doesn't look any more like him than her own kid does."

Chapter Thirty-nine

I felt my red-haired Irish temper flare up. I could even feel my blood pressure rising. I was outraged. Appalled. Furious. For a moment I couldn't even speak. I took a couple of deep breaths. "I need to call my husband." I hardly recognized my own voice. "Thank you for your honesty, Tricia." I turned and walked down the stairs to my aunt's living room in search of some aspect of sanity. I couldn't bear to involve her in such garbage. I put my sweet baby back into her carriage, said a pleasant goodbye, left Aunt Ibby's house, and walked more or less sedately to my own home. I didn't, couldn't tell Ella what was going on. I realized that, after all, she needed to be shielded from some of the world's ugliness.

Once inside the back door, with Ella still dozing comfortably in her carriage, I called Pete. I don't recall exactly what I told him, but it was enough to bring him bursting into the sunroom within minutes. He held me close for a long time, not speaking. When he did speak his voice was gruff, angry, not quite like I'd ever heard him before. "Tricia may be right about Shirley. She could be a crazy woman. A dangerous crazy woman. I'll put a tail on her right away so we'll know where she is. Then I'll talk to her son and see what he knows about all this."

Why do you want to talk to him? I wondered. He's the man who is almost stalking me. He may be as crazy as Shirley is. But I didn't say it aloud. It was time to depend completely on my professional law officer husband. He spoke again, his tone almost normal. "Tonight I'll hook up that baby monitor. I don't want Ella Marie out of our sight for even a second. I need to get back to work and get the tail on Shirley in motion. I'll try to get home early. I'll pick up take-out. Italian okay?"

"Italian would be wonderful," I told him, and hooking up the pink monitor made a great deal of sense to me. Even if the thing had been a gift from Shirley, it was appreciated. The way I was feeling at that moment though, I'd probably spend the night right beside Ella Marie's crib, eyes wide open. I could sleep some other time. I sent the video I'd made over to Marty at the station. It wasn't even noon yet, and again, the day stretched out before me, pretty much empty of anything meaningful to do. The buzzing of my phone was a welcome distraction—particularly when the caller ID showed Rhonda's number. I grabbed the phone, hoping that the buzz wouldn't wake my dozing darling. "Hi. Rhonda. What's going on?" I whispered.

"Marty says to tell you thanks for the video. It's

going to clean up just fine. Doan took a look at it too, and he says since you're obviously up and around he wants to know if you're ready for a small assignment."

I moved to the other end of the room, still speaking softly. My answer was sincere, but hesitant. I'm never sure what Doan's definition of "small" might be. "I guess I can," I said. "What is it?"

"It's another pre-Halloween idea he's dreamed up. You know how Salem is famous for the beautiful doorways? Like the Samuel McIntire ones on Chestnut Street? There are even books written about them, and postcard pictures of them."

I knew what she meant. I had one of the books. "Great minds," I said.

"What does that mean?"

"There are some pretty nice ones here on Winter Street," I told her. "I was talking about them to Ella Marie just this morning. Most of them are decorated for Halloween. Except mine. Is that what he's thinking about?"

Most anyone else would question me about talking to Ella Marie on the topic, but Rhonda didn't. "That's right," she said. "He'll send Francine over to pick you up and you can do a stroll down Chestnut and grab the best ones. How's this afternoon for you?"

"I'm not sure. I need to find someone to watch the baby." The very idea of being separated from her brought a pang of something like fear.

"Call me back. Howie can do it if you can't."

"Okay." I called my aunt, of course. I wasn't about to hand this over to Howie if I could help it.

"I'd love to," she enthused. "I'll come right over."

"I'll feed her and put her to bed," I promised. "She won't be any trouble."

So that's how I happened to be happily employed for part of the afternoon, in my green WICH-TV jacket, which once again fit me. I'd already made out a pink sticky note reminding me to return Scott's jacket. I was excited to be working with my favorite videographer, Francine. My mind was only slightly pained by some separation anxiety, but I knew that Ella was in excellent hands. The filming went well—the doorways were gorgeous, as expected.

Pete, as he'd promised, came home early, bringing Olive Garden, complete with plenty of that good bread. I told him about the doorways shoot and how good it had felt to be doing it. "As long as you feel all right," he said. "Having a baby must be pretty tiring." I assured him that I felt as good as new. "You look as good as new, that's for sure," he insisted.

After dinner, he got to work on the monitor. The directions were reasonably clear, so it didn't take long. "This is really cool," he said. "We can even watch it from our phones," he marveled. The camera fit nicely beside Ella's crib with the receiver at the foot of our bed. It was focused so that both the crib and my rocking chair should be visible. "Let's test it." We propped up our pillows and lay on the bed, focused intently on the screen.

"What the heck is that?" Pete sat bolt upright. So did I. What we saw on the screen was surely not our baby. It took a moment to register what the yellowish blob was. O'Ryan had positioned himself darned near on top of the camera.

"He doesn't want us to see Ella," I said. "I don't understand."

"He doesn't want *someone* to see Ella," he said. "Someone who can see her—and us—on a cell phone."

"Someone who gave us the monitor." I stated the obvious. "A crazy lady who gave us the monitor and who thinks I was sleeping with Bernie Bingham."

Pete went into the baby's room, angrily yanking the cord, disconnecting the monitor, then consoled me. "I have a tail on the crazy lady, day and night."

"They trade cars all the time," I complained. "How do you know whether she's in the Bentley or the Range Rover? How do you know you're not following him?"

"We track her phone," he answered.

"The phone she uses to watch our baby?" I was angry.

"Probably the same one," he said. "Anyway, I've made an appointment with the son to meet me in my office first thing tomorrow morning. I think it'd be a good idea if you came along with me to see what he has to say about all this. I don't want to leave you and Ella alone here until this is all cleared up. Hugh must know that his mother is suddenly behaving erratically."

Chapter Forty

If there was anything I didn't want to do, it was have a face-to-face meeting with Hugh Bingham, even in the confines of a police station with Pete by my side. Once again, I called upon my willing aunt to babysit. We dropped Ella off, along with bottles of both breast milk and formula, plus plenty of diapers and cute onesies. O'Ryan was waiting at Aunt Ibby's front door before we got there.

We met in Pete's office. He'd given a don't-disturb order to the desk sergeant. I sat as far away from Hugh, and as close to Pete as I could. I couldn't bear to even make eye contact with the creep. I focused on a round bronze city of Salem seal on the wall. Interesting. It was all about the spice trade. Nothing there about witches at all.

"I called you here, Mr. Bingham, because your mother has made some quite irrational comments to others lately.

In addition to that, she's made a provable attempt to spy on my personal household. Have you noticed any—um—disturbing changes in her behavior lately?"

"You mean since Bernie died? Sure. She's a different person now." It was a flat, unemotional statement.

"Your father's death made a profound impression on her." Pete's comment was made in a similar tone of voice.

Hugh lunged forward, pounding his fist on the table. "You still don't get it, do you?" There was an urgency in his voice I'd never heard before. "Lee wasn't the first one to find Bernie's body. I saw it before she did."

"Go on." Patient cop attitude.

"I think my mother give Lee that shawl and sent her downstairs. I wanted to stop her, what with Lee being pregnant and all. I didn't want her to see—well—what she was going to see." He looked down at his hands, now folded in his lap. "But at least I'd picked up the knife. Stashed it away safely. Lee didn't have to see that."

"You handled the knife?" Pete questioned. "Didn't you realize that there might be fingerprints on it?"

"Sure. That's why I did it."

"You already knew who the killer was," I said.

"Of course I did. Don't you get it?"

I got it, all right. So did Pete. The faithful son was protecting his mother.

"Do you want to tell us about it now?" Pete asked.

"Yes. I guess I need to." He shrugged. "Bernie had come over to our place to try to work her for more money. His little side chick, Tricia, had been there earlier and told Mother all about Bernie supplementing his income by banging all his rich lady tennis and ski clients and how she didn't mind at all because he shared all the money with her. To be brief, my mother minded. A lot. She never got over loving him, you know. That's why she didn't mind paying the alimony or bailing him out of jams."

"But she knew he was living with Tricia," I pointed out. "He certainly didn't pretend to be celibate."

Another shrug. "She still considers Tricia just a plaything," he explained. " 'That vacuous twit,' she calls her. She'd always believed that Bernie still loved her too." Sad smile. "Apparently, they still had sex once in a while. He used to sneak in through the cellar door. I think he must have told her it was over between them. Maybe he'd met someone else. I don't know. But he made the mistake of turning his back on her. Walking away. The knife was right there. Just back from the sharpener's. He probably never knew what hit him."

"I must have come in just after—after what she did." I thought back to that moment. "She was at her desk. She looked beautiful. Made up perfectly. Dressed to the nines. Not a hair out of place. Calm as the proverbial cucumber," I remembered aloud. "She offered me a chocolate. She gave me her cashmere shawl to wear." The enormity of the situation hit me. "She knew exactly what I was going to see when I went down there."

"So it was you who put the knife into the candy box, Mr. Bingham?" Pete reasoned.

"I had to get rid of it in a hurry," he said. "I heard the door chime from upstairs and I was afraid someone might come down. A health inspector or maybe one of the workers. People come and go up and down those stairs all the time. If I'd had more time I was going to shove him into the old tunnel behind the coal chute. That way I figured he'd be a skeleton by the time anyone dug him up."

He was probably right about that. "But you came back later and got the candy box," I said.

"I had to. Besides the murder weapon inside, it also had my bloody prints on it."

I nodded. "You wore a candymaker's uniform and a mask." At least now we knew who Chocolate Box Man was. "Does Shirley know you've been covering for her all this time?" I needed to know.

"We've never discussed it at all. I think she knows, but then—she seems to be what I think they call 'detached from reality.' She talks as if his killing is a big mystery."

"She can be very convincing," Pete acknowledged.

"I'm so sorry she involved you, Lee. But still, she's my mother and I didn't want her to go to jail—especially for ridding the world of that rat bastard."

"You've decided to tell us about her now," Pete said. "Has something changed? Is there an urgency now for some reason?"

"Yes." He looked down at his hands again, twisting his fingers together.

"Why?" Pete insisted. "What's changed? Is she about to leave town?" He stood, his body tense.

"She doesn't know I'm talking to you. She's probably quite sure I'd never betray her." Eyes downcast. "I wouldn't if I didn't have to. Bernie was a no-good scum. Nobody's sorry he's dead."

"But you're willing now," Pete said. "Why?"

"I'm afraid somebody else is going to get hurt."

"Because of Bernie?" I asked. The question slipped out. This was Pete's case. None of my business. Pete didn't acknowledge my nosy query. I'd slipped quite ungracefully into field reporter mode.

"You're afraid Shirley is going to hurt someone else?" he prompted.

I had to lean forward to hear the mumbled words.

"Lee," he said. "I'm afraid it might be Lee." He spread his hands in a hopeless gesture. "I've tried to keep an eye on her." He looked at me. The look was pleading. "I've tried to protect you from her, Lee, I really have."

"I understand," I said. And I did. I'd been trying for weeks to avoid the man. I'd altered my route to work, hoping I wouldn't encounter him on the common. I'd ducked into doorways, hidden behind trees, closed my draperies so he wouldn't see me at my window, tried to lose him in traffic. I'd thought of him as a creep. A stalker. And someone to fear—even though I denied it. All the while he'd been trying his best to protect me from his mother—a woman he loved unconditionally. What a dilemma Hugh Bingham had faced every day since Bernie's murder. He wanted to protect his mother. She had, after all, rid the world of a man with no apparent redeeming value. He had no intention of ever revealing her as the killer, seeing her go to jail for what amounted to doing society a favor. But her recent fixation on me had thrown the proverbial monkey wrench into the picture.

"I caught her looking at her phone," he said. "Looking at you in your rocking chair nursing your little baby. I was so angry I yelled at her! I mean, I didn't really care that she killed Bernie, but spying on you with that monitor she gave you—that was unforgivable." His face reflected his anger. "She promised she'd stop, then she told me that you must have figured out that someone's phone was connected to it besides yours and that you'd unplugged it. Is that true?"

"Yes," I said.

"She said something about the cat ruining the picture anyway. That didn't make any sense, but of course she was delusional by then I guess." I chose not to comment on O'Ryan's clever move. "She was so annoyed anytime I criticized her—*unjustly and harshly*, she said. I swore I'd never forgive her for that time she borrowed my car and deliberately ran it into a chain-link fence. Then, naturally, she paid to have it fixed." A puzzled headshake, then a fake chortle. "I pretended to take a run at her precious Bentley, just to show her that I could do it if I wanted to." He twisted his fingers again. "She just laughed at me. She knew I wouldn't really do it. She knew I loved her too much."

There were real tears in his eyes.

Pete reached for his phone. "You'll testify to what you've just told us?"

The answer was a soft "I will."

Chapter Forty-one

There was no point in pretending that Hugh Bingham's assessment of his mother's behavior wasn't accurate. It was time to arrest Shirley Parker for her ex-husband's murder. Pete called for a stenographer to take his statement. I figured that since she was already being tailed, they always knew exactly where she was and it wouldn't be difficult to make the arrest. Pretty soon this would all be over. Pete called for a uniformed officer to give me a ride back home so I could retrieve Ella's carriage and pick her up from Aunt Ibby's house. I'd still have plenty of time to get ready for the promised afternoon baby shower with the girls from WICH-TV. He dropped me off at the front door. I thanked him and waved goodbye as he pulled away from the curb. I knew he didn't have time to act as a taxi for the boss's wife, taking time away from much more important duties. I hate being a pest!

I'd barely put my key into the lock when the Range Rover pulled into the spot vacated by the police car. Hugh Bingham jumped out of the vehicle and pressed himself against my back. "Open the door," he growled.

But how could this be happening? Was I becoming delusional too? I knew that Hugh was at the police station making a statement. "I have a gun," he whispered. I believed it. I felt the cold muzzle in my ribs. I turned my head, to better see his face. He looked deadly serious. I did as I was told, terrified by what was happening, yet grateful that at least my baby was safe with my aunt.

But wait. There was something wrong about him. His face? His voice? It hit me. This person was not Hugh at all. It was Shirley. Her face, free of makeup, was so like his. Her hair was pushed up under a knitted cap. I'd seen that jacket on him before. The padded shoulders had changed her body image, in much the same way Scott's green jacket had changed mine. The boots were his too, with heels that made her an inch or so taller. I turned the key, pushed the door open. She shoved me inside so hard I sprawled onto the floor. She kicked the door shut behind her, then spoke again, this time using her own voice.

"Bitch." She aimed one of the boots at me. I rolled out of the way and got to my feet, my hands raised above my head, my eyes on the gun. I realized then that there was a silencer on it. I'd seen a silencer before. Pete had one for his personal weapon. "I think I knew it was you the minute you walked into my house with your phony story about putting my chocolates on television," she snarled. "You're just the type he liked, rich and beautiful." She laughed, a chilling, hideous laugh. "You're thinking they can track me. You're thinking that that dumb cop husband of yours will come to your rescue. Forget about it." She came close to me—pushed the gun with its lengthy silencer against my forehead. "This was Bernie's own gun, you know. Isn't that appropriate? I got it back after my lawyer got that jewelry store owner he held up to change his story about Bernie being armed. Money is a wonderful thing—and they say it can't buy happiness." A childlike giggle. "Nonsense. It's bought me plenty of happiness. It's about to buy me some more."

She backed the gun away a fraction of an inch. "I bought the silencer all by myself. I was darned sure I'd need it for killing you. At first I was going to kill you with the chocolate knife. I had it all planned. I haven't been able to think of anything else for days."

That would explain why I saw Jim's photo with the missing knife in the vision. She was planning it even then.

"The gun, this gun, Bernie's gun is a much better idea, but it's sure hard to get you alone." She furrowed her brow. "You always seem to have people around you. Why is that? Because they like you? Because you're rich and pretty? That's what Bernie liked about you, I suppose." Her voice then changed again to the gravelly growl. "I'm rich and pretty. Why wasn't I enough for him? Why did he always wander off looking for other women?" She pressed the gun into my forehead again—harder than before. "He was never true to you either, you know. Not a loyal bone in his beautiful body."

Could I reason with her? Under the circumstances it was certainly worth a try. "Shirley," I said. "Please listen to me. I never had an affair with Bernie. I'd never even seen him before until the day I found his body. I'm happily married to my husband. We have a new baby. Please think of the baby. She needs me."

Did I dare try to grab for the gun? Not a good idea. It might go off. I had to be careful. Nothing she said was rational. She didn't respond to my words. I realized that she wasn't registering them at all. She was in some different place in her mind.

"They can't track me, you know. Not at all. They'll be using that cell phone trick all the cops use. Bernie taught me a few things about cops." Another smile. A little more pressure with the gun. "That phone is safe, riding around in the Bentley," she said in an ordinary, conversational tone of voice. "I told my mechanic that my car had a terrible rattle. I told him to drive it around until he found it. Brilliant, aren't I?"

She kept talking. "After I kill you, I'm going to go down the street and grab Bernie's baby." She took the gun away from my head and cocked her own head to one side in a fake thinking pose. "Of course, that means I'll have to kill the old woman too. And maybe that brainless ninny Tricia. Oh well . . ."

"You'll never get away with it," I told her, furious now, and not trying to hide it, gun or no gun. She meant to kill me. To kill my aunt. To steal my baby. "She is *not* Bernie's baby. A simple DNA test will prove it. Don't make this any worse for yourself than it already is."

"Oh, I'll get away with it," she said. "I have plane tickets to—never mind. Do you think I'll tell you where I'm going? I have fake passports for myself and an infant female child. It's wonderful to be rich. Money can buy just about anything." She motioned with the gun. "Get in your bedroom. I know exactly where it is, you know. I saw it on the monitor. That monitor. What a lovely gift. All pink and pretty."

I walked toward the bedroom. She was close behind me. "Lie down on the bed and close your eyes. It will be just like going to sleep—except that there'll be a lot of blood on the pillow—and no one will hear a sound." Again, the laugh.

The bedside table was blessedly close to the head of the bed. Using only the slightest hand motion, I reached for the fob and pressed the panic button. Immediately, bright flashing lights shone through the window while the horn blasted and a siren screeched at an earsplitting pitch. Two yowling cats streaked into the room. I heard feet pounding and the back door bursting open. The woman with the gun whirled toward the sounds. The cats attacked her at once, teeth bared, claws extended. Michael, in overalls and wielding a wicked-looking pitchfork, took a few seconds longer.

The cats had gone for her face, raking nose, cheeks, and eyes. The pitchfork had pinned her right wrist—with the gun-holding hand—to the floor. Shirley screamed an agonized scream. I jumped from the bed, kicking the gun away. Dark blood spurted onto the rug. I remember thinking, "Oh dear, the pitchfork must have pierced an artery."

Things moved very fast after that. I called 911. More sirens. More flashing lights. Police cars. An ambulance. Even a fire truck.

Then Pete was there, holding me close, murmuring comforting words. I knew we were okay. All of us.

Chapter Forty-two

Naturally, the planned baby shower with the girls couldn't—didn't—take place exactly the way we'd all pictured it. It didn't take place at my house either, even though I'd had the bedroom carpet replaced. It happened in the far-from-glamourous break room at WICH-TV, and it was not your traditional, pretty-in-pink, all-girl event either. And it was way bigger than had been originally planned! All of the female contingent at the station showed up. Those who were on the air or on camera ducked in and out as time allowed. Buffy Doan was present, of course. So were Francine, Marty, Therese, Rhonda, River, and Wanda, along with an assortment of women from the sales department, the secretarial pool, and the housekeeping staff. There were guys there too. Pete was my escort, of course. Scott Palmer wasn't about to be left out, and neither was Old Jim or Phil Archer. Buck Covington dropped by, and so did Mr. Doan. Some of these folks had already attended Aunt Ibby's shower but happily joined the group anyway, some bringing gifts again. Wanda, using her fully operational WICH-TV on-site kitchen, served an amazing fall-themed apple cider cake to rave reviews.

Baby Ella, because of the extraordinary outpouring of loving gifts, had way more outerwear, onesies, bonnets, hoodies, and booties than any child could be expected to wear. We were able to make a significant donation to the woman's shelter where Trisha had recently been so unhappily housed.

My association with WICH-TV remained friendly. It was a bit more casual than it had once been, but it was surely still a part of my life. There was indeed time to be a mommy and time to do some freelance work, both on and off camera. The things that interested Salem, the things that Salem talked about, did not stop being of vital interest to me—or to the people who watched my occasional appearances on the station. Not all of those things were cheerful happenings like baby showers, cat reunions, red barley candy lollipops, and chop-your-own Christmas trees. Some were sad, bad, disturbing things, like a chocolate heiress on trial for murder, and for attempted murder. Like a man having to testify before a jury about the mother he adored— those were the things that Salem talked about, worried about, wondered about.

I had to talk about those things too, sitting beside Michael Martell on WICH-TV's late news with Buck Covington. The city, the state, and apparently the whole country were interested in how the man Scott Palmer had once dubbed "your friendly next-door murderer" had overnight become "my friendly next-door lifesaving hero!" Michael was astonished by the outpouring of prayerful support he received from viewers, and from readers of newspapers who'd picked up the story, and from talk radio programs all over America. Perhaps it helped to assuage the heavy burden of guilt I knew he still struggled with. I hoped so. Frankie still lives with him and shows no sign of moving on. But with Frankie, one never knows.

Michael's wonderful garden continues to thrive, and his Fenton Bishop *Garden Club Mysteries* series does too. Ella's planned swing and slide set has already been erected in our backyard, and there's a tire swing attached to a low branch of the maple tree in anticipation that someday Peter Donald might want one. We also have a "someday" set of plans for a tree house.

Michael's transition from "murderer" to "hero" is well-known now around the country, and another person not famous but deserving of praise is Hugh Bingham. For such a long time I tried hard to avoid him, mistrusted him, and even grew to fear him as a possible stalker. All the while he was doing his best to protect me, and Pete and I are forever grateful.

Shirley Parker has been tried for the murder of Bernie Bingham and for the attempted murder of me— Maralee Mondello. As was expected, the Parker fortune had relied on the expertise of the usual army of top-flight defense attorneys. Shirley was found not guilty of either crime by reason of insanity. There are a number of secure mental institutions in Massachusetts where women in Shirley's position can be cared for.

Again, the Parker wealth came to the fore when Hugh opted for a private psychiatric hospital in Vermont for Shirley's care and hopefully for her eventual recovery. Bernie's prepaid funeral that Shirley had arranged took place as scheduled, even though she couldn't be in attendance. Earl and Hugh and Trisha were the sole front-row mourners, although there was a good-sized representation of media, both regional and national, in the rear of the funeral home.

Chief Whaley wasn't entirely satisfied with the way things turned out for what's left of the Bingham family. Hugh was able to get away with paying a *very* hefty fine for an "obstruction of justice" charge because he didn't report his mother's guilt earlier. Chief wasn't exactly thrilled with that "not guilty by reason of insanity" decision either.

Casa de Chocolatte is no longer producing boutique candies. The candy making equipment has been sold to other confectioners and the mansion itself has been returned to its original status as a private home. There is a small, discreet "For Sale" sign on the lawn facing Washington Square East. There have been no takers so far.

Scott Palmer has produced an ongoing documentary predictably called *The Chocolate Shop Murder*, complete with interviews with everyone he could find who'd talk to him about Bernie's death—including Tricia Violette, who, along with Bathsheba, had become quite the popular personality on the show, even though the producer had to keep a ready finger on the bleep button. Scott invited me to participate in person. I declined with thanks, but gave him permission to use any of my relevant videos, photos, or program clips. He says, once again, that he owes me one.

Hugh Bingham has moved away from Salem and has accepted a business administration teaching position at his small Vermont college alma mater. He adopted Shirley's black cat—who is no longer called "Blackie," but answers to his new name of "Magic." Hugh's home in Vermont is close to the hospital and he's able to visit his mother frequently.

It was probably foreseeable that I'd continue my association with WICH-TV. Doan did indeed like the evergreens idea, and I have a couple of other programming thoughts lurking in the back of my mind. Being a wife, a mom, and a TV freelancer seems to be working out nicely for me. I think my long association with Aunt Ibby, who raised me, managed a household, excelled as a cook, maintained a part-time job at the library, and always had time for friendships along with the occasional adventure, is and has always been a true inspiration.

Since Ella's birth the visions have been rare, and thankfully none of them lately have been of the frightening variety. River says that marriage and motherhood may have changed my metaphysical profile, and that my creativity has been noticeably heightened. That's good, but I'm afraid it hasn't extended very much to my kitchen abilities, so Pete and I, with Ella in a high chair, still eat out fairly often.

O'Ryan and Ella have already established a special rapport. When she's asleep, we've sometimes observed him sitting quietly nearby, just looking at her with what seems to me like cat adoration. When she's awake, she always greets him with a smile. He's taken to walking along with us when, with Toby on his leash, we cross the common to join the other moms and babies. He gives the other littles a few polite glances, but always remains beside the carriage, ready to step between Ella and any admiring stranger who might approach too closely.

Here in Salem, with fall leaves in glowing colors, and visitors from everywhere on the globe coming to enjoy all of the history and mystery our city has to offer, I feel blessed in our comfortable home on Winter Street, with my wonderful husband, beautiful baby, good friends, and family nearby.

Life is very good.

Acknowledgments

Here's to the writers of books for children—the writers with the ability to engage, to charm, to teach, and, perhaps most importantly, to instill a lifelong habit of reading.

Some of the most popular have survived for more than a century: Lewis Carroll's *Alice's Adventures in Wonderland* (1885); Louisa May Alcott's *Little Women* (1868); Johanna Spyri's *Heidi* (1880); L. M. Montgomery's *Anne of Green Gables* (1908); Anna Sewell's *Black Beauty* (1877).

Some of the great mid-century books might include C. S. Lewis's *The Lion, the Witch and the Wardrobe* (1950); E. B. White's *Charlotte's Web* (1952); Maurice Sendak's *Where the Wild Things Are* (1963), and surely Roald Dahl's *Charlie and the Chocolate Factory* (1964).

Great ones of more recent vintage will certainly be topped with J. K. Rowling's *Harry Potter and the Philosopher's Stone* (1997); Louis Sachar's classic *Holes* (1998); and a spate of *New York Times* bestselling series, like Sara Shepard's *Pretty Little Liars* (2006 to 2009), Francine Pascal's *Sweet Valley Twins* (1983 to 2003), and Ann M. Martin's *The Baby-Sitter's Club* (1986 to 2000).

Today's kids have a veritable feast of book adventures awaiting them. As a mystery writer and long-time mystery reader, I gravitate to that genre for children too. Look for *The Swifts: A Dictionary of Scoundrels*, the first in a new series of fun mysteries for middle-graders. Kekla Magoon's *The Secret Library* is a delightful fantasy/mystery/adventure for middle grade readers. There's a new *Sweet Valley Twins* title—this time a graphic novel for kids—*The Haunted House*. A nonfiction paperback with a lot of appeal is Kirsten Anderson's *Who Is Taylor Swift?*—a well-written biography of one of the most popular musicians of the twenty-first century. For the littles, try *Just One More Sleep* by Jamie Lee Curtis. Waiting isn't easy for children. Measuring by "sleeps" helps the time pass.

Read to your children! Read to your grandchildren! Introduce them to the library. You'll find some wonderful stories from generations of writers, just waiting to be discovered—to begin a lifetime of reading for pleasure for a new generation of readers.

Recipes

BETSY'S SOUTHERN SWEET TEA

1 gallon water (divided use)
3 family-sized tea bags (Betsy uses Lipton)
2 cups sugar
¼ teaspoon baking soda

Boil ½ gallon of the water on stove in a large pot. Once it comes to a rolling boil, pour it into a 1-gallon pitcher. Add the three family-sized tea bags and the baking soda to the pitcher, making sure the teabags are under the water. (Baking soda helps keep the tea from getting bitter.) Set a timer for 15 minutes and then take out the tea bags. Don't squish them; just let them drip into the water. Add the sugar and stir the mixture. (It's okay to use Splenda if you're cutting down on sugar.) Add the other ½ gallon of cold water and stir again. Chill in the refrigerator before serving.

Serves 16 one-cup servings.

PENNY PARKER'S ORIGINAL CHOCOLATE FUDGE

1 cup milk
2 ounces (2 squares) unsweetened chocolate
   or unsweetened dark chocolate, cut up
2 cups sugar
1 teaspoon corn syrup
Dash of salt
2 tablespoons butter
1 teaspoon vanilla
1 cup chopped walnuts (optional)

Place the milk and cut-up chocolate pieces in a saucepan over low heat and stir until the chocolate is melted and the mixture is smooth. Stir in the sugar, corn syrup, and salt. Cook it gently, stirring from the bottom of the pan to the top, and use your candy thermometer. When it reaches 236°F (a little of the mixture dropped into cold water will form a soft ball), remove it from the heat and stir in the butter. Cool it, without stirring, until it's lukewarm. Add the vanilla and beat it until it is thick and no longer glossy. If you are using walnuts, now is the time to stir them in.

Spread the mixture into a buttered 8-inch buttered square pan and cut it into squares.

About 1¼ pounds of fudge.

AUNT IBBY'S SLOW-COOKER BEEF BURGUNDY

6 bacon strips, diced
1 boneless beef chuck roast (3 pounds), cut
   into 1½ inch cubes
1 can (10 to 12 ounces) condensed beef broth
1 small onion, halved and sliced
1 medium carrot, sliced
2 tablespoons butter
1 tablespoon tomato paste
2 cloves garlic, minced
2 big sprigs of fresh thyme
½ teaspoon salt
½ teaspoon pepper
1 bay leaf
½ pound fresh mushrooms, sliced
½ cup burgundy wine
5 tablespoons flour
⅔ cup cold water

In a large skillet, cook the bacon over medium heat until crisp. Remove it to paper towels, then brown the beef in the drippings and drain. Put the beef and bacon into a 5-quart slow cooker. Add the broth, onion, carrot, butter, tomato paste, garlic, thyme, salt, pepper, and bay leaf. Cover and cook on low until the meat is tender, 7 to 8 hours. Add the mushrooms and wine. Combine the flour and water until smooth and gradually stir into the cooker. Cover and cook on high until thickened, about 30 to 45 minutes. Discard the bay leaf and serve over noodles.

Serves 8.

WANDA'S APPLE CIDER BUNDT CAKE

One 15.25-ounce box of spice cake mix
   (Wanda uses Duncan Hines)
1 cup apple cider
½ cup cinnamon-flavored applesauce (Wanda
   uses Mott's)
3 large eggs
¼ teaspoon cinnamon
1 tablespoon brown sugar
1 teaspoon good-quality vanilla

For the topping:
2 tablespoons cinnamon
¼ cup sugar
¼ cup butter, melted

Preheat the oven to 350°F. Grease and flour a 12-inch Bundt pan. Put the cake mix, the apple cider, applesauce, and eggs into a large mixing bowl and whisk until smooth. Then add the cinnamon, brown sugar, and vanilla to the batter and pour the mixture into the Bundt pan. Put the pan on the center oven rack and bake it for 40 to 50 minutes. It's done when a toothpick stuck in the middle comes out clean. Remove it from the heat, turn it out of the pan, and let it cool on a wire rack for 20 minutes.

Meanwhile, make the topping. In a small bowl, mix together the cinnamon and sugar. Once the cake has cooled, brush the entire surface with the melted butter and cover it evenly with the cinnamon-sugar mixture. Enjoy!

Serves 12.

AUNT IBBY'S BLUEBERRY PIE

1 quart fresh blueberries
1 cup sugar, divided
1 tablespoon flour
⅛ teaspoon nutmeg
2 tablespoons butter
Pastry for a two-crust 9-inch pie

Aunt Ibby says the best blueberries are the ones you pick yourself in the wild. If you can't do that, buy local berries if you can. For the pastry, you can make your own or buy the kind that comes frozen.

Preheat the oven to 450°F. Wash the blueberries and drain them well. Then roll out half of the pastry or use the thawed frozen bottom crust to line a 9-inch pie pan, trimming the pastry so that about ½ inch of it hangs over the edge. Mix 1 tablespoon of the sugar with the flour and sprinkle it on the bottom crust. Fill the crust with the blueberries and sprinkle with the nutmeg. Cover it all with the remaining sugar and dot it with the butter. Roll out the top crust and also overlap the edge about ½ inch, Tuck the top crust under the overlapping bottom crust and seal it by crimping the edges firmly together. Prick the top of the pie with a sharp knife to make an attractive pattern to let steam escape.

Place the pie on the bottom rack of the oven and bake for 10 minutes. Move to the middle rack and reduce the heat to 350°F. Continue baking for about 30 minutes or until the crust is golden and the kitchen smells heavenly.

Serves 6.

AUNT IBBY'S PINK CAKE

*The cake for Lee's shower was much bigger than this,
but here's the recipe for a normal-sized pink cake.*

⅔ cup shortening (Aunt Ibby uses Crisco)
⅔ cup butter
1½ cups sugar
2¼ cups sifted flour
2½ teaspoons baking powder
1 teaspoon salt
¼ cup maraschino cherry juice
¼ cup milk
16 maraschino cherries, cut into eighths
5 egg whites (⅔ cup), stiffly beaten

Preheat the oven to 350°F. Grease and flour two
9-inch layer pans. Cream the shortening and butter together until fluffy. Sift together the sugar, flour, baking
powder, and salt. Add the dry ingredients alternately
with the cherry juice and milk. Stir in the cut-up cherries. Fold in the egg whites. Pour into the prepared
pans and bake for 30 to 35 minutes. Remove from the
oven and let stand in pans for 10 minutes. Then turn
cakes onto wire cooling racks.

Pink Icing
3 cups sifted confectioners' sugar
⅓ cup soft butter
About 3 tablespoons of maraschino cherry
    juice
maraschino cherries, halved (optional)

Stir the confectioners' sugar, butter, and cherry juice together until smooth. Once the cake has completely cooled, spread the icing between the layers and frost the top and sides. You can decorate with the halved maraschino cherries, if desired. (For the shower, Aunt Ibby used purchased baby shower decorations.)

Serves 15.

SPINACH QUICHE FROM "THE PLACE"

One 9-inch pastry pie shell
One 10-ounce package chopped frozen
    spinach
8 ounces Swiss cheese, diced
2 tablespoons all-purpose flour
1 cup milk
3 eggs, beaten
½ teaspoon salt
⅛ teaspoon pepper
Dash of nutmeg

Preheat the oven to 425°F. Bake the pie shell for 6 to 8 minutes. Remove from the oven and lower the heat to 350.

Cook the spinach according to the package directions. Drain it well and set it aside to cool. Combine the cheese and flour. Set aside.

Combine the milk, eggs, salt, pepper, and nutmeg. Mix well, then stir in the spinach and cheese. Pour into the partially baked shell. Bake at 350°F for 50 to 60 minutes. Cool slightly and serve.

Serves 4 to 6.

Visit our website at
KensingtonBooks.com
to sign up for our newsletters, read
more from your favorite authors, see
books by series, view reading group
guides, and more!

BOOK **CLUB**

BETWEEN THE CHAPTERS

Become a Part of Our
Between the Chapters Book Club
Community and Join the Conversation

Betweenthechapters.net